## DATE DUE

| | Starcher |
|---|---|
| JCB-8-BH | |
| | |
| | |
| | |
| | |
| | |
| | |
| | |
| | |
| | |
| | |
| | |
| | |
| | |
| | |
| | |
| | |
| | |
| | PRINTED IN U.S.A. |

# SHOTGUN

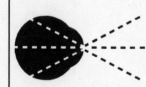

This Large Print Book carries the
Seal of  Approval of N.A.V.H.

# SHOTGUN

## C. COURTNEY JOYNER

**THORNDIKE PRESS**
*A part of Gale, Cengage Learning*

GALE
CENGAGE Learning·

Farmington Hills, Mich • San Francisco • New York • Waterville, Maine
Meriden, Conn • Mason, Ohio • Chicago

GALE
CENGAGE Learning®

**LIBRARY OF CONGRESS CATALOGING-IN-PUBLICATION DATA**

Joyner, C. Courtney, 1959–
    Shotgun / by C. Courtney Joyner. — Large print edition.
        pages ; cm. — (Thorndike press large print western)
    ISBN 978-1-4104-6968-7 (hardcover) — ISBN 1-4104-6968-9 (hardcover)
    1. Outlaws—Fiction. 2. Revenge—Fiction. 3. Brothers—Fiction. 4. Large
type books. I. Title.
PS3610.O976S56 2014
813'.6—dc23                                             2014007248

Published in 2014 by arrangement with Pinnacle Books, an imprint of
Kensington Publishing Corp.

Printed in the United States of America
1 2 3 4 5 6 7 18 17 16 15 14

# SHOTGUN

"You damn well know, I'll do it."

"Major" Beaudine's spit-shined boot was flush against John Bishop's right arm, pinning it down, while he turned the blade in the moonlight to heighten the threat.

Beaudine said, "So, your choice?"

Bishop managed, "You're thinking I know something I don't. I swear, I've told you everything. You got no reason to touch my family."

Beaudine gripped the handle of the long cleaver, saying, "A liar always boils my blood."

Bishop was on the edge of consciousness, trying to take in the faces of the other men holding him to the frozen ground. They were dirty fragments: moustaches dropping into beards, fresh burns, and one curtained eye. Their names were nothing but jumbled noise, while the screams of Bishop's wife and son cut through everything to reach him. Their voices didn't even sound like them anymore, though they were just a few feet away. Bishop cried out, twisting his head to see, as Deadeye and another man gripped him by his ears and jaw.

"Them ears'll come right off!"

Deadeye asked, "Why are you tryin' to look, anyways?"

Beaudine let Bishop know, "They're breathing. I see her little bosom moving in and out, but it's not honorable for you to make your wife and boy pay for your being contrary. Do you understand the penalties, what it means to incur my wrath?"

Exactly fifteen minutes before, Amaryllis Bishop had joined hands with her husband and son for a Methodist grace. John always gently rubbed her fingers with his thumb while his wife asked for blessing, and she flashed her blue eyes in a way that was supposed to be annoyance, but was something else.

Their son giggled as he reached for a piece of chicken before the plate was offered. Mama issued a smiling warning. "I know somebody's birthday is in three days, but it may not come at all, if —"

Amaryllis's voice was cut off when the front door was kicked off its hinges.

"Major" Beaudine and his men exploded

into the house, tossing the dinner table, splintering a bookshelf, and slapping the youngest to the floor. Bishop sprang at the "Major," but heavy fists from behind pounded him down, and Beaudine's heel cracked his ribs with little effort.

Beaudine warned one of the others not to do more. "Show restraint, gentlemen. Our friend is essential to our mission."

He knelt next to Bishop, measuring his words. "I am aware of the gold you and your brother liberated, one half of a million dollars. Don't deny it. The letters he wrote you from prison, finalizing your confidential plans? I wrote them. You know your brother could neither read nor write, and so he trusted me to set down his thoughts. Devlin and I were cellmates, until the morning he was hung. He took me into his deep confidence, which I honor. You have all that money, John, and you need to share. Your brother is departed, but I am here. Death's arrived, and I want paying."

"I'm swearing, I don't know a damn thing about any gold. There's nothing between me and my brother. Never was."

"No, that's not the answer."

"Where's my wife?"

"You must think clearly now, about the gold. Nothing else matters at this moment,

I promise you."

The man with the trimmed moustache and salvaged grey Confederate tunic, who spoke as if he were reading holy scripture, pressed his knee deep into Bishop's back. Bones cracked. Beaudine asked again about the stolen gold.

"If anything happens to my son . . ."

Beaudine pressed his knee again and Bishop couldn't move, his thoughts slipping away with his bleeding.

Beaudine said, "There's a Foster Brothers cleaver with a polished blade on a thirty-one-inch handle resting across my saddle. It's a thing of beauty, but you do not want me to fetch it."

Beaudine put the last of his weight on Bishop's spine, dropping his voice. "You need to concern yourself with gold. Try again."

The outlaws waited for the answer, and Amaryllis swung a pork-fry pan from the Crawford stove, spattering hot grease across the face of one of them, sending him screaming into the cold. Time stopped for a few heartbeats as Amaryllis Bishop scooped up her son, his arms around her neck and their tears mixing on their cheeks, as she whispered a kiss to him.

That's when the first shot was fired.

# CHAPTER ONE: NOTHING DIES LIKE A MAN

Huckie's Saloon, with its caving roof and sides, was a whipped dog cringing in front of the Colorado Mountains, ready to snap. It was the only place John Bishop saw with any signs of life, and he angled his horse toward it.

He was navigating a tough trail winding out of the steeper foothills that led to what was passing for some kind of a town. Bishop's bay horse was cautious with her footing. The snow on the trail wasn't deep, but a layer of ice beneath the white cracked under each footfall, throwing off her steps. Bishop patted her neck to tell her she was doing well as she managed a narrow cut between some tall pines.

There was another rider following, about half a mile back, but Bishop didn't even turn to see, his mind and eyes locked straight ahead, the reins steady in his left hand to keep the bay sure. She responded.

The frozen white was blowing just enough that he had to squint to read the battered sign that declared Huckie's. A pack mule snorted out front, and a mutt scratched at the front door, until someone let it in. There was loud, drunken talk followed by laughter. Bishop figured there had to be at least five in the place, including a cackling woman.

Bishop clenched the reins. His memories from months ago, the ones that beat hell out of him every other minute, had brought him to this place, but now he had to put feelings away. He was going to do this, and had to be clear about it. No backing down.

Chester Pardee liked Huckie's. The drinks and the one woman were so watered and worn that even he seemed like a big shot in the place. He took another swallow of no-name whiskey and tried to fan his cards, but they were too ear-bent to separate. Pardee then studied each of them, pausing for a sip, making a show of what a fine hand he was holding.

Chaney, who had killed someone someplace, was getting tired of the put-on. "You ain't droppin' anything on the table, Chester."

"I like to think my bets through."

"Nobody's got that much time. Play or fold."

12

Pardee adjusted his fingerless gloves, and reached into his pocket for the last bit of paper he had. He'd gotten the coat from a dead man, and it was stained with his fortune, but the money was his own, and he placed an old Union twenty on the torn felt like he was presenting a king's crown.

Chaney said, "The bill's got blood on it."

"What doesn't? I know'd every one of ya and your dirty habits. I say can't none of ya match it."

Chaney nodded. "Things are temporarily lean, but I have twenty-three in silver, and this banker's watch you've always admired. You're being raised, Chester."

Pardee reached into his jacket, and took out a letter that had been roughly folded into five sections, the words smudged by whiskey rings. Too many reads had frayed the paper, but Chester Pardee waved it at Chaney like a red veronica in front of a Brahma bull.

Pardee said, "You know what this is?"

Chaney didn't change his expression. "You jaw about it enough."

"Right, it's a goddamn treasure map. I'll throw ten percent — no, one percent — into the pot. One percent. One."

Chaney said, "You might as well say you wipe yourself with it."

13

"You won't take that much of a chance, Chaney? You ain't a gambler at all."

Chaney looked up from his cards.

The Colorado snow eased as Bishop rode to the hitch rail. He threw his weight to one side, angling his right arm from its special sling on the saddle, almost turning in the stirrup, before dropping to the ground. Here, the snow was slush under his boots, as he listened again to the voices escaping from Huckie's. Bishop rolled his shoulders and said something like a prayer before walking the last steps to the batwings that were banging against the front door.

The glass in the front door had a little split, and for some reason, Bishop almost knocked. Instead, he opened it with his left hand and let the door swing free inside, the glass breaking in half to announce him.

Pardee turned in his chair to see Bishop standing in the doorway. One of the others at the table belched, "You're gonna have to pay for that."

Bishop kept his head down with his arms straight at his side, his black duster a size and some too big, hanging scarecrow loose, but it gave him the freedom of movement he needed. The first time he saw himself, he thought he looked like a specter from Poe.

14

Bishop cleared his throat, but didn't speak.

Huckie's was all whispers and mutterings; guesses about Bishop passed from the drinkers who sat at the old silver exchange counter that now served as the bar, to the laughing whore on the straw bed tucked away in a corner, with the pull curtain above it. Bishop had their attention, until he raised his eyes. The whispering stopped, and then started again, punctuated with loud snickering.

Bishop's face was softly round, and not protected at all by his blond beard — the kind of face that made men like these laugh among themselves before trying something.

"Chester Pardee."

Pardee paid no mind. He slipped the letter back into his jacket, and said to Chaney, "You can't kill me for tryin'."

Chaney said, "Find somebody to stake you, or fold."

Bishop hadn't moved; he tried again. "Chester Pardee."

Pardee said, "It's freezin' in here."

"That's all you have to say?"

"We've got a game, jackass."

Bishop took a single step closer to the table. "Then you don't know me?"

Chaney said, "You lost, Chester."

Pardee said, "Hold up! You say you know

me? Stake me to this pot. I got the cards, amigo."

"You really don't remember?"

Chaney said to Pardee, "I called, that's it."

Chaney laid out two pairs of faces, while Pardee tossed a weak five-high straight on the table. Chaney gave Pardee a smirk with some pity.

Pardee faced Bishop with, "Whatever the hell you're on about, it didn't mean nothin'! You just cost me!"

"Slaughtering a man's family doesn't mean anything?"

"What man?"

The first blast ripped through Pardee's shoulder and sent him spinning out of his chair, spurs catching the edge of the table, sending the whiskey, cash, and five-high flying. Pardee twisted on the bowed floor, screaming out for Jesus, but Jesus didn't make a move. Nobody did.

The whore burst into tears because she'd never seen a shooting up close before; everyone else rubbernecked for a look, not exactly sure what had just happened.

Bishop stood over Pardee, gun smoke drifting from the end of his sleeve where his right hand should have been, but wasn't. Instead, the two barrels of a Greener shot-

16

gun poked from the ragged cuff, which had been singed by the blast. Burning threads danced from the cuff to the floor.

The double barrels were in place of Bishop's right arm, attached somehow at the elbow, and held waist-high steady. He shifted his weight from one leg to the other, keeping the weapon dead-centered on Pardee's chest.

Pardee was still crying out for Jesus as he struggled to stand, red spreading across his jacket. He tried drawing his Colt with fingers that wouldn't work. "You ain't given me a sloppy Chinaman's chance!"

"What kind of chance did you give my wife and son?"

"Jesus Lord."

"I've still got the second barrel."

"Can't you just let me out, Bishop?"

"So you know me now."

"What happened wasn't my doin', I swear. That's not why I was there."

"I can barely see where my wife threw the grease from that hot skillet."

"Please, let me ride out and you'll never hear my name again."

"Beaudine."

Pardee said, "If I live another twenty years, it won't matter. I'm already dead."

Bishop had to shift his weight again, but,

with effort, he kept his voice calm and the shotgun aimed at Pardee's chest, "You wanted to know about gold I didn't have. Well, now I want to know something. I'm counting."

"Beaudine's crazy, and I fell in with his gang. That's all it was: us tryin' to eat. Nothin' personal."

"I'm only going to five."

Pardee stammered through tears, giving up a crossroads where Bishop could look for Beaudine, and kill him, if that's what he intended. Pardee even gave his permission.

Bishop said, "You know what retribution is?"

"It means I'm done."

"If you can get off the floor, I'll let you try."

Pardee didn't move. Bishop said, "I'm not a murderer."

"You're a blessed man, Doc. Better than I'll ever be."

Pardee dropped his words as he grabbed Bishop's left hand, and yanked him forward, slashing him with a rifleman's knife he had strapped to his boot. The blade sliced deep, from earlobe to the corner of Bishop's mouth.

Pardee whooped, "How you like that —?!"

Bishop heaved backwards and brought up his right arm in a single motion. Buckshot 'n' fire erupted from the sleeve a second time, rag-dolling Pardee into a stack of empty beer kegs. Wood and bone shattered together, then settled into silence. Pardee's eyes stayed wide and his grip on his pistol never relaxed.

Everybody froze for a moment, and then the talk started, along with nervous laughter. One old boy said something about a "nice killin' " and spit a stream of tobacco juice that spattered a brown halo around Pardee's head.

Bishop waited for someone to try something, but no one bothered. The mutt in the corner wagged his tail and barked his approval. Chaney, the card player, scooped the poker pot into his hat as Bishop took careful steps to the shattered door.

Chaney said, "You blew both barrels."

Bishop jerked his arm, and the shotgun breeched inside the duster, the sleeve tenting the open barrel. Bishop reached inside the sleeve, coming out with two spent shells and dropped them on the floor. He grabbed two fresh from his jacket, and reloaded, before bringing his arm upward in a motion that snapped the barrel shut.

This took moments, with everyone watching, their eyes wide and "goddamns" whispered. Bishop aimed the rig directly at Chaney's gut. Chaney showed his palms. "Hey, nobody gave a shit about Chester, except you."

"You going to bury him?"

Chaney shrugged while winding his watch. "The railroad's probably put up a price."

Chaney said, "Knowing Chester, they're offering the lowest bounty in history."

Outside, the midnight wind stung Bishop as he checked the cinch on his bay, but his one hand was shaking, and his chest pounded. A lot had led up to this, and in a few moments it was over. Well, Pardee was over, but there were still the others. At least now Bishop knew he could go through with it; he had to keep that in his mind, the knowing, no doubts at all. He had to.

His face was sticky with the wash of blood from his sliced cheek, and as Bishop calmed, he started to feel the pain. The batwings creaked, and a few drinkers poked their heads over the doors. The whore moved to Bishop, holding out a lace handkerchief. "It's clean."

Bishop wrapped the handkerchief around his face to soak the bleeding. He felt the girl behind him tying it off and caught her heavy perfume. Bishop thanked her and she

20

nodded before wiping her wet eyes on her sleeve.

The others hung back on Huckie's porch, watching as Bishop hefted himself onto his saddle, again throwing himself wide and keeping the shotgun clear of any tangle. He played it slow for them, settling against the leather, and sliding his double-barreled right arm into the canvas sling.

The bay was ready to run, but Bishop kept the reins tight around his only knuckles, holding her back.

Old Spitter hollered, "Hey! You busted some good bottles killin' that piece of sheep dip! Plus the door, and a couple of chairs!"

Bishop took fifty from his vest and tossed it. "You're going to tell folks about this, right, friend?"

Spitter gum-grinned. "I'll be talkin' about tonight for the next five years, five months, or five days. Dependin' on how much time I got left."

"God only knows, and I'm obliged to you both."

Bishop brought his horse around slow for that last look, and then heeled her. The bay took off toward the blue-black silhouettes of the rising hills, and the high Colorados beyond.

Spitter whistled with gums and two fingers, but Dr. John Bishop didn't hear it. His horse was running strong into the winter night, knowing where to go, even if his mind was taking him someplace else beyond the hurt — maybe back to his wedding day, or the birth of his son.

Behind him, a rider was charging hard to catch up, a Cheyenne war club in their hand.

# CHAPTER TWO: THE FOX

White Fox kept her body low and tight against the painted stallion. They moved as one, racing down the trail, the snow kicking up around them like bursts of brake steam. She grabbed the horse's mane, fingers tangled in wiry brown, and gently pulled. The painted slowed as the path through the trees widened into an easier slope that led to the "town" just below. It was a mule squat for drifters who still had hopes for the played-out silver strike at Cherry Creek — stop for a drink or an ash hauling, and ride on.

But this was where Bishop had to go, so White Fox had to follow.

She pulled up to watch Bishop's silhouette pause outside Huckie's, say something with a roll of his shoulders, and then go in. White Fox dropped from the painted, and walked him around the burned skeleton of an old barn to a water trough thick with ice. She broke the icy surface with a kick and tossed away the pieces.

The painted inspected the trough with his nose, then drank.

While he watered, she scraped packed snow from his hooves with a six-inch blade. She had the feeling everything in this place was dying or dead. Two loud voices from Huckie's stopped her.

White Fox stepped into the moonlight, craning her neck toward Huckie's to hear. A voice she didn't know was yelling about Jesus. Two shotgun blasts followed; that low rumble mixed with those louder cracks that ring in the air and ears.

The painted lurched as the blasts smashed against the hills. White Fox said, *"Nâhtötse,"* close to the stallion's ear, calming him, before swinging herself on his back, and circling around the far side of the barn. She saw Bishop on his bay, talking to the Spitter on the porch. White Fox dug in, and the painted broke into a run, while Bishop rode off without looking back.

The Spitter whistled loud after Bishop, before looking up to see White Fox charging toward him. It was either an image from some kind of holy book or his best damn whiskey dream ever: the beautiful Cheyenne woman, onyx hair spreading behind her, riding out of the night just to take the old man away. White Fox pulled a war club she'd tethered to her belt and held it high.

Spitter closed his eyes and smiled, thinking, *This is a hell of a way to go, and why not?*

White Fox rode close, swinging the club into the skull of the drunk standing next to the Spitter, creasing his head. The drunk fell forward, the revolver in his hand hot-blasting the muddy snow instead of John Bishop's back, where he had been aiming.

Spitter grabbed the pistol for a trophy, and White Fox threw him a stony nod while the painted galloped toward Bishop. Bishop turned at the sound of the shot, just as White Fox rode up next to him, still holding the war club. They rode side by side for a moment, the legs of the painted and the bay falling into sync.

White Fox said, *"Hetómem."*

Bishop spoke through the bloody handkerchief, "He remembered me."

White Fox pointed to the nearest mountains with the club, and broke ahead. Bishop heeled the bay.

The cave was a huge, yawning smile beneath a jagged slope of blue rock, sheeted by snow and protected by daggers of ice formed by the water flowing from up-mountain. Bishop followed the barely-there trail for more than a mile, guided by a small fire White Fox had left burning inside the cave's mouth, its drifting heat melting hanging icicles. Bishop felt comforted by the distant, flickering orange, even as a raw burning raced across his face and down his right half-arm.

The painted was tied to a Rocky Mountain birch, eating fresh snow, when Bishop reached the cave. White Fox stood just inside, waiting to see if he could get down from the bay by himself. He did, a scream jamming the back of his throat. Fresh blood specked Bishop's sleeve and the shotgun barrels. She took a step toward him that he stopped with a raised hand. He nodded that he could beat it, allowing himself a moment to let the throbbing from his arm and face ease with deep, cold breathing. It didn't.

White Fox slipped herself under his shoulder and helped him to the fire. "Bi-shop."

Bishop smiled at the way she said his name, breaking it gently in two, as if each syllable had a spiritual meaning. She eased him onto a blanket on the cave floor, where he stretched out, propping himself on his right elbow, the shotgun rig resting on his knees.

White Fox pulled off the blood-flecked

duster and folded it carefully, before putting more wood on the fire, sparking the flames. She then opened one of the redware jars she'd arranged around the cave, along with bedrolls, a cook pan, a coffeepot, a lot of ammunition, and a small leather satchel that had Bishop's initials stamped on it in gold.

Bishop said, "You're nesting — Jesus!"

He cried out raw as she peeled the pink handkerchief from the drying blood caking his cheek. White Fox tossed the rag, and dabbed the wound with a soft cloth she'd wetted with melted snow. It was cool, and felt good against the damage.

Bishop said, "Stitches. You know how."

White Fox ran her fingers along the inside of the jar, gathering yellow salve. She smeared the mixture on the wound, then cut a piece of yucca in half, opened it flat, and pressed it against Bishop's face.

She took Bishop's left hand to hold the plant in place and he said, "This won't be enough. *Ma'heo'o Ôhvó'komaestse.*"

Bishop got the words out, but White Fox didn't hear them. Her jaw was set, which meant that she would take care of him in her own way; she didn't need white medicine.

She unbuttoned his shirt, and he automatically leaned forward so she could pull the right sleeve free, gathering the rest around the shotgun rig, then slipping it off. The shirt caught on the hammers, and White Fox yanked it.

Bishop swore in Cheyenne, and White Fox gave the back of his head a gentle slap before allowing him a swallow of mescal.

Bare-chested, he leaned to one side, his back toward her, so she could unhook the canvas strap that was tight across his shoulders and connected to the two triggers of the Greener twelve gauge. The strap dug into him, leaving marks like the bite of a whip, and was connected to a looped piece of fabric that ran down his right arm and anchored to the triggers, so that the action of bringing the shotgun up to waist level would pull on the strap, firing either or both barrels.

The bleeding started around the leather cup that was fit to Bishop's right arm just below the elbow joint. It was a standard prosthetic that rebel and union boys now wore as a battle prize, but had been modified to allow the short stock of the Greener to fit where a metal hook would replace the patient's hand. The stock was secured in the cup with small metal bands that joined the shotgun and prosthetic together as one.

White Fox loosened the ties that held the cup tight to Bishop's arm, and pulled the entire rig away, revealing a bleeding stump. More mescal from the heel of the bottle, and Bishop's head lolled back, his hand still holding the yucca against his cheek as she checked the arm for fresh wounds.

He said, "Nothing's opened up?"

She examined the corrupted skin and muscle that was a knot around the bone, and saw that none of the crude surgical scars lacing it together had ruptured. The blood was smeared from small wounds around the elbow, where the amputation point met the healthy rest of the arm. White Fox swabbed away the streaks of wet red.

Bishop said, "It's not setting right, rubbing raw. I know you don't understand everything, but you did a fine job. I'm the doc, but you're the surgeon."

White Fox dressed the wound with salve and wrapped it, saying, "I still am, Bi-shop."

"Not always, not always."

White Fox allowed the corners of her mouth to turn up, as she settled Bishop down on the blanket. A last bit of mescal and he closed his eyes at her touch treating his wounds.

"Where's my medical bag?"

"Close."

Bishop barely opened his eyes to see the small, black leather bag, age-cracked, with LT. BISHOP embossed in flaked gold on one side. It was Bishop's field kit, blood-stained and heavy with instruments. White Fox had arranged it among the other supplies, but knowing that piece of himself hadn't been lost eased Bishop, and he closed his eyes again.

Bishop said, "You take care of me."

White Fox rested the shotgun rig between the medical bag and the stacks of ammunition, all the time watching Bishop as he drifted, his words folding into each other.

"When your husband stabbed you, I sewed you up. And when he broke your arm? You were a good patient."

White Fox treated the slice on Bishop's face with the last of the yucca pulp. His eyes were heavy with sleep coming, but his thoughts were fighting the peace.

"Pardee had never seen anything like me. Nobody had."

Bishop lifted what remained of his right arm to reach out to White Fox, but he couldn't. She touched the side of his face, lightly tapping the pulp onto the wound so it would dry in place.

Bishop said, "I've watched a lot of men die, but I never killed one. Not even in the conflict."

White Fox lay next to Bishop, pulling a blanket over them both, keeping one hand on his chest.

Bishop said, "It felt different than I thought it would."

White Fox understood but didn't react; she just lay next to Bishop, feeling the still-excited, rapid beat of his heart and quietly murmuring his name until his body eased, and he fell, peacefully, asleep.

# CHAPTER THREE:
## DEADEYE

"Death ain't much of a threat."

The Spitter pounded his glass on the counter of the old exchange station for another pour, while Lem "Deadeye" Wright tried to cut through his jabber. "I got no interest in killin' ya, old man."

"You're the ugliest son of a bitch I've ever seen. You tellin' me you never killed nobody?"

"No, I just ain't interested in you. Yet."

Wright rubbed his white-curtained eye, and took in the rest of Huckie's with an exasperated breath. The saloon was now empty, save for the whore, a deaf miner, and the fat-neck behind the bar. Fat-neck poured the drink that separated night from morning, pocketed his cash, said nothing, and wandered off.

The Spitter said, "He took it in the guts right there."

The poker table had been righted, and the

whore was sharing Pardee's chair with the miner, letting his grubby hands absently roam while she dozed. Wright moved to the spread of dried blood on the floor in front of them, then looked to the shattered door, figuring the distance between Pardee and the stranger who had killed him. He could still smell the shotgun's smoke.

Wright said, "I've seen some things, but nothin' like what you're talking about."

Spitter was getting the last of the shot glass as Wright scraped the red-black stain with his toe. Spitter asked, "Want me to tell it again?"

It was damn late, and Wright's patience was running thin, his sightless eye aching him, but he had his task. Wright said, "Just about the fellow with the shotgun. I got the rest."

"He was younger than you, and a damn sight better lookin'."

Wright let it pass. "You said he knew Pardee?"

"Called him by name."

"And the shotgun was under his coat?"

The whore yawned awake and said, "More like it was a part of him."

"So you rode with that sheep dip, he was a friend of yours? Or some kind of kin?"

Wright let the Spitter fix on his dead eye,

and then, "That why you thought I'd kill ya? To revenge Pardee?"

Spitter puffed out his boney chest as far as it would go, coughed, and then said, "It's happened before. I've done it, and I'm ready for your worst."

"Stand down. Pardee was no friend, no kin. But we were supposed to meet up. Where'd you put him?"

Lying with the empty whiskey crates next to Huckie's outhouse seemed as good a place as any for Chester Pardee, who was supported by mounds of packed snow under his head and back, with a small rise beneath his knees to keep his body straight for burying. Ice locked his hands on his chest as if he were praying, while a comforter of new snow covered him, hiding his open wounds and their stains. Someone had grabbed his boots, and his toes were turning from blue to black to match his lips. His eyes were frozen-open blanks.

Spitter said, "At least he'll keep. We don't got no undertaker here."

Wright's teeth were chattering as he tried to pull apart Pardee's fingers, but they wouldn't give. He said, "You could use one. He don't look natural with his hands like that."

"If you're worried about it, leave me

twenty and I'll make sure they burn off a piece of ground, warm it up for diggin', so he can be planted. If you don't, he could be here 'til the spring thaw."

"I ain't worried."

"So what now?"

Lem Wright squinted his good eye and blew a hole in the Spitter's chest, sending him spinning, and spraying Pardee with fresh red. The sound brought the whore to Huckie's back window, but this was her second killing in less than a day, and she hadn't been the one who had taken the bullet, so it didn't matter to her. Not in this place, not this morning.

Wright stood in the blowing snow, with two dead men, as small traces of morning broke apart the night sky. A few minutes, and there was enough light for him to see to go into Pardee's pockets.

The coat was stiff with blood and ice, but Wright found the letter, and held it close to his good eye with just enough new sun behind him to read it.

Except the page was blank.

Wright turned it over, and then he heard Chaney behind him. "You're pretty quick with that Colt, but I'm dead-center on your head."

Chaney was on his horse, new snow spotting his bowler as he aimed down at Wright. Wright took a few steps back, gun holstered, before turning around.

Chaney said, "There's been a lot of blood spilled, my friend."

Lem was calm. "You want some more? I'll accommodate you. You've got a good chance at a dead shot aiming down from that saddle, but all I have to do is take a half-step to the left, and I can put one in your throat before you'll know what happened."

Chaney lowered his gun, just a bit. "You don't have to do that. We can bargain; seems to me there's more than enough gold to go around."

Wright shook his head. "Christ on a busted crutch, you got the letter."

"I'm one of the few in this dog pile who could read it."

"It's a crock."

"Not according to Pardee. He was a hell of a chatterbox when he was at the poker table, so it's a good thing he was cut down, or everybody in the territory would know."

"We got no money, and all Pardee got was a belly full of twelve gauge."

Chaney touched his false tooth with his thumb, as he always did when considering a situation. "Except this Major Beaudine wants to see you about something, and the

36

man with the shotgun wants you dead. When folks get this worked up, it's always about money."

"And you're cuttin' yourself in?"

Chaney found some of his gambler's bravado and said, "Let's call it taking over Pardee's share. Besides, I'm thinking you need somebody to watch your back."

Wright said, "Or shoot me in it?"

"We'll see how it goes."

Wright half-smiled at the thought of killing Chaney right then. He walked around Huckie's and got on his horse, pulling up his collar against a sharp lash of wind from the mountains.

In less than a moment, Lem had pulled his gun and fired, blasting apart the buckle of Chaney's gun belt. Chaney scrambled to grab hold of his holster, steady his gun, and fire back. He managed to do nothing.

Lem still had his Colt out, and said, "Just so you know how things really are. But I might find some use for you if you want to tag along."

Lem turned his horse around, and started for the miles of white that lay between them and Cheyenne. His back was a perfect target, but he never flinched.

After a few minutes, Chaney fell in alongside, his gun belt slung over his saddle, but

37

the pistol within reach. Lem said nothing to him, and neither of them looked back at the dead men lying together in the blood-pink snow, waiting for someone to give a damn.

# CHAPTER FOUR:
# THE MAJOR

Major Beaudine called the young woman by her Christian name, even though she claimed it was something else.

Beaudine said, "Being truly coy is an attractive and vanishing art, Miss Nellie, but you don't have to be that way with me. Certainly not now."

Knowing better, she didn't protest. She would listen, call him "Major," hand him his cooled julep, keep the pipe filled, and then listen more. Sometimes he would pause to emphasize a phrase, looking for a reaction. If she reacted correctly, then he would chuckle because they'd shared a moment. She always tried to react correctly, because she didn't know what would happen if she did not.

Beaudine heard her call him "a man of power."

They would lie together, and he allowed her questions, even when they touched on painful memories. He'd answer them as well as he could, even helping her take notes so she'd have them for her newspaper articles.

Beaudine knew she'd try to be impartial, but lying next to him, her body tangled close, her questions whispered, the best she would be able to tell her editor was that her impression of Major Beaudine was "tainted. In a sweet way."

Beaudine spoke without looking at her. "People don't understand how two such as ourselves could ever be brought together."

"Unlikely, but not unheard of."

"You're a woman of fine character."

"Not all would agree."

"Because you're consorting with the enemy?"

"You're teasing this Pennsylvania girl."

"Victory was yours."

Beaudine heard her quiet laugh as she pressed herself against him and said the words, "The more I know about who you are, the more I'm fascinated."

"I don't want to be another object of curiosity for the unwashed."

"What you tell me in confidence remains so; what you want the world to hear, I'm honored to help you."

Her hands stayed on his shoulders, massaging them, while her breath kissed behind his ear. "Tell me."

Beaudine shut his eyes and said, "I've been torn by conflict; seen too many men die, too much blood. It changes you forever, from what you were."

"What were you before?"

"I recall mopping the floor in a house of ill repute. Can you even dream such a thing? A sensitive lad forced to associate with that kind of society, then becoming a decorated officer, commanding troops in the field? It amazes me still."

Without being asked, she handed Beaudine his bourbon and branch and let him sip. "You've done yourself proud."

"You have to send men to their death. It's a Godlike burden, but I feel I wore it well. Every man in my command snapped to his feet when I approached. Once a young private whose weapon misfired, his eye destroyed, stood to salute me. His head wrapped in bandages, but he had to show that kind of respect. He's with me still."

"You have a quality that your men respond to."

"Only the best. I won't abide a liar or ne'er-do-well. The orders I give come from heart and experience, which is why I expect them to be obeyed. It's for their own good, but I've met the defiant, and taught them

41

this lesson."

"I can't imagine anyone defying you."

"One did. Only one."

Her voice was like distant music to him. "You can tell me if it will lighten your heart."

Beaudine allowed himself another cool sip. "It was a man who had committed a crime and had never been brought to justice. I'd been entrusted to see that he paid for his wrongdoing, but he defied me. Wouldn't acknowledge the wrong, and put his family in harm's way. Disgusting."

"What did you do?"

"I took a part of him. It was important that he bleed, hover near death, so he could reflect on his circumstances, and how he brought it all on himself."

Beaudine said that the first shots fired were like thunder claps in the dining room, and had to be shouted over to restore order. His men obeyed commands, dragging John Bishop and his family outside, and waited in the snow for his next instruction. It filled his chest, that power. He remembered stepping on a crystal flute that had fallen to the floor, he could still feel it under his feet, and thought what good taste Mrs. Bishop obviously had.

Beaudine had complimented her, even as

she was dying, "I don't know if she heard me, but if I had been in that home for another purpose, we would have had a lovely talk, I'm sure."

"What was your purpose that night?"

Beaudine said nothing about the liberated gold bars, but only spoke of the weight of punishment, the cleaver in his hand, and the force greater than himself that had brought it down on John Bishop more than once, separating him from his right arm.

Beaudine said, "I admit I let loose the beast."

"Did this Bishop die?"

"He met his god that night, yes."

Widow Kate pounded on the door with bear-size fists until it swung open. She came in, coughing back dust-thick air and trying to clear her painted eyes, "Beaudine, you've been doing a damn poor job of clock watchin'. Find your pants."

Beaudine was sitting on the edge of the cot, its knotted-rope center giving way, his eyes fixed on the pages of the Sears catalog that papered the slat walls and ceiling of the room. Ads for lady's corsets and iceboxes for a fair price surrounded him, their edges curling yellow. There were no windows in this place, just an opening for a stovepipe, and the only light came from a small oil lamp that smoked acrid brown.

Beaudine said, "I've asked that you refer to me by my officer's status."

Kate snorted. "I'm not playing games with you. This place is a trash pile."

A bourbon bottle, neck snapped off, lay empty by his feet, which were laced with blood from stepping on the broken glass. Behind him, a redhead of some age was curled into a corner, her stained nightshirt bunched around her. She didn't utter a sound through her frozen smile.

Beaudine said to Kate, "Madame, do you think I owe you an apology?"

"Forty more dollars. At least."

"Speaking of money in front of a lady like Miss Bly is a true insult. You've interrupted us. Miss Bly and I were having an interview for an Eastern newspaper. She's come a very long way to talk to me, and she deserves my full attention."

"Nellie Bly again, huh?"

The redhead sucked her thumb, while playing with her curls with her other hand. Her eyes were vacant spaces in her wide-white face, and she giggled when Kate asked her if she was hurt.

Widow Kate said, "Whatever he did, you didn't feel it. How much laudanum did you soak?"

The redhead came back with a blank grin.

Beaudine said, "If you leave us now, you won't incur my wrath. We have important work yet to do."

"Where the hell do you think you are?"

"The sanitarium at Milledgeville. And again, please show respect for my rank."

Widow Kate held back a slap and said, "You're in the attic of my house, *Major*! With one of my public girls. You got that?"

There was a moment of thought, and then Beaudine met her glare, saying, "This hospital, and the way you treat a decorated Confederate officer, is a disgrace, and Miss Bly is here to expose these conditions. When her articles appear, there will be a clean sweeping, including you, Madame."

"At least you got that right."

Widow Kate put one of her giant hands on the redhead's face, gently wiping her nose with her thumb. "Look at me, honey. Anything happen that I should charge extra for?"

The redhead settled for a moment with her thoughts. "No. He just talked like a genteel man — and I didn't say nothin' at all. He'd ask a question, and then answer it his own self. Carried on like he was two people."

Her words slurred together, but she made

a point of saying "genteel," and was proud of the choice, before slumping back into the corner of her own world.

"So just the forty." Kate turned to Beaudine. "You're crazier than a shit-house rat. How'd they ever let you out of anywhere?"

Beaudine covered his face with his palms. "You're pressing me to an edge. Madame, you do not want to incur my wrath."

Widow Kate grabbed Beaudine's uniform jacket from a hanging peg. "That goes both ways. Downstairs. You know what happens when you owe the house."

"When my release is secured, my men will be coming for me."

"We'll wait downstairs for them, and if they bring cash, they're as welcome as spring."

Widow Kate held up the grey tunic, seeing that it was pieces of two or three Confederate uniforms of different rank sewn together. The brass buttons across the front were mismatched, and the epaulets looked to be an afterthought. Blood spatter stained one side.

Widow Kate said, "Honey, you need someone who knows what they're doing to take of this. You want to appear your best, don't you?"

Beaudine looked at Kate with calm eyes,

46

"That's part of my battle dress. Every spot of blood is a badge of honor."

Kate took a Bowie knife from the inside pocket before handing back the tunic. She said, "I'll put this in the office with your guns, and they'll stay safe, until you get right with the house."

"You're putting me in jeopardy, Madame. How am I to properly defend Miss Bly and myself?"

Kate took Beaudine's hand, her palm smothering his. "Against what, Major? Against what?"

Beaudine said, "The traitorous enemies who're plotting against us."

The trickle of water from the morning-melted snow laced along the bites of the cave roof, before finding a place just above John Bishop's head, where it rained into his mouth. Bishop leaned back, took a drink, and then stepped away from the cave wall, all the time holding his right half-arm in front of him as an exercise.

Two pieces of heavy scrap iron were laced together with a leather thong, where White Fox had tied them to his arm, just below the elbow joint. The pieces dangled free, clanking together with every move. Bishop strained. The leather gutted tight, as he lifted the weights with the small section of arm that Beaudine had allowed he could keep.

Bishop straightened his elbow, fighting the iron as if he were leveling the shotgun. "You counting?"

White Fox gave her answer with her deep, black eyes: she was.

Bishop lifted again, drawing his arm as close as he could to his shoulder. He lowered it slowly, stopping waist-high and holding. He stole another drink from the ceiling.

White Fox said, "Too much water."

"Who's the doctor, huh?"

She settled cross-legged between the ammunition and medical supplies, wiping the dried blood from inside the leather cup that held the shotgun rig. She soaped the cup, kneading it with her fingers, before folding a small piece of tanned deerskin around the edges. She put her hand inside the rig, gauging its comfort, while keeping a watch on Bishop. Always keeping watch.

Sweat beaded his face, as he held out the scrap iron, his body shaking. Finally, he exploded, "God almighty!"

Bishop and the iron banged to the cave floor. White Fox moved to him, untying the leather thong with a quick pull, releasing the weights.

White Fox smiled and said, *"Koké'ahe."*

Bishop leaned back, catching the stream from above, "I thought my arm was going to come off, 'least what I have left."

"Beaudine is with you."

"Always."

*"O'osó."*

"I'm not wrong. The bastard's the reason we're here." Bishop smiled. "Amaryllis'd be so angry that I cussed."

Bishop took a small mirror from his field kit and examined the deep slice on his face, which was now purple with healing. He said, "He cut everything I had to pieces."

White Fox stood, opening her blouse to reveal a scar that snaked from the edge of her rib cage to just above the curve of her right hip. The raised tissue was ten inches long and a quarter of an inch wide, with the jagged pattern of sutures now flesh-permanent. She ran her fingers over the area, which was still dead to the touch.

Bishop said, "I did a sloppy job there."

"You saved me."

"But that's the reminder of your husband and that night. You can't forget."

*"Tóxetanó?"*

"You haven't taught me that one."

"Good memory — what makes you sing.

49

Bad memories are a fog."

Bishop shook his head. "You act like you don't understand," he said, then held out his right while White Fox fitted the shotgun rig onto him.

"I killed a man last night and I'm ready to go after a hell of a lot more. A year ago such a thing would have been unthinkable. Everything's changed."

"Not changed, changing."

With the deerskin lining, the cup fit snugly over Bishop's arm, cradling it instead of rubbing it raw. He leaned forward without being asked, as White Fox fastened the straps across his shoulders before tightening the slack of the line to the shotgun triggers. The rig felt good this time.

White Fox said, "You're not clear. Not yet."

Bishop would have started his old argument, but stopped when White Fox pressed her hand against the back of his neck, just two fingers squeezing, as a signal. He turned as she tilted her head in the direction of the cave entrance, listening.

The wind outside was a low whistle, but someone's words were carried on it, and then lost. They sounded close, though. Bishop thought he heard the nickering of several horses; White Fox was sure.

She leapt to her bedroll, lifted the blanket, and grabbed her short bow and beaded quiver, which she slung over her shoulder. She moved along the cave wall, staying on the balls of her feet as she worked her way to a small outcropping of rock by the entrance. The quiver was tight with arrows as she pulled one, fitted it to the bow, and drew back, waiting.

She threw Bishop a nod; the look told him there was no more time for doubt.

Bishop understood. "Maybe I should forget about Beaudine, my brother, all of it." He spoke loudly enough for his voice to echo through the cave, and to cover the sound of his dropping two shells into the Greener, locking the double barrel.

Bishop stood, bringing the weapon up. "That is the best way to find peace."

He moved his shoulders, adjusting the strap to tighten the slack on the line to the two triggers. He started for the cave entrance, then planted his feet, with the rig waist-high. Whoever was outside was sure to see him.

White Fox approved with a blink of her eyes, keeping her bow and breathing tight.

There was more low speaking from outside, and a few heartbeats. Bow and triggers were ready, when a ragtag soldier charged the cave entrance, brandishing a torch in one hand and a Navy Six in the other.

Ragtag screamed, "Welcome to Hell!"

White Fox let go, and the arrow tore through Ragtag's jawbone, shredding his cheek. His scream choked into a gurgle.

# CHAPTER FIVE:
# DEAD MAN

Just ten minutes earlier, and Captain Creed brought his tall chestnut around to face the men riding with him. He threw an arm toward the cave. "Bishop's hole up with that dog-eater. I can smell 'em. Earn your pay."

Ragtag, in Union blues, grabbed Creed's reins to lead him to a small slope, just to the side of where the cave split the mountain face. Creed kicked at Ragtag from his stirrup, keeping his voice low. "*Their* horses!"

Ragtag quick-stepped to the tree where the painted and the bay were tied, while Creed's other men cleared the snow in four small areas about ten feet from the cave entrance. They worked in joined silence, their leathered faces covered by rough wool scarves and with collars turned up. Ragtag led the painted and bay away, the horses nickering.

It was a bright, clear morning with no warmth to be felt, just bitter cold, even as the sun threw diamonds off the snow and ice. This was the kind of February that had strangled everything on Creed's place, with no hope of resurrection in the spring. But Creed didn't blame the weather or the Almighty for his plight; he blamed the man in the mountain.

Creed eased back on the cantle of his hand-tooled saddle, taking off his amber-lens glasses to rub his sightless eyes and saying to no one, "I know this country just by its feel."

One of the men, with a Colt double-action pistol tucked in a belt loop, moved to Creed quietly. "We got her the way you wanted."

Creed responded, "You better."

The man with the Colt whistled a blue-bird's song, and two others cut a bulging canvas sack from the back of a horse, and hauled it over. They slit the sack as they would a hog's belly, then pulled out a scorched red, white, and blue flag of the Tennessee Volunteers.

The burned tatters were held with respect, even as others were yanked from the canvas one after another: shredded sections of the Stars and Bars; the Georgia "Cummins White Cross," with its field of red now torn in half; bloody shreds that had once been infantry banners.

Creed said, "Whatever you've got, bring it here."

Colt unfurled a dark blue flag that had been punched with bullet holes, and held it up to Creed, who ran his fingers across the large white star in its center.

"Bonnie Blue."

"You don't have to do this, sir. We can cut some branches."

Creed said, "Burn them."

His men heaped the battle colors and banners onto the cleared areas of frozen ground. Jugs of kerosene were tossed from a pack mule, and the fuel was poured over the piles of torn cloth. The air bent with the smell of the kerosene, and the men fought their hacks. A boy choked and spit. The last bit of fuel was dribbled onto the old flags, but the men said nothing as they looked to Creed for his reaction. Colt almost spoke, but held back.

Creed adjusted his glasses, pushing them up on a nose that had been deformed by frostbite, and finally said, "At your ready." Colt lit a torch, then passed the flame to the others as they checked their weapons. A fat gut with a plaid kerchief, who'd always crowed that he was Creed's cousin, pumped a shell into the chamber of a Winchester and took position to the side of the others.

Ragtag almost danced in place, ready for Creed to give the signal.

Creed waited, his blind eyes fixed on a memory, and then he ran his hand across his grey beard, lightly tugging on his chin.

That was it. A torch was put to the fuel, the flames sputtering in the chill before catching and racing along the kerosene trail to each pile of flags. They burst into flames.

Fat Gut, his stomach sucked in, shouldered his rifle while the rest of Creed's men stood as a firing squad, pistols aimed at the cave.

Creed said, "Bring him to me."

Ragtag threw his head back with a wild howl, before charging the cave, a Navy Six in one hand and a torch in the other, screaming, "Welcome to Hell!"

Ragtag's cry was cut dead short. Then, the echo of him from the cave died, and there was no sound from anywhere except for the sizzling of the kerosene pools.

Creed backed his tall horse a few steps, which was the cue for his men to move away from the flames, but to keep their guns aimed beyond them, into the cave's mouth. Fat Gut let out his breath and then dropped to one knee, his Winchester steady on some shadowed movement.

Creed called out, "Dr. John Bishop, this is

Captain Dupont Creed! Don't come out? You're going to roast alive! I don't give a rat's ass about the squaw. She can cook."

Inside the cave, the growing flames kept John Bishop and White Fox low against the outcropping of rock that offered protection. Ragtag had hold of Bishop's ankle and tried to speak without a jaw. His words were sloppy nothing, as he swallowed hot smoke and the blood that wasn't pooling around him.

White Fox readied her second arrow.

Ragtag's fingers opened slowly around Bishop's ankle. Bishop reached down for him as if to help; it was a doctor's instinct to give aid, even as Ragtag tried to aim his Navy Six at Bishop's face, but couldn't.

White Fox said, *"Nâhtötse."*

Bishop knew the meaning and pulled back his feelings. Ragtag made a final sound with his tongue and his eyes stilled, as Bishop stepped over him and braced himself against a small rock shelf. He extended his right-arm rig toward the growing flames blocking the cave entrance.

The heat hard-slapped Bishop, but he found his first target behind the moving curtain of fire: It was the man with the double-action Colt, his dark shirt outlining him against the hot orange-white.

Bishop took aim, bringing his shoulders together to tighten the slack on the trigger line. It was a natural movement now, and the rig was feeling right to him. He glanced back at White Fox, who lowered her bow barely a quarter inch. Smoke from the burning flags sanded her eyes, but she would not blink.

Creed shouted, "John Bishop! It's been twelve years, and you know goddamn well —"

Bishop pulled the trigger-line with his shoulders, blasting through the fire to the man with the Colt and knocking him back onto a mound of snow, where he lay holding his pouring stomach.

Creed's men opened up.

The bullets screamed into the cave, sparking off the walls, spitting rock and ice with each hit. Their echo brought each ricochet back twenty times, piercing the ears.

A slug tore by White Fox's face as she released her arrow steady, hitting one of Creed's men in the throat, sending him spinning into a fire pile. The kerosene-soaked flags pasted themselves to his flesh, instantly swallowing his head and shoulders in flames, killing his cries for help.

Bishop swung the rig to the other side of

the cave opening and fired again, blowing apart the shoulder of a crouching hired gun before White Fox's arrow punctured his eye. Hired Gun flopped onto Fat Gut, who threw him aside, and racked off four rounds from his Winchester.

Fat Gut's voice was a banshee's scream, and louder than the shots he fired. A flaming arrow whipped into his leg just above the knee, opening a red geyser. His scream became a sob.

Creed shouted, "You're gonna taste hell now or later, Bishop! Your choice!"

The layer of thickening smoke tied Bishop and White Fox to the cave floor, wet with blood and melting ice, even as she let fly another arrow at Creed's men, splitting the flames.

In response, muzzle flashes could be seen through the heat and choking grey. Again, the slugs careened from stone wall to jagged ceiling, and back again. Bits of lead splintered into White Fox's back and creased Bishop's thigh. Neither cried out.

Bishop stayed on his back, cooling the shotgun barrels with a handful of snow, before breaching them. The smoke from the fires was heavier now, churning the air in the cave from grey to black, as Bishop fumbled for his twelve-gauge shells. He reloaded, his tears stinging him, then snapped the rig shut, his chest heaving. He fired both barrels toward the cave's mouth.

There was no specific target, nothing Bishop could see. Someone cried out. Bishop's eyes were lost to their whites as his throat seized, strangled by the heavy smoke.

White Fox scrambled to him, turning Bishop on his back and opening his mouth with her fingers, when the lasso dropped around her neck from behind, and was pulled tight.

White Fox spit, *"Mé'anéka'êškóne!"*

A yank on the rope silenced her.

# CHAPTER SIX:
# BLOOD AND TRUST

Chaney could feel Lem Wright watching him from his spot a few paces behind him. They'd been riding all night, guided by a bright winter moon, and Lem had slowed his horse, letting Chaney get farther ahead but keeping steady behind him, like he was planning an ambush. Instead, Lem did nothing; even if he wasn't going to make a move, Chaney hated his watching.

He'd tied his gun belt together with a small piece of rope, so at least his holster was back on his hip, but it kept slipping and this compromise to his draw edged his nerves. Chaney pushed on, trying not to ponder it, but he was the one who was supposed to have the winning hand, holding all the cards. Somewhere he'd lost his advantage.

Dawn broke in streaks of orange as the horses angled down the small, snowy grade to the road that led directly to the Overland

Trail. Chaney looked over his shoulder to see Lem dozing in the saddle, his curtained eye locked open as he slept. The reins were slack in Lem's hands, but his chestnut mare followed Chaney without prodding, while the eye did its job watching. Always watching.

The eye looked back at Chaney from behind its white film, darting on its own as Lem started to snore. Chaney turned away with a shudder, wishing he had a decent bottle to kill the queasy feeling. He swore like he was praying, getting up his nerve to try something, but brought his thoughts back to Major Beaudine's letter and its life-changing promise.

Chaney thought, *Hell, I know where to go; I don't need that ugly son of a bitch at all.*

Suddenly, Lem was riding beside him and yawning. "You could've shot me and left me in a drift. One good snow and they wouldn't find me for three months."

"That's not what was in my mind."

"Sure it was, but you couldn't tell if I was sleeping. I can't see out of this damn thing, but it does have its uses."

"You were snoring."

"And you still didn't make a move."

Lem's statement was just a fact, said in a flat way that hit Chaney in his guts. He was losing his bluff. Chaney brushed the snow from the rim of his bowler, and said, "I thought we were trying a partnership."

"Oh, building trust so the other fella doesn't know he's being suckered."

Chaney said, "I know you ain't no sucker, Mr. Wright. You made that mighty clear."

"Glad to hear it. So who'd you sucker to get that fine Denver saddle?"

Chaney straightened. "Barbed wire salesman from Jackson Hole. It never ceases to amaze me what folks will chance when they're sure they have a winning hand."

Lem shook the ice around in his canteen, considering something, before taking a drink to wake up. "And they never know you're beating them until it's too late?"

"That's how I eat."

"Not lately. I know broke when I see it."

Chaney said, "Like most of the country. So why'd you come to that dog pile? To team up with Pardee, or kill him?"

"I hadn't decided."

"I was gonna blow his guts out, take his stake."

"But the man with the shotgun got there first."

Chaney tried a push, asking, "The man you know?"

Lem said, "He was just a fella Beaudine

told us about."

"Holding a chest full of Army gold?"

"You read the letter, you talked to Chester."

Chaney said, "I surely did."

Lem's voice dropped. "Then what the hell you asking me for?"

"To see if Pardee was bluffing; he'd always try to bullshit his way out of a hand. So he was telling the truth about the gold."

Lem gave Chaney a dose of his eye, "None of us will know a damn thing until we get to Cheyenne; that's the point, ain't it?"

Chaney flicked his tooth with this thumb, figuring the best way for the conversation to go. "There's a pot on the table? I'll try for it, but I know the odds of catching a bullet instead. Like I said, you made that real clear."

This was good enough for Lem, who handed Chaney his canteen. The ice-cold metal numbed Chaney's fingertips, but the water tasted good and clean going down. Chaney knew enough not to drink too much, or else he'd cramp up. He handed the canteen back to Lem, in case that was his plan.

Chaney said, "Tell me about Beaudine."

Lem didn't respond, so Chaney tried, "Did you meet in the war? That what happened to your eye?"

"My eye was lost during a conflict. I'll let Beaudine tell ya the rest, if he's of a mind."

"Pardee said you all came together at the territorial prison on the Wyoming border. That nobody in Beaudine's Raiders ever did no military service, 'cause you were all locked up."

Lem pulled his horse to a near stop, and Chaney knew he'd overplayed his hand. "You ask questions you think you know the answers to; that's clever, but not too smart."

"You said Pardee was full of shit, but maybe not this time."

"I know what I said."

Lem put a period at the end of his statement, allowing that they'd ride in silence for a while. Lem kept his hand on his pistol the next few miles, forcing Chaney to do the same. Chaney's fingers ached, and he jumped every time Lem made the slightest move, which is just what Deadeye wanted.

The road widened, and their horses stepped around the ruts left behind by a thousand wagons meeting the Overland. Ghosts of schooner canvas, bits of wagon tongues, and shattered wheels lay frozen in the blue-black ditch that ran beside the road these last miles into Wyoming. The pieces reminded Chaney of grave markers.

The two continued riding without speaking, although Chaney kept clearing his throat. Lem offered no more water.

After an hour, Lem noticed his first Wyoming cottonwood, standing bare against the grey sky, and said, "That man with the shotgun?"

Chaney coughed, and said, "What about him?"

"At Huckie's, he let you go. But now you're with me, so next time, he's going to cut you in half, which'll give me a chance. Thanks, partner."

Chaney mumbled something. He'd bought into this game and now was wishing he was out of it. He should be someplace like Kansas City, holding a middling hand, bluffing his way to a small pot to cover his hotel and drinks. That was what he knew, what he liked. Not these stakes.

But there was still the chance at the treasure — more damn money than he'd ever know. Who could give that up?

Chaney couldn't help himself, and glanced over his shoulder to see who might be riding up from behind, maybe with a shotgun sling on their saddle. Lem couldn't help himself, and laughed like hell.

# CHAPTER SEVEN:
# BROTHERS IN BLOOD

White Fox twisted, angling her back to the flames as she was dragged through the burning kerosene pool, the rawhide lasso biting her throat. She tucked her muscular legs in, bending at the knee, and then sprung forward with all of her strength, pushing herself closer to the two cowboys who were pulling her, forcing their line to slack.

She could hear Creed's voice above the shouts and cries of his men. "You've done well! Tend the wounded, then take a moment to enjoy victory."

The rawhide loosened, and White Fox clawed, pulling it over her head as Creed's men bulldogged her around the waist before tossing her into a small, slushy snow bank away from the cave's mouth.

"You ain't goin' no place, *nésé'kêhá'e*!"

White Fox's neck whipped against the frozen ground as she rolled into the snow, keeping her face away from Creed's men. Her long black hair shielded her movement as she turned her head just enough to see everything in that moment when the shooting finally stops — pools of fire and blood, hired killers lying wounded, and others dead.

She wasn't yet twenty-five, and couldn't count how many like these she'd left bleeding.

Creed brought his horse a few steps closer to the cave's mouth; smoke poured from it like a grey scream. His men kicked snow onto the still-burning flag piles while, feet away, another died with his buckshot-ripped stomach pouring through his fingers. Nobody gave their dead amigo a glance, even as they stepped over him.

Creed used his saddle as a pulpit, calling out to his flock, "You've earned your pay and my respect, but remember why we're here!"

Someone said, "Long as we get ours."

Creed adjusted his glasses and said to anyone close, "Did the dog-eater survive?"

The one with the lariat said, "Squirrelly as hell and took some of yours with her. Turn your head, you can spit in her face."

"That won't be necessary."

White Fox raised her eyes, meeting Lariat,

who thought he was clever misusing "bitch" in Cheyenne. Wobbly on his feet, he was coiling the rawhide, red spreading from the wound he'd gotten above the knee. His hands were shaking, and his smell stung her nose.

Creed said, "Where's the prisoner? Where's Dr. John Bishop?"

Lariat said, "Close."

Lariat smiled toothlessly, cocking his head toward Bishop, who was lying in the snow beneath the Rocky Mountain birch where the painted and the bay had been tied.

White Fox saw that Bishop's right arm was almost behind his head, with the double-barrels of the rig leveled naturally at his temple, so that if he moved his shoulders hardly an inch, the triggers would be pulled.

But he wasn't moving, at all.

White Fox couldn't help whispering, "Bishop."

As if in response, Fat Gut bellowed, White Fox's arrow still protruding from his leg. He grabbed his Winchester and aimed it at her, pumping off an empty chamber, and then bellowed some more, because she refused to react.

Instead, White Fox kept her eyes on Bishop, waiting for him to stir, or speak. There was nothing. For a moment, she felt

relief that the rig wouldn't go off acciden-
tally, and then fear that Bishop was still as
death. Her hands stayed around her neck,
massaging the feeling back into it, but ready
to grab the next lariat they tried to slip over
her or a knife from the boot of one of the
*mé'anéka'êškónes,* if he got close enough.
She counted how many of Creed's "bastard
sons" were left, and figured which ones to
kill to get to Bishop and a horse.

Lariat checked the pockets of the dead for
cash, pried guns from their hands, and
inspected their boots, yanking off two pair
that caught his fancy. He kicked at Bishop's
boots, waiting for White Fox's reaction
before throwing his head back in a Georgia
howl.

That's when Bishop's left hand moved,
barely making a fist. Barely.

White Fox saw his fingers closing, and
drew herself in, muscles tightening. She
thought Bishop had murmured something,
his lips just parting, forming a word. She
couldn't hear him, but watched for another
sign of life, while slipping both arms out of
her buckskin jacket without notice. She sat
up, arms out of the sleeves, palms flat
against the ground, ready to spring.

Creed called, "Where's the boy?"

The youngest of the bunch, all straw-white

hair sprouting over a wide face, ran from the cave and dumped Bishop's field medic kit, blanket, and some ammo onto the wet ground in front of Creed.

Smoke from the fire smeared him, and he coughed, "Right in front of you, sir."

"Ragtag?"

"They really killed him, sir. I never seen worse."

"What did you find?"

"There weren't no gold, but I think I got the valuables you wanted."

Creed looked down from his mount, sensing the boy's expression. "You're a good man, follow orders. You understand this is about a lot more than money."

Lariat yelled, "What about this fancy gun rig?"

Creed said, "Bring it to me."

White Fox watched Lariat draw a blade and crouch next to Bishop. Blood soaked his pant leg and the knife wasn't steady as Lariat cut through the straps holding the shotgun in place. White Fox bit her lip as the trigger lines caught on the knife before being sliced. First one, and then the other; Lariat hadn't checked the breach and didn't know what the hell he was fooling with. He yanked Bishop forward roughly, his head lolling, before pulling the rig away from his

71

half-arm.

Bishop flopped back onto the ground, as Lariat struggled to his feet, pockets bulging with the other guns he'd stolen, holding his shotgun trophy in the air.

Lariat was weaving when he crowed, "Bastard won't be usin' this again!"

The buckshot wound was bleeding Lariat dry, and he managed a few steps before his leg gave way, dropping him dead. The shotgun fired, blasting the rotting top of a tree stump. Creed's men ducked.

White Fox sprang from the snow bank in a burst of ice 'n' white, as she leapt for Bishop's leather medical bag. Her moves were whip-fast, her body a blur, as she grabbed the bag, swinging it wide to smash one of Creed's men in the temple with its hard corner. Dazed, he stumbled backwards, even as she took two gigantic strides toward Bishop. Pure grace and speed.

Creed shouted, "Tell me what's happening!"

White Fox jumped over Lariat, grabbing one of the stray pistols around him. She turned about, and dropped to one knee, leveling the Colt on Creed.

The boy said, "Sir, she's set to kill you."

One of the men said, "Ride like hell, Cap'n. We'll punch ten holes in the bitch before she gets off a shot."

"I might be blind, but I know our dead belong to her. Nobody makes a move, unless you want to join them."

Creed let his words echo for a moment, before calling out to White Fox, "You think you're going to get out of this? You're not. Savvy?"

White Fox stood, her skirt torn almost to the waist, the gun perfectly leveled from her naked hip. Blood and melted snow had pasted the shreds of her blouse to her body, outlining her flat belly and the curve of her breasts.

Creed's men traded snickers and made gestures, shrugging off how many of their own she and Bishop had just killed.

White Fox let the fools be fools. "Bi-shop is mine."

Creed said, "You're both my prisoners. I know you understand."

White Fox took two steps to the side and one of the men fired. The shot ripped the mud at her feet, but she only turned and knelt by Bishop, dumping his medical bag. One of Bishop's eyes opened.

Creed said, "Is she hit?"

The boy said to Creed, "No sir, didn't even flinch. She's doin' somethin' to the prisoner, like a doctor would."

Creed wiped the grit from his eyes. "I wonder if she'll leave him blind."

Creed heard one of his men cock a hammer. "The next man that shoots without my order'll be executed! We came for prisoners, not corpses."

The device White Fox placed on Bishop's face was made of yellow celluloid shaped like the breast of a rooster, and it fit snugly over his mouth and nose, sealing them. The mask was attached by rubber tubing to a small brass and wooden cube, with a music-box-style cranking mechanism on its side. She attached a small leather bellows to a nozzle on the side of the cube, and cranked the handle, expanding the bellows and pumping air through the cube and into the mask.

Bishop's eyes struggled, the lids sticky with soot, as his lungs heaved, and he spit charcoal-streaked phlegm into the mask. She reversed the crank, drawing the fluid out of the mask, then pressed the bellows to force air in.

One of Creed's men said, "That's a long way 'round just to kill somebody."

Creed said, "You're a fool."

More brackish fluid erupted from Bishop's mouth as White Fox worked the small machine, until Bishop's lungs swelled with new air and released. White Fox tore the mask away, and pushed hard on his chest, forcing out the pockets of smoke still trapped inside him.

The boy said, "I've never seen no miracle before."

Creed kept his head locked toward Bishop and White Fox as if he could see them, and said, "This is no miracle, boy."

Blood sprinkled Bishop's chin as his chest racked. White Fox pulled him forward, and wrapped her arms around him and clamped them together in a fist in the center of his back. She yanked her arms inward, forcing more smoke from his lungs.

Bishop gulped for air, struggling for breath, his lungs burning.

White Fox called, "Water!"

Fat Gut screamed out, "They almost killed me, Cousin! Why the hell you helpin' 'em?!"

Creed said, "Because we're not finished."

Creed handed the canteen from his saddle to the boy. "Give him all he wants."

"Yes, sir."

The boy tried a salute, his hand tangling in his stalks, before taking the canteen. He hitched up his tattered pants and stepped around two bodies, trying not to look at the faces with mouths and eyes locked open.

He stopped a few feet away from White Fox, before looking around at Creed's men, their guns aimed right at him. A couple of them were smiling.

The only sound was the hack ripping from Bishop's chest.

Creed said, "Give him the water!"

White Fox snatched the canteen from his hands. "Hold him."

The boy slipped an arm around Bishop, propping him up. "I swallowed some smoke in the cave myself. It's god-awful."

Bishop drank, coughed, drank some more. He looked to White Fox, managing, *"Eamet-anéné."*

# CHAPTER EIGHT:
## COFFIN MAN

Resurrection, Wyoming, was the kind of place that Chaney loved and Lem Wright hated. It was a new border town, being built from the mud up. For Chaney, that meant rail workers and teamsters who could be stupid-drunk with their pay, and ladies who had set themselves up to take as much as they could.

Fresh-cut lumber, glass, and wet paint were everywhere you looked, and the air was full of the noise of saws, men, and working animals. To Chaney, it was music: the sound of cash being made.

But for Lem Wright, Resurrection was something blank, with no tradition or history. The kind of place "that might be something someday," but wasn't yet, and likely he wouldn't live to see it. New places reminded him of his own mortality.

So it was all right that Lem and Chaney guided their horses past the freshly painted porch of a feed store, to Gutterson's Funeral Parlor. The name was scrolled on the front window, with a discreet crucifix and Jewish star tiny in the corner of the glass.

Lem tied his horse and went for a close look at the symbols. "Wonder who buries the Chinamen?"

The window, backed by purple drapery, bloated Lem's face, but was kind to his wandering eye.

Three old women in mourning black stepped from Gutterson's, and Lem moved aside, taking off his hat in elaborate fashion, and half-bowing his head. One of the women was crying, with the other two at her elbow, offering comfort.

The crying woman stared at Lem's face long enough to get out some words. "My Edward was injured in the war, too. Thank you for your brave sacrifice."

"You're welcome, ma'am."

She began sobbing again, guided off by the other two. Chaney watched all this, flicking his tooth with his thumb, thinking what he could do with a widow's bank account, when Lem's voice snapped him back. "Ready to take care of some business?"

Chaney joined Lem by the front door. "Haven't said a damn word in four hours. I got distracted."

"I've been deciding if we should stop or not."

Chaney slipped his hand inside his jacket, an obvious move for a weapon, before asking, "Why this place?"

"So you can meet another one of your partners."

Lem opened the door to the funeral parlor, gesturing for Chaney to proceed. Chaney held back, keeping his hand out of sight, ready to draw. Their words were steam in the air.

The pretense meant nothing to Lem. "Your gun belt's comin' apart, partner. Better take care of that."

"In case I haven't told you, thanks for your brave sacrifice."

Lem stored his response for later. Chaney kicked the snow from his boots before going in.

The sun sliced the dark of Gutterson's in long slivers, landing against a small wooden pew, a rude coffin set up on a pair of saw horses, and paper flowers knitted into a wreath. What Chaney could make out in the rest of the room was unfinished: bare walls waiting for paint, against which there were two new rugs neatly rolled, floor planking, and some nail kegs. Ten raw coffin lids were stacked against the opposite wall, with prices scrawled on each. The prices had been crossed out several times, replaced by higher ones.

Lem said, "Howard! Show your worthless ass!"

The response was a dog barking up the street. Lem started for a small door at the back of the parlor, with Chaney following. Chaney regarded the empty pews and coffin, and Lem said, "That's what you have to look forward to." He continued into the backroom, adding, "Me too."

The back room was less finished than the rest of the place, with tools, scrap wood, and several bodies lying in rows on the dirt floor. The bodies were wrapped in heavy cloth, with lengths of rope securing the necks, arms, and feet like so much packed meat.

There was a slapped-together box in the middle of the floor, with a man laid out inside, his huge arms folded on his chest. His mouth was smothered by a drooping moustache that laced into muttonchops along his jowls, covering most of his pitted face.

Lem Wright looked into the box, which was just slightly smaller than a piano crate, then turned to Chaney. "You know a dead man can still break wind?"

The man in the coffin sat up. "You want me to show ya?"

"I think you already did. Jesus, Howard."

Howard said, "Those boys are just going a little ripe. Get me the hell out of here."

"You could stuff a family in that thing."

"All of them, or maybe just me."

Howard held out his tree-trunk arms, as Lem shouldered him from the crate. Lem bellowed in pain as Howard's weight almost pushed him to the floor. Howard swung his legs over the side, with Chaney steadying it as best he could. The wood buckled.

"Jesus is crying, hurry up!"

A couple of bent nails tore into Chaney's hand, prompting Howard to say, "I ain't much of a carpenter."

Lem said, "Then what the hell are you doing here?"

"There's so many killin's, with all the crews comin' in. The coolies and the Micks and the Jews all want a piece of each other. Old man Gutterson can't keep up, so he hired me on."

Chaney regarded Howard's work, sucking the blood from his thumb and forefinger. "A gunny'd be nicer."

"Pulled up the floor for the boards, got a stack of bags for when we run out. One more team of railroad men, and we're good for at least five shootings. That's money, man. I gotta finish this one and two more before tomorrow."

"What about those fellas?"

Howard nodded toward the five on the floor. "Teamsters got ambushed outside of town. Nobody's claimed 'em, so we'll dump in the same hole. I'll give ya each ten if you help me dig it."

Lem said, "Sounds like you're doing all right."

Howard held up a pair of iron pliers and a small chisel. "Between their teeth fillin's and whatever Gutterson misses in their pockets, yeah, I'm stayin' out of jail."

Lem said, "Better that than dead."

Chaney said, "Especially if you're handling the funeral."

"It's probably a toss-up."

Lem looked at Howard and said, "We're going to see Beaudine."

"Why tell me? I don't got to do nothing with that crazy son of a bitch. Ever."

"Howard, Chester Pardee got himself killed."

"That's no surprise. Good riddance."

"By John Bishop."

The chisel hit the floor, and Howard knelt to pick it up. Lem was right beside him. "Bishop survived, and he tracked Pardee down and shot him."

Chaney said, "He ain't lying."

Howard crossed himself, then pulled a crooked, square-head nail from the side of the coffin crate, tearing through the wood planking like it was paper. He spit.

Chaney said, "I was with Pardee, read Beaudine's letter."

"That letter meant squat then, and means double-squat now."

Chaney said, "It might mean a hell of a lot of money, if it's true."

Howard looked up from the coffin, leveling on Chaney. "But it ain't. You don't know shit about this, mister."

Lem said, "Don't get riled. He's riding in with me."

"I don't like guys who flap their gums. You two do what you want, I got men to bury."

"Who's gonna bury you?"

"I ain't too worried."

"About dying?"

Howard said, "We make our choices in this life, and I'm at peace with whatever happens. I brought it on myself."

Lem smiled, "That's straight from the prison preacher."

"Go to hell."

Chaney said, "I'd rather die rich than

poor. But you've got guts to face what Bishop's carrying — a double-barreled shotgun, like it's growing right out of him. If I've ever seen the Angel of Death, it's him."

Howard said, "Then you ain't seen shit," before bringing the hammer down on the square head, missing, and pounding into the coffin's side, splitting the green pine in half. He hollered from his guts, grabbed two pieces of the crate and hurled them across the room with amazing force. The wood broke apart, crashing into the pile of corpses and tearing open their burlap shrouds.

Chaney took a step back, and Lem reached up to put hands on Howard's huge shoulders. "This is the time to think, right? Hear me, Howard? Calm down and listen to what we're sayin'. We need you. If John Bishop's coming, let's take care of it together, and not have him pick us off when we're not looking. Doesn't that make sense?"

Howard looked to Lem. "You scared, Deadeye?"

Lem said, "No, but I hate unfinished business. Beaudine got us into this."

Howard nodded. "Uh-huh. The Raiders. Just a gang of thieves."

"Yeah, shitty ones. Thieves and fools."

Chaney said, "Maybe Beaudine was right about all that gold."

Howard moved on Chaney. "You keep talkin' like an expert 'cause you read a letter? I was there when it was written so don't tell me shit! If Bishop's alive, then he's coming for us for what we done. And we deserve it."

Lem got Howard to sit down before Chaney said, "Or maybe he's out to protect what's his. You boys could have been right all along."

Howard barked, "There's no gold, no payroll, no cash."

Lem said, "Either way, we've got to finish this. You want to stay here, building coffins, waiting for death to come through that door? Or ride to Cheyenne, maybe cut it off? If nothing else, you really wouldn't like a chance to drop Beaudine?"

Howard said, "I'm trying to keep peace in my heart, and you're tempting me."

"Maybe you could finally break the Major in half with your bare hands? You'd like that, Howard, I know you would."

Howard spit again, kicked away the remains of the box, moving to the pile of bodies. He regarded the corpses for a moment, and then looked to the heavens for a sign, a message. The dog down the street started barking again.

Howard said, "The end's comin' no matter what I do. Might as well enjoy it, I guess. First, help me bury these fellas."

Chaney said, "They're dead. What difference does it make what happens to them now?"

Howard threw one of the corpses over his shoulder. "That's what I've been sayin' to *you,* jackass."

# CHAPTER NINE:
## EYES OF THE DEAD

Creed sat command-high on his chestnut horse, doing a blind man's inspection of the shotgun rig, pulling the trigger line, and testing the straps that secured it. He shucked the spent shells, holding the gun next to his ear, snapping it shut, listening for rattles. There were none. He measured the stock with his palms, then ran his thumbs over the end of the barrel for sharp edges or sloppy job where it was sawed off. He gave his silent approval of the gunsmith.

Creed held the rig out in front of him, sensing its weight. "Just move your arm and it fires?"

Bishop's words were a strain, even as White Fox spread cinnamon oil on his lips with her index finger so he could speak. "My shoulders."

"Do all the work yourself?"

"There was a smith, followed my design."

"Damn clever, but that's you, Dr. Bishop."

Creed hung the rig on the saddle horn, while dropping from his tall horse. The chestnut sensed Creed's every move before he made it and adjusted, patiently helping his blind master.

Creed scratched behind the horse's ears, "Where's the boy?"

"Here, sir."

The straw-haired boy led him around the dead, the smoky kerosene pools, and the bloody snow, to the little clump of trees where Bishop was lying. White Fox, next to him, rose up on her knees, but her hands were always on Bishop's chest, protecting him.

One of Creed's men shouted, "She's startin' somethin'!"

Bishop said, "No, she's not. And you men don't either."

Creed was standing over Bishop now, and the doctor's gaze locked on to Creed's amber glasses. Creed cocked his head, sensing the moment, and nodded to Bishop in formal recognition. Spread out a few feet behind, Creed's men casually waited to shoot, guns resting on hips but with hammers back.

Creed said, "Let me see that thing she was after."

Bishop said, "Your men need to stand down."

"Apparently, you didn't leave many."

"I see a lot of guns."

Creed ordered, "Holster weapons!"

Some of the men obeyed. The one bleeding from the head didn't and Bishop said, "There's still one."

"And always will be. You fought a good fight, but you're my prisoners, Doctor. Maybe you better explain to her just what that means."

White Fox said, "I know."

"Then toss away that pistol you had aimed at me."

She threw the gun, with Creed listening for it to land in a bank of snow with a pillowed thud.

Creed said, "I'm entitled to inspect all spoils, even if I can only see them with my hands. Your latest invention, Doctor, the one that saved your life."

"She saved my life."

Creed laughed, "Bullshit. Go ahead, boy."

The boy reached down for the breathing device lying next to White Fox, then stopped. Her eyes cut him.

He swallowed. "Ma'am."

Bishop asked, "What's your name, son?"

"Hector Price, sir."

White Fox kept her other hand hidden in the field kit, clamped around a scalpel. Bishop squeezed her arm, and she let the knife go.

Bishop said, "It's all right. *Otséeme.*"

She smiled to herself at being called "brave" and handed the device to Hector, who held it out so Creed could turn the small box over and over, fingers tracing its edges. He fit the mask onto his own face, drawing deep.

Bishop said, "Turn the crank."

Hector turned the crank, as Creed continued with the mask; then the captain took it off, saying, "I feel my blood pumping."

Bishop said, "Pure oxygen. The crank draws the air into the device which filters it through a cell filled with purified water, and the bellows pumps it out through the mask."

"How'd you come to this?"

"Remember the fire at Lynchburg? Our men choking to death, and there wasn't a damn thing I could do about it."

"So, you're still a soldier."

"Still a doctor."

"And you carry your weapons with you."

"You never know when you'll need them, Captain."

"You were an officer, and proud to display your rank on your field kit. Maybe I can't see, but my vision's clear."

Coming up out of some bloody slush, Fat Gut screamed, "What about the bitch with the arrows? She killed near half of us! And me!"

"You survived." Creed handed White Fox the breather. "Be grateful for that."

Bishop said, "I remember you saying that before, after a skirmish on the other side of the Shenandoah."

"Because we have history."

Bishop looked at all the guns ready for him, and the men behind them. "I might even recognize some of these faces, under the scars."

"Scars you left them after our battles. These men have stayed loyal, all these years. Unlike you."

"Revenge?" Bishop let the word hang in the air before asking, "How long have you been tracking me?"

Creed said, "Not long after you struck out on your own. You're wanted for killing the gunsmith who made your rig. He was married to the squaw? That's reward money, and who better to collect? Obviously, I can't read signs the way I used to, but you weren't hard to find. Not if you keep using that rig."

"And when are you going to kill us?"

Creed took off his glasses, to wipe them

with a handkerchief from his pocket. His eyelids were heavily corrupted with raised tissue, and the eyes themselves seemed solid black, but were actually blood-flecked purple. Blinking was a slow impossibility.

Creed faced Bishop's voice and said, "No one has more cause than I do."

Bishop said, "But you're holding back."

"You know me, Doctor. You know there's a strategy."

"Hell, yes."

Creed let his words go flat. "I have some planning to do yet."

"You're still riding Pride. He's about the finest animal I've ever seen."

Creed said, "Of course, I haven't seen him in years, but Pride's the one thing I value from my days in command."

White Fox helped Bishop sit up against the tree, and he gestured toward the smoldering piles of cloth with the right hand that wasn't there. "Those fires to smoke us out, they're old flags. You took that Bonnie Blue when we fought those guerillas out of Baton Rouge."

Creed stood at attention. "Damn right. I captured them, so they're mine to keep or burn. I can't see them anymore, so they're nothing but shitty rags."

"No, they have meaning. Every battle you

won, and every man you lost. I know your feelings about them."

Creed dropped to one knee. "Tell me, Doctor, that you're not using a bedside manner with me. Who do you think you're talking to? The only thing that's keeping you and the dog-eater alive is I haven't given the final order. You've got a lot of tricks in that bag of yours — you have my eyes?"

Bishop said, "I did my best."

Creed pulled himself to his feet on Hector's arm. "You know how I lost my sight? What a fine field medic Dr. Bishop was? He was with the Virginia Volunteers. He saved hundreds of lives, but not my eyes. That was beyond him."

Bishop hacked, his throat still burning, even as White Fox let him drink from a water bag. It went down cool, but there was still a taste of gunpowder and fire in his mouth and nose. That hot-metal taste brought the sound of screams and a battery of cannons back to Bishop's ears.

John Bishop looked at the dead men sprawled around the entrance to the cave, the light afternoon snow beginning to shroud them. But it wasn't the memory of their screams he was hearing.

It was the screams of Captain Creed, as he worked to remove the Howitzer shrapnel from around his eyes. Bishop slit his lids, and dabbed away each sliver of torn metal. It took hours, because Creed would stop him, and insist he help one of the other wounded, even as he cupped his hands over his eyes, to hold back their bloody wash.

Bishop said, "The Battle of Buffington Island. You wouldn't let me put you under."

"I was in command."

"You were out of your mind with pain."

Creed said, "The pain was hellish for sure, but, Doctor, I was never out of my mind."

White Fox helped Bishop to his feet, and he said to Creed, "It was the infection that took your sight. You'd just been sutured; you never should have crossed that river."

"My men needed me. I didn't matter that I was wounded; it mattered that I lead."

"That river was filled with bodies, disease. You slipped, and your bandages got soaked. Nothing was going to save your eyes after that."

"You know the last thing I saw?"

"You're going to tell me."

"The bandages pained me, and I tore them off while I was in the bloody water. There was a body of a little girl who'd been shot in the throat, just moving with the river. I don't know who killed her or why, but when I went under, her face was right in front of me and I looked into her dead eyes. Then mine were gone, forever."

"Then how am I to blame for what happened?"

Creed kept his hand on Hector's shoulder as he faced Bishop and said, "Because I choose to."

The gun with the head wound yelled, "What happens now? Firing squad? They took out half of us, they got it comin'!"

Creed said, "I think I'd enjoy that, but it doesn't serve the purpose. Doctor, tend the wounds of my men. The boy and your squaw can help. Then we march."

"Where?"

"A blind man can't do much in the world. My ranch was lost, and my pension wouldn't keep a dog fat. So now, I do what I have to do. Just as you are."

Bishop stood, picking up his field kit with his one hand. "And what do you think I'm doing?"

"Going after Beaudine and his gang of egg-sucking gutter trash."

Bishop regarded Creed for a beat, the mention of Beaudine's name pulling him up short. Creed said, "I told you we've been tracking you for a while. You must remember I credit myself with knowing my enemies. I know all about it."

Bishop said, "Is this your get-back for your blindness? Deny me *my* revenge for my wife and son?"

"The world will be a better place without Beaudine's gang. Hell, every one of them deserves to be shot, hung, and shot again."

"So what's your strategy, Captain? What are my orders?"

Creed said, "You have wounded to attend to, Dr. Bishop."

"I need that device."

Creed threw it to Hector. "He means the breathing gizmo, not the shotgun. That rig's mine."

# Chapter Ten:
# Dead Letter

"Brother John,

"My guess is that when you read this, I will be gone. We will have had a little talk, settle our scores, and considered what might have been if I'd taken a different road. I know you feel superior to your older brother, and probably with good reason. I have many thoughts to express, and since I never learned to read or write properly, my cellmate is setting all of this down for me, using the best language in his capability.

"You were barely in long pants when I left Virginia, and Ma and Pa had long before decided you were the favorite. You were smart, took to school, and looked like our father. I hated school and don't resemble either of our parents, and those differences have been between us ever since.

"I was in jail for robbery when you were getting out of school. That was not my first time locked up, but the first time you were able to visit me, which I appreciated. When you were studying medicine, I was on the other side of the law in the wild country, and was then in jail again for the manslaughter of a miscreant. You did not visit me then, but I understood that mama refused to give you her permission, so I hold no grudges.

"With the war came your commission and my own difficulties; I killed my fair share, but was not in official uniform, and so I am now to be hung. That uniform makes all the difference doesn't it? As do the rules, which you have always respected, except that one time.

"That one time is why I now regard you as My Brother John.

"Since my death is now a thing of yesterday, it is my desire that you should keep all of the Army gold that we hijacked together from the troop train coming from Richmond. I don't know why you threw in with me on this, but I am glad that you did, brother. This fortune has always been our secret, and since you were the only one to know its final location, it was also our trust. Despite the end of conflict, the government will never stop looking for that money, and I know you have the strength to keep it safely hidden. I thank you and respect you that you did not spend it, as I knew you would not, but now all of it is yours to do with what you will.

"One half of a million dollars is a great deal of money, John, and I am facing the hangman with at least the good feeling that after a life of doing wrong, I helped a good man provide a special life for his wife and son.

"I look forward to the day when we are joined again on the Streets of Glory.

"Your older brother, Devlin Bishop."

Widow Kate read the last paragraphs aloud a second time, then leaned back in her overstuffed velvet chair, her fat fingers locked together in pause. She wiped away a small moustache of sweat before speaking.

Kate said, "That's what you've been chasing all these years, Beaudine?"

"Pilfering that letter from my jacket was a foolish mistake. I remind you, again, of my rank and the consequences of disrespect."

"Oh, no disrespect intended, but you should be glad I read it. You owe me quite a sum, and this gives me some hope of being paid."

"Madame, you'll get yours."

Beaudine sat opposite the large, dark oak desk that hid half of Kate's massive body, adjusting himself on a stack of fine silk cushions that had been sewn to the seat and back of a finely carved rocking chair. Like the desk, the chair was highlighted with streaks of lamé, while the rest of Kate's bordello office was all silk wallpaper, carved ivory dragons, and Chinese vases on thin pedestals. Heavy drapes killed the sun, and the oil lamps around the room burned low.

Kate removed the glass flute from the small lamp on her desk, turning the flame down to a blue burn as she said, "The chance at half of a million dollars in one fell swoop is a hell of a thing, if it's there. I've had my chances to grab quick fortunes, but let them pass. I prefer to amass my fortunes a few dollars at a time. That way, I know it's real."

Beaudine leaned suddenly forward. "Now you don't think it's real? Dev Bishop was my cellmate."

Kate smiled, shaking her head. "I know you wrote the letter, Major. It has your exaggerated flair."

"You compliment and offend at the same time."

"One of my many talents."

Kate took a jade pipe from her top desk drawer, and held the bowl over the lamp's flame. Her concentration was total, her thick fingers now delicate instruments, as she felt the pipe's temperature before opening a small ivory pillbox and removing a pea-sized dollop of opium to drop into the pre-heated bowl.

"My third husband was a sea captain who introduced me to the ways of the dynasties. I learned a lot from the Chinese, not the least of which was how to run this place. They know their business."

After a few moments, the green-yellow started to smoke, and Kate took a long draw on the pipe before leaning back in her chair and allowing the feeling to wash through her.

Kate judged Beaudine's dark expression and said, "The girls have no idea I allow myself this. If they did, they'd assume I condoned use for the non-injured, not understanding the discipline it takes to control your consumption. Fighting the tiger keeps me strong. Do you understand, Major?"

"As a matter of fact, I do, given some of my extreme hospital experiences" — Beaudine's voice was drifting — "and the soldiers I know prefer opiates to whiskey. Miss Nellie Bly, who I had an interview with earlier, will be writing extensively about the problem for *The Pittsburgh Dispatch*."

Kate said, "That wasn't Nellie Bly, Major. Remember where you are."

"I do — I do — but you interrupted us, while we were discussing dire issues. Some of which concerned you directly, Madame. That wasn't appreciated."

"There was no interruption, no Nellie Bly. Just one of my whores and, a crazy man." Kate added after drawing on the pipe, "Maybe not all his fault."

Beaudine studied his boots, the ragged edge of his sewn-together tunic. He cleared the air with a wave of his hand. "I get lost sometimes, Madame, but I always find my way back. Always."

Kate said, "That's why I allow you to bed here."

Beaudine bowed his head. "I know, truly, that I never had the chance to talk to Miss Bly, and tell her of the terrible conditions in the hospitals where I was a guest. But I should have, really. That would have been valuable."

"I agree."

"Hospitals and prisons, that's been my life. Did I say anything to that girl? Do anything unseemly?"

Kate put another match to the pipe. "You were a gentleman in your session, and if you said anything to Thelma, she'd forget the next minute. She's a sloppy girl. Swills laudanum like it was fresh cider and thinks

I don't know it. Doesn't have the character to indulge and still keep her wits about her. Not like me."

Beaudine nodded to Kate and said, "Some are born to lead."

"And some are born to stay on their backs."

Laughter ripped Kate, flesh jiggling, before she drew deep on the pipe and closed her eyes as the feeling kissed through her. Her eyes were still closed when she said, "That gold shipment is real, not a flight of fancy, or something for you and Nellie Bly?"

"Real as death."

"Why don't you have it yet?"

"The good doctor John Bishop wouldn't cooperate."

"Did you kill him?"

Beaudine's voice lowered. "He was — destroyed."

"That doesn't say it, and you didn't get the money."

"There's tracking to be done. My men will be joining me, and we'll set off on our mission. That's the last question, Madame. I've already given one interview today, and your tone is grating."

The Colt Lightning was in Kate's hand instantly, her flabby arms steadying the gun directly at Beaudine's head by resting on a large dragon carved from a solid piece of jade.

Beaudine said, "Threatening an officer is a very serious offense."

"Living in that head of yours must be a hell of a thing. I'd hesitate killing you, but I'll shoot. Or, you can come upstairs with me for a moment."

Beaudine stood. "I understand. Opiates have poisoned your reasoning."

"No, they just keep my aim relaxed. After wards, I wouldn't mind having a little late supper, since you're spending the night."

Kate moved around the desk as Beaudine stood. He didn't put his hands up, but kept his eyes on the Colt pistol following him. "Are you really that worried I won't be paying your whore her piddling amount?"

Kate said, "This is the problem, Beaudine. You can't follow the path of a conversation: we're talking about something bigger than what you owe. Understand? Come on. Let's see if you can make it upstairs without straying."

Kate opened her office door. "Major."

Voices, mild groans, and laughter from the other bedrooms drifted about the hallway in a mix as Widow Kate and Beaudine made their way to the small set of curved steps that led to the attic bedroom. She kept the

Lightning close to his spine, and he buttoned his tunic and flattened his lapels before going up.

Kate said, "Your session was fine, and I trust you'll pay what you owe. It's what happened afterward that's a problem."

The cramped attic room was the same as Beaudine had left it, except the redheaded girl was lying on the bed, night clothes shredded, her head cocked at an impossible angle with deep purple bruises smothering half of her face and the sides of her neck. Kate stood behind Beaudine, close enough to see a shimmer of sweat on the back of his neck, but there was no other visible reaction, even as she gently prodded him with the barrel of the gun, poking his ribs. He ducked under the doorframe to enter, then took a few steps to the bed.

Kate said, "You claimed you forgot something and had to come back up. Remember?"

"No, I do not."

"But that's what you told me, *Major.* Then the girls and I heard the screams, and found this."

Beaudine bent down, brushing his fingers across Thelma's strawberry curls. His mouth went slack, as he leaned just an inch from her face and blackening lips, before looking back at Kate. "It's the one I knew as Nellie."

"You can call her any name you want, it don't make no difference to the law."

Beaudine swallowed his words. "You're trying to hoodwink me, Madame. It's not appreciated."

"But we all heard it. Thelma screamed at you, disobeyed orders, and you set her straight. Now the Marshal likes to stay over when he's riding through the territory; would you like him to know about this and the treasure, or should we keep today's interview between us?"

Beaudine stepped away from the corpse, his fists clenched. "Is this supposed to frighten me?"

"No, but your loss of freedom might. Your gold quest will be a damn sight tougher if you're in a jail cell, waiting for the hangman."

"I've been there, and now I'm here."

Kate met Beaudine's hard look. "Don't act like I haven't taken everything into account. I'm not one of the dog-tail felons you ride with. I'm talking real business — are you up to it?"

Beaudine slumped against the doorjamb, his shoulders and arms sagging with all that he was carrying. He looked to Kate, rubbed

106

his temples. "My mind's swimming, and that's a dangerous thing."

Kate said, "I've got just the cure for that downstairs."

"You have me at a disadvantage now, Madame, but tomorrow won't be the same. All this betrayal will come into focus, boiling my blood. I'll be hell-fired for sure."

Kate eased Beaudine out of the room, pulling the door shut behind them, "We'll see."

The coffee had cooked down to acid-brown when Lem poured himself a cup. Howard pulled a new shoe from the coals of the campfire, and Chaney struggled with his horse's left hind leg until Howard shoved him aside, straddled the shank, and nailed the shoe into place.

Lem tipped his coffee. "Tubal-Cain from the Book of Genesis, the first blacksmith! I bet you could give him a run for his money, Howard!"

Chaney said, "You got the strength for it."

Howard gave the horse a pat. "Takes more than that. You have to know your animal, which you don't. If he'd walked one more mile on that shoe, he'd be lamed for sure."

Chaney offered, "Then I'm obliged."

Lem said, "See? It's a good thing you're here."

Howard looked to Chaney. "Yeah, so why are *you* here?"

Lem countered, "Come on, we talked that through. It never hurts to have an extra gun."

Howard said, "Or target — what you got painted on your back?"

Lem finished the coffee. "It's all going to depend on Beaudine, and if we want to carry on."

Chaney said, "I thought that was Bishop's call. He raised the stakes by coming for your bunch."

"That's true, and if I had more than forty dollars to my name, I'd say the hell with Beaudine, the hell with Bishop, the hell with it all."

"But now you're thinking about the chance of that gold."

"I'm thinkin' about death, and the money. And wondering which we're going to find first. Just wondering."

Howard drank some coffee, then spit it into the fire and said, "You're not all in, Lem?"

"Hell, yes, I am. But I'm feelin' better now that there's three of us."

Howard said, "And the law."

Chaney looked to Lem, who was grinning. "What do you mean?"

"He means this." Howard took a bent deputy's badge from his pocket, and pinned it on his torn vest, directly over his heart.

Lem snorted a laugh. "He got it when he was leg-breakin' agitators for the railroad, just to keep things nice and legal."

Howard said to Chaney, "See, I'm not just some big, dumb, son of a bitch. I'm the law."

# CHAPTER ELEVEN: INTO THE STORM

"You gotta be shittin' me!"

Hector was propping Fat Gut by his shoulders as Bishop pulled the chrome instrument from his med kit. Gut winced when he saw the thing: it was tong-shaped, with a metal clamp mounted between curved scissor blades that opened wide enough to fit around the top of Fat Gut's leg, while the clamp extended to grab hold of the arrow shaft that protruded eight inches out of the calf. The snow was falling heavier now, sticking to the open wound.

Bishop said, "This instrument's designed for removing bullets, but it's adaptable. Unfortunately, I only have this left hand, and can't perform the procedure myself."

Fat Gut "what the hell" squinted, and then Bishop added, "It won't work without two hands."

Fat Gut yelped, "Then who in tarnation's gonna do it? And I don't get no painkiller or nothin'? I know you got powders!"

"Your ambush broke everything we had. Maybe one of your buddies has a bottle in his saddle?"

One of the hired guns wiped his nose and said, "Creed don't allow nothing. Thinks it keeps us sharp. Bullshit."

Creed called out, "Where's the boy? Where's Hector?"

Hector made some noise, his nose buried in Fat Gut's shoulders, propping him up for surgery, as Bishop tightened the metal clamp around the arrow. His moves were left-hand clumsy, but the instrument locked into place. Hector strained against Gut's rolling weight, "I'm here, sir!"

"Front and center."

Bishop countered, "I need him, Creed, if you want your wounded tended. I'd bet you still have that bottle."

Creed took a bottle of Evan Williams pre-conflict bourbon, wrapped in oilcloth, from his saddlebag. The hired guns spit and grumbled, as White Fox stood directly in front of Creed, fixed on his amber glasses as they were being dotted with fresh snow. "*Eó'ó'éne vo' êstanéhotame.* Do you know its meaning?"

Creed sniffed the air, then handed her the bottle. "Dr. Bishop wanted this. For medicinal use only."

Bishop took stripped bandages, antiseptic, and scalpels from his bag; suddenly he was a field medic again, prepping, but with only his left hand. White Fox sat next to him, holding the bottle just out of Fat Gut's reach, as she waited for Bishop to give the nod.

Fat Gut said, "That bottle's for me!"

Creed said, "That's not coffin varnish, it's fine sipping whiskey, with a history."

"You claim that about everything, 'cuz."

Dr. Bishop checked the clamp, the tongs on the instrument, the leg's torn muscle and flesh. Fat Gut grabbed for the bourbon again, but got nothing. White Fox fought her smile.

Fat Gut let it out again, "Come on! I'm dyin!"

Bishop said, "Well, you were trying to kill me."

Fat Gut snorted like White Fox wasn't there. "Just her. We had orders to take you, but you ain't the one who shot me."

Creed said, "Doctor, I expect you to do your duty."

Fat Gut wiped his mouth and said, "There's your orders, Doc," before nodding toward White Fox. "I've left 'em dead and wishin' they was dead. Had some fun, too.

But not this time, huh? Not with you?"

White Fox looked to Bishop, her eyes solid, black pools with blood red around the iris, a circle of fire. This only happened in moments of rage, just before exploding. Just before.

Bishop watched the moment pass, White Fox never looking away from him. Then he said to Fat Gut, "You're damn lucky."

"Quit stallin'! Fix me up!"

Creed said, "Conduct yourself properly, or I'll order the doctor to let your leg rot."

Bishop said, "Give me a Winchester shell."

"Spent. More in my pocket. Can't move my arm."

"Boy?"

Hector reached into Gut's pocket, pulling out two cartridges. White Fox took the bullets, pulled away the brass and emptied the black powder around the shaft of the arrow, just below the clamp. The arrowhead wasn't barbed, but it had sliced beneath a muscle and had to be cut free from the tissues before removal. Fat Gut grabbed the bottle of bourbon like he was wringing a chicken's neck.

"Drink. Your captain got that bottle from Ulysses S. Grant."

Hector gulped air. "Is that a true fact?"

Fat Gut took three long pulls, wiping the

rest from the scraggle of his beard. "He's told me a hundred times."

Bishop said, "That's a true fact. Creed knows Grant."

One of the guns fashioned a cigarette, lit it. Bishop looked up just as he flicked the match away. "Got another light?"

"Sorry."

"Then come over here."

Creed said, "Whatever needs doing."

The gun sauntered over, a Morgan-James long-sighted rifle slung on his back. He stood by Fat Gut, snickered, and blew smoke into the light-falling snow.

Bishop looked up at the gun. "What do they call you?"

"My given name's Epiphany. My Christian name's Fuller."

Bishop said, "Mr. Fuller, when I tell you, put the cigarette to the powder on his leg. It's going to pain."

Fuller said, "I never cottoned to this son of a bitch anyway."

Fat Gut screamed with spittle, "I ain't lettin' that darkie do nothing to me!"

White Fox grasped the tongs, Bishop positioned the scalpel and said, "Now!"

It all happened at once. Fuller put his cigarette to the black powder, flaming it around the wound, as Bishop cut the arrowhead free. White Fox threw her weight against the clamp, forcing it to pull the arrow from Fat Gut's leg in a single motion. Blood was a fountain, spraying her, before the powder burned over the wound, sealing it.

There was a meat-sizzling, even as snow cooled the wound, and Bishop swabbed it with iodine. Hector grunted as Fat Gut slumped back, unconscious.

Fuller pulled Hector from under Gut's massive weight. "Come on, tadpole, before he crushes you."

Fat Gut's head hit the ground, his mouth sagging.

Bishop said, "He'll be out for a while."

Creed said, "Take care of these other men, then we'll get him on his feet. We're moving before the sun sets."

"The snow's going to get worse."

"Then you and the dog-eater better work as fast as you can, because you've got a long walk."

The gun known as Fuller rolled the last of his makings and popped it in his pocket before untying Bishop's bay and White Fox's painted stallion. No matter how he moved, his sniper's rifle stayed perfectly slung across his broad shoulders.

The snow was a straight curtain now, still light, but not melting when it reached the ground. The kerosene pools and bloody slush around the mouth of the cave were again pristine white, and the dead were in a neat row beside the tree line. Lariat was face down, to hide his twisted expression.

Fuller led the two horses to where Creed was now sitting atop his chestnut, away from the few men who were still being bandaged by White Fox, as Bishop guided her. The doctor inspected every dressing, and Creed listened for his approval.

Fuller said, "They're almost done. I've got the horses. The snow makes it look like nothing's happened here. It's all brand new again."

"What about the boy?"

"Helping your doc friend."

Creed said, "That's a prisoner."

Fuller reached into Creed's saddlebag, found a match to go with his last cigarette. He struck it against Creed's stirrup. "He's gold to me, Creed."

"You're forgetting yourself, Fuller."

"I ain't forgetting nothing. I've been with you since Richmond, and I always appreciated that you saw my blue uniform, instead of my black skin. You were always blind to that, now you're blind for real."

"But still in command, here."

"You're not an officer anymore. We're just trash the army threw away, the ones who should've been killed, but weren't. We're the walking dead, and now we got a shot at real money? This ain't about loyalty, Captain — it's about leaving my kids something. Without my uniform, I'm just another runaway slave with a gun, so this better work out."

The acknowledgment of rank pleased Creed. "You'll always be a soldier; a fine sniper with a good eye. Maybe I can't see it, but I know your skills. Conduct yourself with discretion, and you'll be rewarded."

"I can keep my mouth shut, but one way t'other, I'm getting mine."

Creed finally said, "We all will."

The colorless sky and white earth met somewhere, forming an empty void, barely broken by the distant sketch of a mountain or the dot of trees, all obscured by blowing snow. A hanging fog turned any landmarks into grey-blue ghosts, as Creed's prisoners trudged through the building cold.

Behind them, they left hoof prints in furrows of snow that were being filled in from the sky, while ahead there was only blinding white.

Bishop and White Fox led the group, the bay and the painted stepping high out of the snow and coming down through a frozen crust, almost to the knee. White Fox's hands were tied at the wrist behind her back, while Bishop's left was knotted to his saddle horn.

Creed and Fuller rode side by side, the painted and the bay tethered to Fuller's horse so Bishop and White Fox couldn't break away. Fuller's Morgan-James hung in a scabbard by his leg.

The rest of Creed's men followed in line, some bandaged, their weapons casual on their laps, ready to shoot Bishop or White Fox, or anyone, between the shoulders. Hector was the last rider, sharing his horse with Fat Gut. Gut was still dazed from the surgery and heaving into the frosty air. Even when he waved in the saddle, he held onto his Winchester like it was precious treasure.

Everyone kept their faces low, the horses angling slightly to the side, against the beating wind as they trudged. Bishop pulled up, and the other riders stopped behind him, the animals bobbing their heads, snorting. Hot breath hung in the air.

Bishop called out, "Why are we setting the pace? We'll freeze before we get anywhere."

Creed said, "When I want us to move faster, we will."

"Then where the hell are we going?"

"You're heading in the right direction, Doctor. That's all you need to know."

"You can tell?"

"I can tell."

Bishop said, "Then how about this: are we wanted dead or alive?"

"There's a price to be paid. Now move."

Bishop looked to White Fox, who kept her gaze straight ahead, seeing something beyond the yawning white. Snow hung on her eyelashes and lips, and she didn't meet Bishop's face when he asked if she was all right. She just gently heeled her painted, starting the trek again. Bishop did the same.

The group followed in line, with the hired guns muttering. Fuller looked back from his saddle and said, "You boys want to see some shares, I'd keep my opinions quieter than that."

One of the guns said, "The house slave never has to worry about nothin'."

Fuller cocked the Morgan-James, the metallic click of the hammer hidden by the howling wind, and was drawing it from its scabbard when Creed said, "Rise above it."

Fuller regarded the blind man who'd heard the weapon, and said, "You've been grinding about the doc for years."

"But I waited, and now is the time. Be patient, and you'll have your time, too. Should I make that an order, Fuller?"

Fuller glanced over his shoulder at the seven men behind him — bloodied, bandaged, with guns instead of sense. The ones Bishop and White Fox hadn't killed. He'd ridden with some of them for years, knew who they were inside, and usually let their talk pass right over. But now he was going to have to share money with this bunch, maybe a lot. He threw them a strained grin that one of Creed's men returned, full-tooth. Easy target.

Fuller's eyes narrowed, even as his grip relaxed on the Henry, letting it slide back into its place. "No need."

Bishop said, "Sounds like trouble in the ranks."

Creed didn't raise his voice. "It's handled."

"Like the time we crossed into the Ohio Valley? You'd been pushing the men for days, they could barely stand, and that's when the attack came. We lost a lot that day."

"You lost a lot."

"Most were passed saving, Creed. And none died by my hand."

"You mean the one you have left?"

Bishop said, "We've both seen miracles on the battlefield, but there sure weren't any that day."

"I don't need your voice of conscience. I learned a long time ago that doctors aren't gods."

"Neither are officers."

Creed let the words settle before he said, "Even a blind man could hit a target as close as you are to me."

"Wouldn't that lessen our value? Or is it 'dead or alive'?"

Creed chose his words. "I haven't decided."

Creed felt Fuller's hand on his shoulder for a bit of reassurance, and said nothing. They all rode on for a few minutes, the snow cutting harder, before Bishop said, "In case nobody's told you, the sun's going down."

# Chapter Twelve:
## Reunion

The three-story house, with the lattice protecting each floor, looked as if it had been plucked from a tony street in St. Louis and dropped in the middle of nowhere. Years of weather and living in the hard country had left their mark on this beauty, but she still stood tall, the lamps in each window welcoming strangers as they approached.

A soiled dove, with tight, blond curls pulled the Navajo blanket closer to her shoulders as she watched the three riders tie their horses to the hitch rail in front of Widow Kate's. The night was damn cold, with her unmentionables sticking to her skin, but at this moment she liked it better on the porch than being curled up in her warm bed, with nowhere to run.

She seemed to Lem Wright to still be of schooling age when she asked, "Is you the law or customers?"

Howard said, "The law."

Soiled Dove dropped a pinch of snuff behind her lower lip, sticking it out while she thought, then said, "Good. There's been too much trouble tonight."

Chaney took out his small-handled Colt, and Howard sniffed, "Borrow that from your granny?"

Howard pushed around the horses and opened his coat so the Dove could see his deputy's badge pinned over his huge belly, "Look at me, little girl. What the hell's the problem?"

She blinked twice at Howard. "That crazy man killed Miss Kate. I had to get out."

"What crazy man?"

"The one who never pi-roots, just talks. He was a general or somethin.' "

"What room's he in?"

"He was in Miss Kate's office, but I dunno now."

Lem smiled at the girl. "You forgot your shoes. Your toes'll freeze off."

The Dove moved the snuff with her tongue, wiggling her grubby feet. "I guess I wasn't thinkin'."

Lem Wright tucked the blanket around the Dove's feet, then held open the large door with the stained-glass Chinese symbol for "love" in its center, keeping his gun hand

123

ready over his Remington New Model.

Lem's dead eye fixed on Howard and Chaney. "Time for the reunion."

They went inside, while the Dove rubbed her toes and started a song she didn't know all the words to. Lem drew his pistol, and was careful not to let the door slam behind him.

The blood pooling around Widow Kate soaked the Persian rug, casting it purple where she was lying. Her body was balled together next to her comfortable chair, hands clamped against the side where the blade had slit deep. Kate's eyes were closed, and there was no reaction when Beaudine nudged her with his boot. A few of the line girls peered silently from the office doorway, while the only one saying anything was doing it in shrill Chinese.

Beaudine was unfazed as he wiped the blood from the ivory letter opener before slipping it in his pocket; the staring eyes, the Chinese accusations, weren't reaching him at all. He moved quickly, snatching up carved jade and cast-gold trinkets, then stuffing his coat until it bulged. He gave Kate's pipe a deep sniff, tasting the opium residue in the back of his throat, before noticing Howard, Lem, and Chaney standing just feet away.

Beaudine waited for a sign of respect from his men until Howard offered, "Still crazy as a shit-house rat?"

Beaudine said, "I hear you build coffins for heathens," as he opened the drawers of the large desk, dumping out letters, paper work, ledgers, and more onto the floor.

The Chinese girl started yelling again, and Howard thumbed his badge at her face. "Get upstairs. I might even see you later."

The Chinese girl dry-spit, "Yeah, without paying," but the line girls all backed their way up the front stairs as Beaudine kept rifling, smashing an abacus against the floor, then tearing through the bottom of a drawer, bloodying his knuckles.

Beaudine's face was washed with sweat, his words strained, "That cow has cash hidden somewhere, and she's not keeping any secrets. Not now."

Lem Wright said, "Nobody ever gives it up easy, do they?"

"Always a joke, Deadeye."

Beaudine grabbed a box decorated in filigree and topped with a two-headed dragon with ruby eyes. The ornate heads were locked in battle, and when he pressed down on one of them, the lid sprung open, revealing another stash of opium. Beaudine dumped the pure on the desk, then pocketed the box.

Lem said, "Is that why we're here? Robbing a whorehouse?"

"You're here for gold, the letter." Beaudine nudged Kate again with his toe. "Kate tried to include herself in our plans, and had to be dealt with. The cleaver's tied to my saddle, and she's damn lucky I didn't want to brave the cold to get it. Is that Betsy?"

Howard had his Remington New Model out, the hammer back. "You remember."

"She doesn't look like you've taken very good care of her, or yourselves."

"She still shoots."

Beaudine ripped aside the drapes, revealing bare walls. "But can you?"

"You dragged me into somethin' 'cause we shared a cell one time, and I'm still not one dollar richer, but my soul's poorer."

"Not much I can do for your soul, but you're closer to that Bishop gold now than you know."

"By walking into another killing?"

"I was defending what's ours."

Lem said, "We've been through a hell of a lot, but we made it. You've got one minute to tell us what this is, and then I ride out — clean."

Beaudine studied him. "You giving me an

order, Deadeye?"

Lem's gun was leveled. "A choice."

Howard kept the Remington New on Beaudine's chest, the grin on his face spreading. "I know I ain't that bright, but I'd say you got less than a minute, by that clock on the wall?"

"Or Betsy screams?"

"Oh, I'll bust your back first. Then, when *you're* screamin', I'll let Betsy do her job."

Beaudine stepped around the desk. "Bishop survived his punishment."

Lem said, "I know. He cut down Chester, 'cause he was after you. I missed him by a couple of hours."

"I'd say that was fortunate for you both." Beaudine looked beyond the guns to Chaney. "I didn't recruit you."

Lem said, "He was with Chester and figures to take his place. Probably be of more use, if this ain't another bullshit run."

"Bishop still has the gold he stole with his brother, and we can get it."

Howard said, "Jesus save me, I wanna bust you in half."

Beaudine continued, "An officer of my acquaintance will be taking Bishop prisoner, and will deliver him. To us."

"Here?" Lem's voice raised.

"A two-day ride into the hills to the old

Goodwill strike. We'll need supplies, and some extra guns. Kate should've ponied cash, but she gave us plenty to barter with."

Lem said, "You still haven't said exactly what we're walking into. I like to know what to carry, what to load."

Beaudine gave his words mannerly import. "You were always thorough, Deadeye. My co-officer, Captain Creed, thinks he has a right to an equal share for delivering Bishop, but we'll disabuse him of that notion."

"Bull — !"

The rest of the word was the scream of Howard's giant fist crashing into the top of Kate's desk, splitting the wood nearly in half. He raised Betsy like a club to smash across Beaudine's head, but instead took a deep breath they all could hear, and turned the gun around in his palm, aiming it again at the major.

Howard's hand and voice were shaking, his chest heaving, "I made a promise I wouldn't swear or kill no more, but you're pushin' me with this; this part of a million dollars, that ain't real!"

Beaudine said, "Howard, I know what it is to be out of control, but I'm about myself right now, and you need to be the same. This money is real. You know that."

"What makes it more real now than that

night with the doc and his family?"

Beaudine looked straight down the barrel of Howard's gun to his flicking eyes. "All of these people who want a piece, like Madame Kate on the floor. Doesn't that tell you? I wrote that letter for Dev Bishop, believing every word. Men facing death tend to be truthful."

"John Bishop wasn't."

Beaudine corrected Lem with a scolding. "Bishop refused to cooperate. There's a difference. After that night, I never stopped looking. You scattered, but I stayed with it, and every time I turn around, there's someone new who wants a share, because they knew that gold was someplace. And the doctor's the key to the moneybox."

Lem said, "He didn't give it up before, and now he's got nothing to lose, so why would he tell?"

"Because there's only one thing he cares about now — us. He'll bargain."

Lem smiled. "The gold for the chance to wipe us out." He put his hand on Howard's arm, lowering his gun. "This Creed will deliver?"

"He will, but won't be alone."

"This half a million is gonna have a lot of blood on it."

Beaudine pocketed one last jade trinket.

"What half a million doesn't?"

Chaney finally said, "Maybe everyone here, if Bishop uses that double-barrel rig. I've seen it, you haven't."

Beaudine looked down on Chaney. "You're new to me, and not impressive at all."

Lem cut him off, "He'll be more use than Chester was. At least he's seen Bishop, the way he is now."

Chaney said, "So did Chester Pardee."

Beaudine straightened his collar. "Then it's up to you to be properly prepared. You want some kind of a share of this? You're going to earn it." He walked out of Kate's office tall and straight, ready for a parade.

On the front porch, Soiled Dove was rubbing her feet with both hands, as Howard and Chaney swung onto their horses. Lem took a torch from a barrel by the front door, watching Dove as he lit it.

Dove's lower lip protruded, more snuff filling it. "That's a courtesy for the boys who ride in at night. The good customers."

Lem got onto his horse with the torch. "I'll come back, and promise to spend a fortune."

Howard punched the air with a giant fist, and said, "I'm back-slidin'. Five minutes with Beaudine, and I don't have a Christian feeling left. There's lumber 'round back. I could make that dead woman a coffin. It won't take long."

Lem said, "You're wanting to do it is enough to keep your soul safe."

Chaney said, "I figured we'd be given a map or something, not drafted into another war."

Lem turned his eye on Chaney. "Another? I didn't know you served. Thank you for your sacrifice."

Lem snickered at his own joke, making Chaney feel like a fool, again. Chaney let his fingers dance on the Colt he'd just re-holstered, playing with the idea of ending this game right now.

Lem had been watching Chaney's hand. "Stakes getting too high?"

That's when Soiled Dove piped up. "So, you all arrest that crazy man?"

Lem said, "He's coming with us."

"The regular sheriff's away 'til tomorrow sometime, and he's gonna be awful touched up about this. He makes a lot of money from Miss Kate."

Howard said, "You tell the sheriff that we got the killer, and he don't need to bother with nothin'."

"Somebody'll have to step up, take Kate's place," Lem said.

Soiled Dove wrinkled her nose at him. "Maybe me?"

"Maybe. Go on inside, and get warm for real."

Soiled Dove got up, and padded inside as Beaudine rode around the far side of the porch, sporting an officer's hat that had been stripped of its braiding, and his many-grey tunic, newly sewn together. Even made of bits and pieces, Beaudine was again impressive, with the long cleaver tied behind his saddle, the blade wrapped in butcher's paper.

Beaudine said, "How're you fixed?"

Howard was still holding Betsy. "Belly wash and jerky."

"That's going to change."

"Words."

Beaudine looked to Howard. "We've had our wait, but now the Bishop gold is ours for the taking. Are you loyal or not?"

"To you?"

"To the mission. If you have to light out" — Beaudine pulled the cleaver from behind his saddle, and hefted it with both hands — "I'll hold no ill feelings."

Lem said, "What if we turn our guns on you?"

Chaney sat up alert, his hand on the Colt, but again, he was holding back. Waiting. He looked to Lem's frozen eye, to Howard and his clenched fists, and finally to Beaudine.

Everyone seemed ready to pull when Beaudine spoke, his eyes fixed on something none of them could see. "Delivering death is our mission. It's your choice who we deliver it to: each other, or the bastards who're denying us a better life."

Beaudine urged his horse, breaking away from the three. "I know where I'm heading."

Howard, Chaney, and Lem turned their mounts around, guns back in their holsters, or tucked into belts. Lem held the torch for all of them, showing the way.

Howard said, "Shit-house rat crazy."

Deadeye Lem Wright added, "And we're gonna follow."

Chaney said, "For now."

# CHAPTER THIRTEEN:
# THE HEART OF THE ENEMY

"Sir, I'm getting our dinner. I can't be sitting around doin' nothing. Uh, with your permission."

Hector stood at attention before Creed, pointing to a distant gathering of trees that were being swallowed by the long shadows of the setting sun.

After a moment, it dawned on Hector that his pointing was useless and he dropped his arm. "Them rabbits went right for the woods. I can still see their tracks. Must've been five or six. I can get 'em and we'll be eating for the rest of the trek, sir."

Captain Creed said, "Take one of the men with you, and be back in an hour. You can tell time?"

"Yes, sir."

The pocket watch that Creed took from his jacket was a fine, ornate piece, presented to him by his men for his leadership skills. He held it in front of the boy by its gold chain. Hector swallowed air before gently putting it in his palm. "Thank you, sir."

"I expect my watch and you back in an hour, with or without dinner."

The hour bled forty minutes, and White Fox had built a fire to burn low and steady. The fire was obeying, shielded from the wind by a small wall of snow that she'd iced from a canteen, making it solid. Bishop and Creed were beside the flames, as she stood by, waiting for Hector to return from the woods with an armful of rabbits.

Bishop said, "Hector's a good boy."

"Yes. He volunteers for every duty he can. Now he comes up with his own."

"My son was a lot younger, but there's a resemblance of spirit."

"All boys look the same. That's why we give them uniforms."

"They weren't the same to me, Creed."

"Keep telling yourself that. You seem to need it."

Just beyond the fire, the horses and Creed's other six men were dark shapes, outlined by the orange flicker. The six stretched out, assuming positions that favored their bandaged wounds. Their talk was all worn-out sneers.

Fuller took hold of Creed's horse, pulling the bottle of sipping bourbon from the saddlebag, where it was tucked next to the shotgun rig. Little of the bourbon was gone.

Fuller said, "Captain, you think — ?"

"Each man gets one swallow to keep out the chill."

"I'll make sure."

Fuller walked to where the guns were stretched out, and handed off the bottle to Fat Gut, who guzzled deep. Fuller snatched it back, wiped the top, and passed it on to the next.

Fat Gut leaned against his Winchester like a crutch, bourbon wetting his chin. "You're really pushin' it with me, boy."

Fuller said, "No, I ain't," before letting the next one drink and throwing Fat Gut some more words. "I outranked you during the conflict, so I figure I still do. Wanna try? I'll even help you stand up."

Fat Gut rubbed his leg wound, shrugging. "It's too damn cold. Lucky for you."

Bishop watched Fuller pass the bourbon among the hired guns before saying to Creed, "Your bottle's getting some real use. Grant'd be proud."

Creed's voice was in the back of his throat. "I expected better of you than cheap jokes. We're bundled around a campfire, not sitting back in front of a fireplace. Men who served are supposed to have a better fate."

"Who claimed that?"

"It's not policy. It's what you hope for: that sacrifice will be rewarded."

"Like the money you're going to get for us?"

Creed said nothing, just let the flames bounce across the dark amber of his glasses, outlining the edges. Finally, Bishop said, "There's a bounty on me, and I never robbed a bank or a train."

"You killed a man."

"That you said needed killing. You agreed with me."

"I still do, but that don't change what's going to happen."

Bishop felt the piece of arm that remained through his sleeve. "So how the hell do you know about Beaudine?"

Creed took warmth from the fire. "Because he tried to join my regiment. The man'd worn the grey, claimed he had a change of heart. But then we found out he was wanted for strangling some strumpet, arrested right after he'd signed his papers. Not even Southern-born, but claimed he was a plantation owner — with acres of cotton and a hundred slaves — who felt the need to serve. He never served anywhere, except in prison or the crazy house."

Bishop let Creed's words sink in before he

said, "You told me something, Creed, but it's not enough. It's just a hell of a coincidence."

"One of God's jokes — the war connects us all."

"More than the war. I want Beaudine dead."

"I know the feeling."

"You lost your eyes, I lost my family."

"And your limb."

"I don't care about that."

"I wouldn't give it no never mind if I found the replacement you did."

Bishop paused, and then, "You've known me a hell of a long time. You're really thinking you can play with me like this?"

"I'm in command, and you're a prisoner."

The back of Bishop's left hand smashed into Creed's jaw, sending his glasses flying into the fire. Bishop grabbed Creed's blue lapel. "You're talking in circles! Tell me what the hell your intentions are!"

Creed smiled, his scarred-over eyes meeting Bishop's. "Only give the enemy enough information to confuse."

The barrel of Fuller's rifle was sudden, and steady, over Creed's shoulder, pointing right in the center of Bishop's forehead.

One of the guns shouted out, "Problem, Creed?"

Fuller said, "No problem, go back to your bourbon." Then, to Bishop, "Know why I like the Morgan-James, Doc? It's lighter than a Sharps, and balances easy. I still have to load every shot, but that just means I can't waste any. So you let go of the captain, and fetch his glasses."

White Fox stood perfectly in place, letting the wind blow through her hair and the fringing on her jacket, while casting her eyes to Bishop, then Creed, and the rifle Fuller had leveled. She nudged Bishop with her foot and said, *"Ována'xaeotse."*

Bishop released the lapel, but stayed fixed on Creed's face, which showed no movement, no feeling. He then grabbed the glasses from the low-burning fire, the flames snapping at the metal frames, before cooling them off in the snow. Bishop pressed the glasses into Creed's palm. "Not even scratched."

Fuller didn't lower the rifle even a quarter inch.

Creed inspected the lenses with his fingertips before slipping them on. "The Dr. John Bishop I knew would never strike a man in anger."

Bishop took a breath. "He's dead."

Creed said, "Then maybe we should bury him."

"Or each other."

Fuller kept aiming even as Bishop held up his empty right sleeve. "See? Nothing. My temper got the best of me. It won't again."

"But you're smarter than any man here, Doc. That means you can't be trusted."

White Fox looked to Fuller and again said, *"Ováná'xaeotse."*

Bishop said, "That means 'calm down.' "

Fuller held for a few more heartbeats, then rested his rifle on his shoulder. "I know what it means. My mama was half-Cheyenne. Didn't look like her, though."

White Fox unclenched her fists, returning her gaze to the distant trees, which were now sharp black jags against the white, separating the moving snowdrifts from the starless night. The moon fought to break through the heavier clouds, to throw a shred of light on the miles of blanket below, but couldn't.

Creed said, "What about the boy? Do you see him?"

Fuller said, "Not yet."

"It's been exactly one hour."

"I don't have no watch, sir."

"Don't need it; I know what an hour feels like."

Creed wiped his eyes under his glasses. "He shouldn't have gone."

"Hector's chasing rabbits and he ain't alone. You sent that one with the busted head with him, the loudmouth who always cheats at Monte."

"I know all that. Someone needs to find them both."

"You want me to stand guard on these two, or start a search party?"

Fuller half grinned at Bishop, while Creed said, "We've got enough guns for the prisoners. Are they sober?"

"Sober enough."

"I'm ordering someone to go into those woods and find Hector!"

Fuller nodded, about to assure Creed he'd bring Hector back safe, when White Fox bolted. In a single motion, she sprang beyond the firelight, landed in the snow, and then started running for the tree line. Fuller whipped his rifle to his shoulder, pressing his eye against the long sight that was nearly the length of the barrel.

White Fox darted in one direction, breaking into another, then off again. Animal-fast, but she was shadow-boxed by the snow, her back and shoulders coming into brief focus in Fuller's sight. His trigger finger tightened.

A shout ripped from Bishop as he blocked Fuller, grabbing the barrel with his left hand even as pistol shots popped from the other hired guns. Fuller hard-swung the rifle, catching Bishop in the shoulder, knocking him back, onto the fire.

White Fox dove into the trees.

Creed barked, "Sniper, what do you have?"

Fuller focused his sight on the movement he could barely make out along the deep shadows of the woods; it was something dark moving through something darker. Fuller wiped snow from the front of the scope with his thumb, and then pressed his eye to the piece, aiming down. "I'm seeing some shadows, but can make out her head. Your call, Captain."

Bishop said to Creed and Fuller, "Fox can see in the dark. She's not escaping — she's going to find your boy!"

"We're losing the shot!"

Creed finally said, "Don't take it."

Fuller lowered the rifle. "She's gone."

"I recall seeing you pray, Bishop. So you better get to it, begging God to make sure that dog-eater comes back with Hector. Because I am thirsty to have you shot."

Bishop said, "But you have to deliver us alive."

Creed almost smiled. "A dying man still counts as alive, and that gives me a lot of leeway."

The dark was enormous and far reaching, growing out of the ground and towering into the surrounding night, where it met more darkness. Thick, mountainous clouds churned high in the Colorado sky, and let no light escape from the stars or the moon.

Hector sat at the base of one of the huge shapes, straddling the roots that twisted from its trunk into the snow, blowing warmth into his palms. At this hour, the woods weren't trees, just blackened giants, with a hundred huge arms, and standing so close to each other, they formed an enormous wall to the outside. The path between the trees was scraping-narrow, with each tangled access looking like the next and the next. Moving twenty feet in any direction only confused him more, and so he sat, with three dead rabbits and a man's corpse beside him.

Hector blew again into his cupped hands, feeling his own warm breathing against his palms and his face. Even the gloves his mama knit for him weren't helping. He began rubbing the cold-tingle out of his arms when he heard something: that almost-squeak of a foot pressing into the snow. Hector turned; the movement could be right in front of him or a hundred feet away, but all he could make out was the shadowed dark.

To Hector, it sounded like a critter, or a person, or another kind of critter. He tried to pull his pistol from his jacket, but the steel felt colder than ice, and the sight got caught on his pocket. He yanked the pistol, a piece of his jacket hanging from the barrel, but with nothing to aim at. Nothing. There was another footfall, that odd sound coming closer. Hector stumbled forward, pulling his leg away from the corpse folded beside him, and brought the pistol up, whipping it from dark shape to dark shape, wanting to shoot. At anyone, or any thing.

"Hector, put down that gun."

Hector gripped the pistol with both hands to steady it as he aimed blindly at the trees. Then he heard, "I'll take you to camp."

White Fox stood before the boy, holding out her hands. Hector blinked, thinking she was another trick of the shadows. "But you can't talk."

White Fox eased the pistol from him, lowered the hammer, and then slipped the pistol behind her belt. She waited until the weapon was secure, with Hector watching, before saying, "You mean I'm only able to speak my Cheyenne? No. I understand.

Everything. I hate it, but use your tongue when I choose it."

"But why now?"

"You don't speak Cheyenne. And you're afraid."

"No, no, I ain't." Then Hector nodded with chattering teeth. "Jed died. Right where he's laying."

White Fox bent next to Jed's body, which was twisted in an impossible position, his legs tangled in the tree's knotted roots and his head half buried in the snow, a white frosting building on his face.

Hector said, "We got them rabbits and started back. He tripped and that was it. Said he was dizzy, that his head still hurt from when you hit him."

"*Onéstôhóné.*"

"I don't know what that means."

"He was a fool."

"Uh, yes, ma'am."

White Fox struck a match on her leathers, the tiny flame showing the cut between the snow-heavy pines.

Hector said, "I didn't see that. We kept goin' in circles. I was afraid I was gonna end up like Jed."

"I know these woods now."

"But ain't you still our prisoner?"

"Yes."

"You could leave me here."

"You belong at the camp, at the fire. *Néhe'éohtsé'tov.*"

White Fox turned for the tree-break. Hector grabbed the rabbits. "Ma'am, I surely hope you asked me to come with you," he said and followed her, sidestepping the snow-and-pinecone-covered branches that had walled him in.

Fox's movements were quick-sure, weaving around the trees without disturbing them at all while Hector was slapped by the branches as he tried to keep up, icy snow always in his eyes. Every twenty steps or so, he'd reach out to brush Fox's back, assuring himself she was still in front of him. She'd glance over her shoulder and tell him, in her own English, to hold the rabbits high so not to be torn by nettles. Hector did as he was told.

Hector said, "I-I got these right off, like I said. But then we lost the sun, and Jed tripped up. Nobody can see in this dark."

"Me."

"Except you, ma'am."

# CHAPTER FOURTEEN: SNOW BLIND

More than an hour had passed, and the image Fuller saw through the long sight was hazy with cold fog: silhouettes coming out of the shadows of the pines, becoming clearer and clearer with each step, as they moved onto the expanse of snow between the trees and Creed's camp. Fuller lowered his sniper's rifle when he recognized White Fox, with Hector stumbling behind, keeping the rabbits over his head. Bishop stood.

Fuller gulped his laugh. "Tarnation."

Hector broke from White Fox, churning the snow as he ran toward the fire, waving his three trophies. He called to Creed. The captain grabbed Bishop's shoulder and pulled himself up, facing Hector's voice before opening his arms like a father welcoming a son back home. Creed then stiff-backed, froze his arms at his side, and killed the rush of feeling.

Creed's guard was barely down, but it

didn't escape Bishop. "Hector's a good boy, like my son would have been. And Fox made sure he wasn't lost to you."

"That tripe won't work. Your debt'll be paid."

Hector offered Creed a flustered salute. "Reporting back, sir. Uh, mission accomplished."

Creed said, "Not well. I blame Jed for this foolishness."

"We lost Jed."

"Report?"

"Uh, he tripped, busted his head again. He'd been sneakin' from a bottle you didn't know about, sir. He was pretty drunk."

"No more missions, boy. No more losses. Where's the damn dog-eater?"

Hector coughed up his words. "Begging your pardon, sir, but she found me. I know I did wrong for the company, but she didn't. And she talked regular English."

"She's standing with you, Bishop?"

Bishop absently raised his right arm, as if the shotgun were there, to fire both barrels into the blind man. His anger heating, he chose his words carefully: "White Fox is right here with *me,* Creed. And you owe her thanks."

"Sniper Fuller?"

Fuller eyed White Fox as she laced her

fingers around Bishop's left hand, then said, "Hell, yes. The prisoners are accounted for, sir."

That's when Fat Gut screamed from the other side of the fire, "My leg's killin' me, cuz! You've gotta do something!"

Creed said, "Either cure him or kill him. He's been a weight on us too long."

Bishop said, "You giving me an order, Creed?"

"And you both better obey it."

"Want your man treated? I'll need my kit."

"On my Pride."

Fuller stepped around Creed's tall horse, and opened one of the hand-scrolled saddlebags that draped Pride's haunches. He took out the shotgun rig, slung it over his shoulder, while finding the medical bag.

Fuller kept his back to Bishop, making sure he got a good look, teasing him with the rig. The shotgun was less than two feet from Bishop, and he raised his half a right arm as if to reach for the weapon, but Fuller was having his fun. White Fox gently squeezed Bishop's shoulder.

"Sorry, Doc, but that special rig ain't what you asked for." Fuller laughed, then produced the field kit, giving it to White Fox in a deliberate motion. "It's a good thing you came back. The doc needs you." She tucked it under her arm.

Fuller noted the LT. BISHOP in gold across the leather. "I am surrounded by officers." Fuller admired the shotgun before putting it back behind Creed's saddle. "That gun's a hell of a thing. It's a part of you, ain't it?"

Bishop let the words settle. "When I need it to be."

Fuller grinned, but there was nothing friendly there.

White Fox walked by the painted, stroking him along his withers as she moved to the group of hired guns crouched by their own, small fire. The painted snorted, bobbing his head in recognition. White Fox looked to Bishop, who was right behind her. Their eyes met, passing a message he understood.

The guns were snickering something, but it was too low to hear. Bishop stood in front of them, waiting for one of them to jaw something else. Nothing came, so he said, "One-armed man and a woman, and we cleaned your clocks pretty good."

One of them, sporting a fancy blue kerchief, threw out, "But it didn't change nothing. You're here. The squaw had her chance, and she comes back. How mule-ass stupid is that?"

Fat Gut yelled, "Oh, you're a great one,

Doc! Shoot us, then dig the bullets out! My leg ain't nothin' but a lick and a promise, you son of a bitch!"

Bishop and White Fox settled by Fat Gut, who was sprawled on a filthy blanket, his wounded leg stretched out with a bandage newly pink from leaking. Gut was cradling the Winchester, its stock muddy from where he'd been using the rifle as a crutch, sinking it into the wet ground.

"Lose the rifle."

Fat Gut wrapped his paw around the trigger guard. "That ain't happening."

Bishop said, "You have to be able to sit up so I can do this properly. You can't with that thing on your chest."

Gut looked around at the others: two were ready to shoot, casual as hell, and Blue Kerchief wasn't tamping down his hatred for Bishop at all. It read on his face, and Gut liked that, so he let Fox take the rifle. She placed it near the med bag.

Fat Gut said, "Needs more than one hand to shoot it anyways."

That's when the knives came out.

In the light of Creed's fire, Fuller drew his Bowie dagger from the beaded sheath on his belt, while thirty feet away, White Fox handed Bishop a surgical blade. Fuller "ringed" the largest of the rabbits, slicing a notch through the fur just above its feet, separating the skin from the leg muscles. As he did this, Bishop laid the surgeon's blade across Fat Gut's bandages.

Gut sniffed, "You and your squaw gonna operate again? I didn't say nothing about that."

"The wound has to be checked, and I need her hands."

"Her hands and those nice titties. I like them hangers. How about sharing a little? That'd make me feel a hell of a lot better than what you're doin'."

White Fox didn't allow herself a reaction to Fat Gut's mouth. She couldn't. Instead, she held his leg steady as Bishop cut through the last of the bandages, exposing the wound.

"She might just finish what she started. She's taken scalps," Bishop said as he tossed the bandages into a stained pile. "Got a little infection. I'll clean it, but it'll burn."

Fat Gut turned his head away, snorting. "Just hurry the hell up. Do it."

"Never argue with a patient."

By the fire, Fuller tossed Hector the rabbit. "Peel him," he said before casting his eye back on White Fox, as she wiped a surgeon's blade, laid it aside, and handed Bishop another.

Sometime, when Fuller wasn't watching, Fox had tied her hair tight behind her with a leather thong.

A feeling nudged Fuller: it was the bristling he felt when there was an enemy sniper close by, but couldn't be seen. During the war's last days, he'd climbed a tree to take position, and there had been a Reb, perched on a branch and hidden by leaves, loading a Sharps long-range rifle. He'd gotten him with the same Bowie he was using on Hector's rabbits. The Reb hadn't made a sound.

Now, that bristling was back, and White Fox was the reason. Fuller was ready for her move, prepared to shoulder his weapon. He said to Hector, "She talks English?"

"Better than me."

Creed barked, "Fuller, you can't skin a jack faster than that? Boy, stop the jabber and get the meat on the fire!"

Hector said, "Yes, sir!" as he peeled the fur down the big one's legs to its belly, where it gathered in folds. Sniper Fuller ringed the next jack, cutting quickly, and a little deep, before grabbing the last one, its blood sticky between his fingers.

White Fox tore a shirt into clean strips, and Fuller whipped around at the sound. The bandages, scalpels, and Winchester were set out between her and Bishop, who was daubing Fat Gut's wound.

Creed barked, "Doctor, finish up your business!"

White Fox regarded the blind man shouting orders before saying, *"Exanomóhtá?"*

"Yes."

Fat Gut winced. "What the hell's that?"

Bishop looked up from the arrow wound. "She asked, am I prepared?"

The scalpel was a flash from White Fox's hand into Blue Kerchief's throat, the blood-jet around the blade instant as Blue fell back, firing his pistol wild into the sky.

Bishop grabbed the Winchester in front of him, pumped it with his left hand, and blasted the next hired gun who was reaching. The slug sent him spiraling off his feet, his pistol not clearing his holster. He hit the ground red, calling for his ma.

Fox grabbed the scalpels, then busted Fat Gut's lower teeth with her heel, cracking his jaw sideways.

It all took less than a minute.

Fuller turned, swinging his rifle around on its strap, bringing the sight to his eye, just as Fox leapt on the back of her painted. Fuller thumbed the hammer. Easy kill shot.

Chaos exploded.

The painted reared wild, his head whipping from side-to-side, with Fox hanging on, turning the animal on Fuller. The horse's huge legs smashed Fuller square in the chest like two pistons, tossing the sniper clean off his feet, hard into Creed and Hector, shattering ribs, and Creed's dark glasses.

Screams and gunfire polluted the air.

One of Creed's men used Fat Gut for cover, blasting at Bishop and White Fox from behind Gut's huge belly, scorching his shirt. Gut screamed himself raw, as Bishop fired a single shot from the hip, missing Gut and hitting Creed's man between the eyes.

Bishop was in motion, didn't look twice at the dead.

He cooled the barrel of the Winchester in the snow, before using it to snag the handle of his kit on its sight. Gut's broken-teeth-screams never stopped as Bishop charged to Fox and the horses, the kit dangling from the rifle.

The painted chopped air with his legs, while Fox swung him around, kicking wild. Her weapon. A Creed man opened up with a revolver, and the painted bucked at him, shattering his arm to nothing. He went down shooting and screaming.

Captain Creed shouted blind: "The prisoners! Report! Goddamn you!"

Bishop yanked at Pride's saddlebags, grabbing for the shotgun rig. A slug ripped past his ear.

Fuller struggled to his feet, reaching his rifle.

White Fox called above it all, *"Asêsta'xêstse!"*

Bishop leapt onto Creed's Pride, just as White Fox and the painted bolted. Both animals ran for the open snow, the prisoners tight on their backs.

Creed's voice strained, "Shoot them, goddamn it!"

Hector had his pistol raised, both hands shaking. "I — I can't shoot her!"

"I sure as hell can!"

Fuller's words stretched into a howl as he brought up his rifle, pressing against one of his busted ribs. He steadied on his target, and fired. The hammer dropped, and the ball ripped from the Morgan-James in a spit of flame. Fuller's jaw clenched at the recoil, fighting the pain of the weapon slamming back into him.

The targets kept moving.

Captain Creed stood, hands deep in his pockets, listening for a scream. What he heard was the sniper's shot echo and die, above the cries of his own men.

■ ■ ■ ■

A river and half a mountain away, on a trail that was little more than a finger poking through a frozen hillside, Lem and Chaney ate the last bit of their beans and jerky supper, while Howard shuffled a poker deck with massive fingers. Beaudine watched, drinking thick coffee.

Chaney said, "Look at the top card."

Howard turned over the four of clubs. "Shit."

"That's your card?"

"How'd you do that?"

Chaney took back the deck. "I can do it as many times as I want. That's my business."

Howard lunged, grabbing Chaney by the lapels. "You're cheatin' me!"

Lem eased the giant back. "How can he be cheating you when there's no money bet? You didn't lose nothing!"

Howard settled back, wiping the sweat from his face.

Beaudine threw the last bit of coffee into the fire. "When you go into battle, you better bring more than card tricks."

"I got more." Chaney spit out a chunk of hard gristle, and then drank deep from his canteen. Deadeye Lem laughed without making a sound.

Howard said, "I guess this ain't your style, is it?"

Chaney coughed. "I've done my time on the trail, but we're supposed to be eating better than this. Isn't that what you said?"

Beaudine took the long cleaver and a small wooden box from behind his saddle, and sat by the fire. He looked at Chaney as he opened the box, removing a Carborundum sharpening stone, and began running it against the cleaver blade. The sound of the stone against metal seemed to be Beaudine's answer.

Lem said, "You can't ask questions like that, gambler. You have to have faith, like the next card you draw is the one that gives you the winning hand. Only you can't cheat."

Howard snorted. "Winning hand. That's almost funny."

Beaudine didn't stop sharpening. "The troops are always impatient before the attack."

Chaney said, "We're not a troop. I've never been in any army, and they say you haven't neither."

Beaudine kept sharpening. "We were all denied that glory, but we won't be denied

158

this. Chaney, if you're not a coward —"

"Coward has nothing to do with it."

"If you're not a coward, when we find that Bishop gold, you'll eat like a king for the rest of your life, however long it lasts."

"We got the extra rifles, ammo, and dynamite from that dry goods store." Chaney looked to Howard, who was tightening the cinch that held the crates of dynamite on a small pack mule. Two rifles were bound in cloth, and fit tight between the cases.

Chaney wiped his mouth. "But you didn't let us take any extra food."

Beaudine gave his response some pause. "You mean more whiskey, and that cake. A captain, a brother in arms, advises that a fighting unit runs best when it runs lean. I agree. You have a full belly and a purpose. *That* is doing better than most."

Lem raised his one good eye, tickled that Chaney had gotten caught up in Beaudine's obscure logic. He took a drink of Clinch Mountain whiskey and offered some to Howard, who shook his head. Lem had a little bit more, before: "When this Creed delivers Bishop, I don't know who the hell you think you're getting. The doc isn't the same man he was that night."

Chaney, under his breath: "No bullshit."

Beaudine held the cleaver out, inspecting

the edge by the firelight. "You failed in your mission before, so I pray none of *you* are the same." Then he laid the cleaver by his side. "I know I'm not."

# CHAPTER FIFTEEN:
## BLOODY DAWN

They were running like hell.

White Fox leaned into the painted, her belly almost flat against his back, her face aligned perfectly to the side of his neck, holding on tight as they cut through the first row of pines and frost-bare shrubs that bordered the deeper woods. With her ear pressed to him, White Fox could hear the pounding strength of the painted's heart and lungs.

If White Fox glanced over her shoulder to check Bishop behind her on Creed's Pride, a low-hanging branch would smash her clean. So Fox kept down, the trees barely brushing over her, not catching her hair, and she sensed that Bishop was riding fine.

Bishop was handling Creed's horse well, keeping him near the painted, but with enough room to judge where Fox was leading next. The reins were knotted around his left hand as he kept the Winchester tucked under his right half-arm, barrel-down into the stirrup, so as not to catch a passing limb.

Every slight motion Fox made, Bishop did the same, as she guided them through the woods, along the narrow trail she'd broken to find Hector. It was pure instinct, her knowing the cuts, slopes, and the icy bends, all in darkness.

They pushed their rides, gaining speed, dodging trees, their hooves just missing roots and tangles. The crack of distant gunfire split the air, and White Fox deliberately slowed, angling her ride too close to the base of a huge Colorado oak. The painted's legs half-skidded in the snow, and she fought a fall from his back, but Fox was still in control and the horse did as she wanted, before breaking into a hard run.

Creed's Pride stayed tight behind the painted, its legs more sure, keeping Bishop steady as they rode deeper into the dense black of the woods, leaving behind a mess of tracks for their pursuers to find.

At the camp, Fuller swung his pinto around as one of Creed's hired men fired more shots into the solid black of the woods.

"What the hell are you shooting at?" Fuller asked as he checked the ammunition in his jacket pocket. "They're running, and you're wasting shells! Grab some fire!"

The taller hired gun pulled a burning branch from the campfire, then mounted up. The other, shorter gun opened Blue Kerchief's fine jacket, liberating the pearl-handled Colt that was still holstered on his hip. Kerchief's blood smeared Short Gun's hands as he stuck the weapon in his waistband before grabbing the reins of Bishop's horse. The bay bucked as soon as Short Gun hit the saddle, not wanting him. The horse snapped twice more, then seemed to calm.

Short Gun howled, "The doc's got a hell of a ride! I want this one after we've dealt him his justice!"

"They're prisoners, and they need capturing! That's the order!" Creed shouted.

Fuller touched his arm for his attention saying, "I'll shoot to wound."

"I heard you miss once already."

Fuller let the officious criticism go, turned to Hector. "Boy, you ride with the captain, take him along the tree line. Try and find your way over the hill. We'll meet on the other side of the woods come sun-up, *with the prisoners.* And watch yourself, there's nothing darker than Colorado midnight."

Hector saluted Fuller as Fat Gut tried to stand and talk through his busted, bloody teeth. "Wha' da thell am I supothed to do?

163

D'at bitch got my Thinchester!"

Creed buried his anger under his words. "They took my Pride! One drop of that animal's blood is worth more than all of you put together."

Fuller gave a quick, "It's all cash to me, Captain!" and rode out, followed by the hired guns. The taller one rode with the torch, its flame showing the tracks of the escape running through the deep snow to the trees.

Fat Gut limped to a horse, but couldn't raise his leg to mount. "Boy, yuze got da' thelp me."

Creed turned to Fat Gut to blind-stare him down: "You've been a burden your whole life, and now you're worse than useless. If I didn't need every pair of eyes I'd tell the boy to blow a hole in you and be done with it."

No one moved.

"Get your horses! Move!" Creed's shout carried across the open snow, dying as jumbled noise just as Fuller rode to the edge of the tree line. He signaled for the gun with the torch to throw a light on the broken spot between the pines where White Fox and Bishop had run their horses.

Fuller made a slashing gesture across his throat for silence. He waved for Torch to stay close before they rode through the break. The only sound was of the horses cracking the snow's icy crust or snapping twigs, as they followed the tracks left behind by the prisoners. Fuller picked up the pace when he had a bead.

Short Gun kept Bishop's bay horse a few paces back, as he ducked beneath branches and swatted pinecones away from his face. The swat sounded like the slap of a gun being pulled from its leather.

Fuller whipped around in his saddle, his Bowie ready to throw.

Short Gun rocked back in his saddle. "Goddamn, boy!"

"One or t'other, your mouth is gonna get you killed." Fuller replaced the knife. Short Gun nodded, clamping his hands over his mouth to show he wouldn't make another sound.

Fuller gaffed the pinto, breaking into a run. Torch followed, with Short Gun hanging back, until Bishop's bay horse galloped ahead on its own, as if it were searching out its rightful master.

Down the trail a mile, the woods were thickening into a maze, and White Fox held on to the painted's neck, slowing him. The shimmer of icicles on the trees was the only light that Fox could use as she turned painted toward a grouping of tall scrubs, marking where she'd found Hector.

Right behind her, Creed's Pride was running close. Bishop pulled back, breaking Pride's full-out run, stopping where Jed's twisted body was still lying. The horse stood in that spot, as if at attention.

The night's snowfall had tried to shroud Jed, while above him jags of ice fell from the high branches, bashing his face as if he'd been in an after-death brawl. For that moment, the hot breathing of the horses, and the crack of the icicles dropping was all that could be heard.

White Fox stepped over the corpse. "When I looked for the boy, I found the way out. Around the trees."

Bishop said, "The eye of the cat: *Ka'eeséhotame?*"

Fox allowed herself a half smile. "The gun."

They pulled the rig from Creed's saddlebags, a pocket of snow pelting them from the tall trees. Bishop shed his coat and shirt, and Fox fit his half-arm snugly into the prosthetic cup, then tightened the straps across his shoulders until they bit his skin. Bishop tied off the trigger line, with just enough slack to bring the double-barreled chest high. The gun was breeched, with only one shell loaded.

White Fox slipped Bishop's shirt and coat over the gun rig, her hand touching his chest to feel the steady beat of his heart. She nodded.

Bishop buttoned up with his left. "I didn't see their faces this time. At all. Just the eyes, so I could tell when they were about to make their move."

"Good."

Bishop then reached into the saddlebag for the twelve-gauge shells, but found nothing.

The posse was at the edge of the woods, where Fox's trail wasn't so distinct. Fuller halted the pinto to read the mess of horse tracks in the snow in front of them: nothing but mud and slush, sloppy in all directions. Torch stood in his stirrups, trying to make heads or tails: "I can't tell a damn thing. Maybe they doubled back."

Fuller said, "No, they're ahead of us, looking for a way out," and he kept moving, the others following.

Beyond the posse's view, Creed's Pride stood by Jed's body, lifting his legs in place, as Fox searched the rest of the saddle for shells. Reaching far into one of the leather pockets, she found a linen handkerchief tied neatly around a small object. The handkerchief was clean, with initials L.R.C. sewn into one corner. She loosened the knot, revealing a Union Army Medal of Honor awarded to Captain Dupont Creed tucked between the linen folds.

White Fox held the medal out in her palm.

Bishop said, "I was there when they gave it to him," before snapping shut the shotgun's breech, the left barrel loaded.

Fox dropped the medal back into the pocket. "No ammunition."

She stepped from Creed's Pride as splinters of orange flame spread across the surface of the icicles around her; bits of color reflected against the black pines.

White Fox and Bishop turned to see the torch, burning tiny-orange in the distance, but coming steadily closer to them. Bishop tossed her Fat Gut's Winchester. She checked it, pumped a round into the chamber, all the time watching the progress of the three-man posse.

Fox said, "I know places for us."

Fuller, Torch, and Short Gun reined in where the muddy trail was divided by the massive Colorado oak, its knotted branches blocking their way like giant arms. Horse tracks circled the base of the tree, and then seemed to lead off onto both of the trails behind it, going in separate directions.

Fuller recognized the Cheyenne trick, smiled, looked to his men: "They're not supposed to be together. These woods are too deep, they haven't had time to clear 'em." Then to Short Gun, "Follow that side south, we'll take t'other."

"But I won't be seeing nothing."

"You'll see us, and so can they. I got the doc's ammo, and that bitch can't hide in the dark if she's shooting."

The Torch and Short Gun exchanged looks about the black sniper, then split off.

Short Gun rode easily under the tree limb, and followed the left cut into the dark. Fuller and Torch ducked below the branches to get around the oak on their side. Fuller signaled for Torch to keep the flame high, as they veered right, keeping to the trail White Fox had used.

Deeper in the woods, Fox grabbed the reins of both horses, and led them down past a thick barrier of trees, holding the Winchester tight to her side. She tied the painted and Creed's Pride to a scrub pine, then crouched behind a large, ice-coated tree trunk that had been snapped in half by some forgotten storm. She braced the rifle and narrowed on her target.

Fox made no sound.

Fuller and the Torch seemed to be a few hundred yards or so down the trail, but riding closer. The flame of the torch danced off the Winchester's sight, as Fox narrowed her aim.

Following the trail, Fuller said to Torch, "Make yourself a good target."

"You don't give me orders, boy."

"You want to answer to Captain Creed?"

The Torch didn't say another word.

Bishop ran low, holding the rig to his chest, before rolling down a sloping grade, and coming up behind a spreading blue fir, its branches a perfect cover. He lowered the rig, keeping his elbow crooked so he was aiming from the waist, while watching the posse move toward White Fox's position.

White Fox held Fat Gut's Winchester steady against the tree trunk, her eye on the torch's flame as it vanished behind the silhouette of a tree, and appeared again moments later, bringing Fuller closer.

Then, the flame held steady. The riders had stopped, letting Fox make out the shapes of Fuller and one other man: just highlights, and the glint off their rifles. Two rifles. Fox tightened her trigger finger on the Winchester, counting the seconds.

Bishop watched from his position, and flexed his shoulders, drawing the shotgun's trigger line in tight. Bishop knew the posse should be bigger than just two. Fox's trick had split them up, but where were the rest?

Bishop held his breath, waiting for the sound of a horse and rider coming down the small cut, to where he was hidden.

Waiting.

Fuller stepped down from his horse, and walked ahead, his footsteps breaking the snow. Torch was about to dismount, but Fuller hissed, "Stay there! Hold that thing higher!"

Torch did as ordered, telling Fuller to go to hell.

That's when the slug from the Winchester blew a hole clean through his chest, knocking him out of his saddle. The Torch, and the fire he was carrying, hit the ground, dead.

The fire sizzled to nothing in the snow, leaving darkness.

Fuller dove to the ground, Torch's chest wound a bloody geyser, soaking him. He wiped the blood from his eyes and took aim through his long sight, ready for the next shot.

Fox cracked off another round.

The flashes from the Winchester were spears of light that tore the dark, giving her away. Fuller eyed the flash, and zeroed in on the shadowed shape in the distance, half hidden by a fallen tree. He fired, yellow flame erupting from the Morgan-James, followed by a low thunder that pounded the ears.

The woman's scream that came next was a sudden burst of pain.

Bishop tore from his cover. *"Ma'êhóóhe!"*

There was no answer. Bishop waited, heart pounding. His eyes narrowed, watching Fuller's silhouette in the action of reloading, bringing the rifle to his shoulder and aiming where White Fox was hidden.

Bishop's heart was against his ribs.

The sniper drew his breath first, then tightened his finger against the trigger. That's when the Winchester cut the dark again with a second shot that hard-spun Fuller to the ground.

Before Bishop could move, there was a pistol in his side from behind, and a nasal voice with a thick accent from the hills: "Doc, you're done. Your squaw and the slave killed each other, so now it's just us. Come on, I'm takin' you prisoner. Hell, I'll even let you walk alongside your own horse. I got it tied up yonder. Can't ask for more than that."

Bishop turned, the left barrel of the rig protruding from his sleeve and snug against Short Gun's stomach. Short looked to Bishop and said, "But, you doctored me up one time. Saved my life."

The blast blew out Short Gun's side, and he stumbled back against the blue fir, shooting near Bishop, into the ground, at the air, before collapsing. Bishop stood over him, watching his life soak into the muddy snow.

Short laughed, then blood-choked, "She's still dead. Settling up for that bitch wanting my hair. At least, we did that."

Dawn didn't come easy. The heavy clouds of night refused to break apart with the sun, draping everything in dull grey. It was the kind of light that cast no shadows, but you could feel sticking to your skin.

Hector guided his horse, with Creed riding tandem, down a small grade near an orchard that had been beaten by the snow: rows of apple trees stood dead in the blowing drifts.

Creed kept his hands on Hector's shoulders, making sure he had enough pull on the reins. "He was bred from the same stock as President Grant's own Cincinnati. Grant had Cincinnati all through the conflict, and never allowed anyone else on his back. I did the same. No one ever rode, fed, or watered Creed's Pride but me."

Creed rode on for a few moments. "Until now."

Hector said, "Pride won't do for anyone else the way he does for you, sir. You'll get him back."

"I can't see him anymore, but he's still the finest-looking animal there is. That I know."

"Yes, sir. All sixteen hands."

"That's right. Sixteen."

Hector stopped at the edge of the orchard, the thick woods breaking into distant pieces a few acres away, where the trees surrendered to this stretch of flat land. Hector shielded his eyes against the dull white to see any other riders.

Fat Gut galloped from behind, almost colliding with Creed and Hector, before pulling his swayback to a stop. Keeping his hand over his broken mouth, he chose words he thought he could pronounce. "I can't thee — make out — no one."

Creed said, "You in the right place, boy?"

Hector nodded, even though Creed couldn't see it. "Yes, sir. I think so."

"Either you are or you're not."

"No, sir, the other side of the woods. Yes,

I'm sure."

Creed put a hand on Hector's arm. "Fuller said he'd meet us with my Pride. And the prisoners. You understand what that all means, boy."

"I do, sir. He'll be here."

Fat Gut spit pink, and tried again. "Did th-u — ever tell about de damn thorse?"

Creed said, "He knows."

"Ain't d'at your'n Pride?"

"What is it? Boy?"

Hector couldn't answer Creed right away; he was taken by the sight of Pride, running hard from the edge of the woods, the deep snow erupting around his every footfall. Glistening black against the acres and acres of white that met the grey sky.

The rider on his back had the reins clenched in his left hand, the right sleeve of his jacket pinned back.

"It's Pride, sir! And Bishop's on him!"

The bullet fired from the woods ripped through the rider's neck, sending him off the saddle, his foot catching the stirrup, his dead weight finally slowing Pride down. The horse dragged the body to the orchard, cutting a red furrow through the white.

Creed shouted for his horse, as Hector galloped to the orchard. Fat Gut hung back, as he saw Fuller following Pride's tracks out of the woods, his rifle across his chest, and his jacket a soak of dried blood.

Fuller actually nodded to Fat Gut as he rode to where Hector was helping Creed down from the saddle.

Creed said, "Pride?"

Fuller got off his horse with, "I never shot a horse I didn't mean to. He's fine. And I guess I am, too."

"The prisoners, do you have them? Bishop! Answer me!"

Fuller turned the body over with his foot. The slug had torn through Jed's neck, taking the bottom part of his face with it. Perfect sniping. After swearing under his breath, he had to admit, "No, sir. Just the wrong dead man."

"Report!"

Hector said, "That's Jed. I'd swore he busted his neck."

Fuller slipped his rifle bandolier over his head, and handed the weapon to Hector. "He did. Bishop used him as a decoy so they could escape through the woods. Almost worked, too."

Creed started through the snow, his hands palms out, reaching. "You failed."

"They outmaneuvered us, sir."

"But you're reporting that the prisoners are gone."

"Again, I said almost. The two idgits bought the farm, but I got the woman. Heard her scream after I shot. I took a bullet, and passed out. Not more than five minutes. I came around, and saw your horse running through the trees, with Doc Bishop on him."

"Not Bishop."

Fuller opened his coat, and pulled at his shirt that was caked with blood that spread from a flesh wound just above his hip. White Fox's shot had passed clean through, and the cold had stopped the wound from opening further while freezing a curled snake of blood around his waist.

Fuller got the words out — "No, sir. That's my report" — before finding the ground. Hector took the rifle as Fuller lay down, eyes closed, the snow offering him comfort.

Creed spoke, with Fuller blind-feet away from the tip of his boots. "My Pride, with the wrong man on him? The only thing that's saving you right now is that horse."

Creed turned on his heel and started with purpose in the opposite direction, one hand sweeping the air in front of him.

"Captain?"

"Quiet!"

Creed kept walking a few steps, then

stopped to listen. "Stay away from me, boy! No help! Mouths shut."

Creed heard a snort, and started for it. "So you followed the decoy? Damn foolish." Creed's hands found his horse, and a feeling of relief ran through him as he climbed onto Pride's back.

Humiliation spotted Fuller's words as Hector helped him to his feet. "I lost a hell of a lot of blood, but it got your Pride back. Sir."

"Not all of it, sniper."

# Chapter Sixteen:
## The Price of Flesh

The stream was a slash of freezing black through a gentle slope of white-frosted hills, the running water showing up its stony bottom like a magnifying glass. Miles away from the thick woods that had hidden them, surrounded by emptiness, anyone who might be riding after Bishop and White Fox would be an easy target in the morning light.

Bishop crouched, refilling the breathing device with fresh water. Fat Gut's Winchester was within reach.

Bishop dipped the mechanical box into an icy shallow, then attached it to the rubber tubing that was hanging free from the mask covering White Fox's mouth. She was on the ground, lying next to the saddlebag they'd lifted from Creed's horse, with Bishop's medical instruments spilling from it.

The bay and the painted stood by, nosing the cold ground.

Fox rolled onto her back, her head lolling, while she tried to catch her breath. The air caught in her throat in sharp little stabs, as if she'd swallowed broken glass. Blood dotted the snow around her right ankle.

She tugged on the strap holding the mask in place, but Bishop pulled her hand away, attaching the rubber tubing, "I know you hate it, but don't move. Just be still and breathe. That's all you have to do, *háo'omóhtahe.*"

Fox dropped her hand.

Bishop cranked the device, drawing the oxygen from the fresh water into the mask. The small leather bellows expanded, then contracted, forcing the air into Fox's lungs. Fox coughed, her body jerking forward, but she drew deep breaths through the spasms, and then laid back, her air flowing naturally.

He kept a steady motion, turning the handle, watching Fox's cheeks flush and her breathing relax. He said, "You saved me with this instrument, nurse. It's only right that I do it for you."

White Fox unhooked the strap that held the mask into place. "Not a nurse."

Bishop put the mask in his med bag. "Sorry, warrior."

*"Ho'toveotse."*

"You're not weak."

"You carry the box because I'm too weak to breathe. *Ho'toveotse.*" White Fox spit the last word, as if she was cursing her own name.

"No, I've told you, it's called asthma. We don't know the cause, but your lungs close up. *He'poná?* Is that right?"

"*He'poná.* In the chest."

Bishop balanced the small box on his leg, and wrapped the tubing around it with his left hand. "I built this contraption for soldiers in the field, but carry it in case we need it. And we did. We. Not just you." He put that into his field kit also, and then put all of his gear into a saddlebag pocket. The bay was steady as Bishop buckled everything down tight.

Fox shook her head. "It shames me."

"You were strong enough to get us out of the woods, to take a bullet from Fuller."

White Fox rubbed her blood-wet ankle. "That was nothing."

"You got our horses back."

The bay lifted his head, snorting his comment, as Bishop pulled a piece of linen from the medical bag. "This should work. You prepped it." He wrapped the ankle wound. He tied it off. "Just a crease. I heard you scream. I didn't know what happened."

Fox retied the bandage. "Trying to get the

181

sniper to stand. And I did. You were afraid for me."

"So, you're not weak."

When Fox stood, the painted came to her immediately. She swung onto his back without help. "You want Beaudine?"

The question seemed like a challenge to Bishop, but he looked into her eyes for a reason. Without her saying another word, she was giving him a way out, if he wanted it.

He understood and offered, "That's my cause."

"You got one man, and there will be many more."

"I'm ready. *Exanomóhtá.*"

Fox said, "Good. How do we ride?"

The bay pawed the cold ground, waiting, as Bishop tucked the saddlebag into place. "Pardee told me where Beaudine was going to meet his men."

"You trust this?"

Bishop mounted, slipping the shotgun rig into the specially made sling that hung alongside the saddle's leather fender. It felt good. "He was afraid of dying, and too small a man to try a lie."

*"Ho'toveotse?"*

*"Ho'toveotse."*

Fox managed a rare smile. "You talk good. Now."

The grey light of morning died, as large snowflakes drifted from the dark clouds that had rolled in over the mountains. The wind picked up, carrying distant thunder with it.

Bishop gently urged his bay, and the horse moved with trust and speed. White Fox was instantly, and naturally, next to him. They rode together in understood silence and with purpose, following the stream down a sloping hill, to the snowy valley beyond.

The dynamite was packed tight, the new, smaller sticks making perfect bundles of three for Howard to lay out on the ground. He pointed to the logo of the Nobel Dynamite Company on the lid of the crate. "This is their new stuff. It's got that nitro-glycereen."

"What?"

Howard turned to Chaney. "Think I didn't know words like that?"

"I feel safer that you do."

"Maybe you better stop making me feel like a fool."

Beaudine stepped between them. "You're the best at what you do, or you wouldn't be riding with me." Then, to Chaney: "Better prove you can earn your share, boy."

Chaney said, "Yes, sir. Major."

Howard snorted his anger as he continued with the dynamite, setting the bundles next to each other on a blanket. His thick fingers played lightly across the explosives like they were piano keys, as he put them in perfectly even rows.

Chaney grabbed a coil of fuse, bringing his knife to meet it. Beaudine stopped him. "You don't cut 'til he knows where he's going to plant."

Howard was watching and burst, ripping the empty dynamite crate apart, and hurling the pieces toward one of the buildings, breaking some already broken glass. His chest was heaving, lips drawn over his black gums as he faced Chaney and shouted, "You got that boy? You have to do what I say!"

Chaney stayed still, his hand close to his Colt, and managed a half smile. "I know any one of you could kill me at any time. I know."

Howard said, "Damn right," anger rattling his words. Then he scrubbed his face with a pile of dirty snow, letting the cold feeling wrap his head, before shaking like a wet dog, bits of frost flying from his beard.

Beaudine said, "All right? Found your way back to us?"

Howard spit. "Look around. Half the damn mountain could come down on top of us. It's already blasted to hell."

"That's your professional opinion?"

Howard nodded. "Pro-fessional."

"Good. Creed's got a lot of men we have to bury." Beaudine turned to Lem. "Dead-eye, dig in. And find the right place for this one."

Lem Wright nodded to Beaudine before tying his horse to a half an upright piling that stuck out of a massive gravel pile as if it were growing there. The upright was like the other broken pieces of wooden construction that had been left behind by the Goodwill Mining Company, as a sign hitched to a rusty chain so declared.

This nothing.

What was left of Goodwill was a deep pit, a scar blasted into the side of a small mountain. Along the edge of the pit, supported by tar-soaked rail ties, was a narrow, roofless shack that led to the shaft of the silver mine. Twists of steel that had been tracks into the shaft for the mule-drawn carts, curved out of the mine's mouth as fossilized tentacles, another useless reminder of a dead end.

Below the mine entrance, piles of jagged-black slag were pushed up against a few

185

small buildings, their windows shattered and doors busted down by the weight of the mine's waste.

Behind an outhouse, rows of wooden markers made up a weed-choked graveyard for the miners who hadn't made their fortune. The markers, all without names, were bent crooked by the icy winds that tore through the small canyon and were trapped there to beat the final remains of Goodwill silver into nothing.

Everyone in this part of Colorado knew Goodwill had been a false strike, and they'd cleared out as fast as they'd arrived, when the silver rush took the companies to Leadville. The few who'd stayed behind had ended up shooting each other, or freezing to death.

Lem said, "Major, if I can get on top of the old shaft, I'll pick off Creed's last riders as they come in. Howard sets off the dynamite, takes out some more, and the canyon's sealed. Then we'll clean up the ones who're left. I'll put Chaney in one of the outbuildings."

"He's with us on your say-so."

"He's with us because he smells the gold you've been touting. He's been having second thoughts, but if the gold's really close, he'll pull a trigger. I've seen it."

"So you trust him?"

"Not for one minute."

"Then if he's sacrificed, it's no loss. But we have to make sure to take all of Creed's men, so Bishop'll be ours. Alone."

Lem turned on his heel, his eyes fixed on the rim of the section of mountain that had been blown away. "We'll be trapped in here, too. Who picked this place?"

"Captain Creed."

"Perfect for a massacre."

Beaudine stood with his arms folded, staring at the entrance to the old mine, at something or someone that nobody else could see. Gone.

The body of the Döbereiner's lamp was jade, with a golden snake circling the base and opening its mouth where the small flame was lit. Soiled Dove held the head of the dragon pipe at an angle, catching the fire in the bowl so that the opium glowed, and then handed it to Widow Kate as the smoke began to curl.

Widow Kate drew the grey in slowly before John Bishop held out his left to inspect the ornate pipe. White Fox stood by, enjoying the waft of smoke as Bishop held it under his nose, nodding approval.

"This should keep the pain away."

Kate exhaled, "Then you should prescribe a little for yourself. Fine grade, direct from China, and Lord knows you could use it. Push me closer."

Soiled Dove, her hair now spit-curled and wearing a freshly laundered primrose, pushed the wicker wheelchair, with Kate overflowing, around the desk to where Bishop and White Fox stood.

Kate said, "We don't need nothing between us."

"Including secrets?"

"That depends on your attitude, Doctor. Lock the door."

Bishop nodded courteously to Widow Kate, the bloodstained coat draped over his shoulders shifting as he moved to the door, and threw the bolt. He kept the rig against his chest, the double barrel tucked into his shirt like a broken arm in a sling.

Bishop said, "No one in, or out."

"Privacy's important in matters like this, so we can feel free to speak our minds, come to an understanding. Like this beautiful — is it Cheyenne, and maybe something else? She could be thinking anything."

Fox, barely covered by her rawhide jacket, her legs and hips bare through torn leathers, met Kate's stare, but not her smile.

"Honey, if you ever decide to go into business, I pray it's for me and not against me, because I'd be broke in a week." Fox didn't even blink. "You may hate the thought, but the fact is my customers would love to sample something like you. And we could charge 'em a fortune. I'd even make a special deal as long as you could stand it. That's real money."

Fox kept her face locked, but Soiled Dove frowned at the offer. Kate swatted Dove's hand, saying to Bishop, "She understands every word, right?"

"You can bank on it."

"No offense meant, honey, but you don't get anywhere without asking. I can't stand, so you sit. This meeting's eye-to-eye." Bishop settled on a small loveseat, sinking into the satin cushion. Fox held for a purposeful moment, before sitting beside him. Soiled Dove gave them each a snifter, then gifted Bishop's glass with a splash of Napoleon brandy.

Kate said, "To fight back that freezing cold."

White Fox covered the top of her glass with her palm. Dove looked to Kate, who shook her head.

"My comforts bring me enjoyment, and make my convalescence a little more bearable." Kate swatted Dove's hand again and was wheeled a little closer. "Doctor, we've got quite a bit in common."

Bishop sipped. "Beaudine."

"Look here."

The bandage was a large patch, wrapped in linen that went completely around Kate's middle, and was tied in the center of the acre of skin that was her back. Folds of flesh bulged beneath the cloth, straining the cotton that covered the wound, shifting the bandage from its place. Kate snickered as she held open her blouse for Bishop to see, her flesh rolling with her.

"It'd take more than some letter opener to get through all that. I played possum and let him do his crazy-ass business."

Bishop leaned forward to examine her. "Who attended you?"

"A sawbones who likes to have his fanny spanked. Did a nice job, so I gave him two free nights. He'll be back."

"Soon, I hope. Keep it clean. What sent Beaudine over?"

Kate snapped her fingers for her dragon. "Because I told him I wanted a percentage of your gold, Dr. Bishop. The major would tell anyone who'd listen all about it, and you. You're his favorite subject of conversation when he gets going."

Kate held the pipe to her mouth as Soiled

Dove lit it. "And since you got yourself that fancy rig, well, you're a famous man. One of my old girls works Huckie's, and the word's been spreading. You even made the paper."

"And I'm sure they got the facts right."

"I'd say you're on the run now? Need some help?"

Bishop let Kate draw. "I don't have any gold. Nothing."

Kate coughed. "Well, there's something going on that you're a part of, but maybe you don't know it. This isn't just about avenging your family."

"It is for me. There's nothing else."

The pipe made a slight hissing sound as Kate drew again. "Beaudine killed one of my girls. Had some kind of a fit, and wrung her neck, but that brain of his wouldn't let him recall it. I guess that's his blessing."

"Where'd they go?"

"Oh, now we're back to business."

"Where?"

"What's it worth?"

"Everything."

"You claim your gold's a myth. I can find that out for myself, and you can bet I will. But if you swear you'll kill Beaudine, then that satisfies our negotiation. For now."

"I've already sworn, but your information

has to be real."

"Here at Widow Kate's, we always guarantee satisfaction."

Bishop lifted the shotgun away from his chest, and held it out for Kate. She smiled. "That's a hell of a thing. No wonder there's talk." Then she looked to White Fox. "And how well does he use it?"

White Fox said, "Well."

"You're building a reputation, Doctor. That's good, makes the men you're after nervous." Kate took a sip of Napoleon, cooling her cough, and then: "Beaudine and three others rode for the Goodwill silver mine north of here, and they're damn excited at the prospect of seeing you."

"Oh, we're expected, just not alone."

"You changed their plans without their knowing? Good. Ready to change them some more?" Kate winced at some sudden pain, and Soiled Dove had the dragon at her lips. Kate eased, her words washing out of her mouth. "You and I, we beat death."

"Nobody beats it."

"There's a reason we're both still here, and it's bigger than that fever-brained son of a bitch. Let me ask, how many died in the War Between the States? Half the country?"

"There are a lot of graves."

"Everywhere. You know, I've had blue and grey take off their boots, lie with my girls. The uniform didn't mean a thing; they were just men and boys, looking for comfort."

"And I doctored a lot of them, and their insides are all the same. That was ten years ago. What's your point?"

Kate leaned forward in her wheelchair, focusing. "That these same men who're shooting at each other are working together on the Colorado Central, or working the mines, or building new towns. And so are their kids, all pushing west. That's a lot of customers and a lot of money going into my purse. That means girls and houses, maybe a hundred, and run 'em all from right here. Or maybe a palace in San Francisco."

"Big plans."

"Everybody has them. What about you, Doctor?"

"I'm thinking about right now."

"It's eating you up. I can see it. Well, I like the future, and I'm not having some crazy toss all I want to do on the fire. Neither of us needs a wild card in the deck."

Kate wheeled her chair around, her hand slipping before she took herself the few feet to a tapestry that covered one wall of her office in ornate red and gold.

"Kill Beaudine, and we'll both move on. How're you fixed?"

Bishop breached the rig, showing Kate the empty barrels.

Kate nodded. Soiled Dove pulled a sash cord that gathered the tapestry up from the floor, revealing a case built into the wall, stocked with pistols of all kinds, short and long rifles, knives, a few swords, and ammunition.

"He missed all this." Kate fished a key from between her breasts, and opened the cases' intricately carved glass doors. "All left by customers, mostly in trade. Some clothes too. You're riding into an ambush, so take all you need. And honey, there's even a little something for you."

Kate removed a long bow, hanging on a hook with a quiver of arrows, from the case. "I've heard tell you're damn good. A cavalry lieutenant wanted an extra fifteen minutes with Delia, and used up his pay. It's not from a Cheyenne, if that makes it easier. Maybe it doesn't."

White Fox took the bow and pulled it taut, testing it for strength. It held tight. Kate shook her head. "If you ever think you want to go a different way, come see me. You'll be my star attraction."

Kate looked to Bishop. "You hardly

touched your brandy, Doctor. You've got hell's own ride ahead of you, and not many pleasures along the way. Right?"

Bishop threw back the rest of the Napoleon in one swallow, and smiled.

# CHAPTER SEVENTEEN:
## CONDEMNED

The insulator shattered as the handle of Fuller's Bowie struck it from the side, the pieces of glass carried away with the blowing snow, exposing the hot telegraph line. Fuller steadied himself on the top of the far-leaning pole, looking as if it was about to snap in half against the iron railhead that was next to it.

The pole shifted in the wind, and Fuller hung on, legs straining, as Hector tossed him a coil of thin wire that was attached to a Morse sending key and receiver on the ground below. Fuller closed his eyes against the freeze, while securing the wire to a bare contact on the pole's crossbar. His hands moved fast; then his fingers numbed.

The brass key spark-jumped. Hector called out, "We got it!"

Fuller shimmied down, dropping the last few feet as Hector settled on an old crosstie, and began tapping a message on the portable field telegraph that fit in his lap.

Fuller pressed his side to ease a jolt of pain and called out to Fat Gut, "You couldn't have done this?"

"I don't climbth!"

Creed and Gut sat their horses, taking shelter behind the sections of oak and rusting tracks stacked at this end of the Colorado Central narrow gauge line. On a siding, an open passenger car, riddled with bullet holes, filled with snow.

Fat Gut said, "I t'ain't never theen tracks this smaw."

Fuller threw Gut a look as he wiped the blade of his knife. "It's the steam engine line that goes through the mountains to the mines. And this here's the only bit of telegraph line for a hundred miles."

Creed said, "A real man knows his own country."

"I knew all thath, too'd! I figgered thit!"

"I don't want to hear your mush! You getting anything, boy?"

Hector grinned back at Creed. "Yes, sir. What's your message?"

Creed ran his hands down Pride's neck, patting him as he considered his words. "No other way to say it. We failed. Tell them the prisoners escaped, and I will recapture, as ordered."

Hector tapped the message on the brass key, then turned to Creed to say, "Anything else, sir?"

Creed cocked his head for a moment, listening through the wind for the quick Morse tones in response, but none came.

"They're not answering."

Hector leaned into the receiver, almost pressing his ear against it. "No, sir. They're not."

"But it went through?"

"Yes. Yes, sir. And I sent it exactly the way you said it, them words. I didn't want to mess up nothing again."

"If you followed orders, you did fine. Let's move."

Fuller yanked on the telegraph wires, but they stayed fast. He tapped Hector on the shoulder. "Give me a boost."

Fat Gut laughed, "That's what yourth good at now, thniper! Monkey climbin'!"

Hector knelt by the pole. Fuller didn't take his boost.

Instead, he walked to his horse and pulled the Morgan-James from its scabbard, being careful with the long sight. Fat Gut wiped his nose on his sleeve as Fuller faced him, while fitting a cap on the rifle's metal nipple and then thumbing the hammer to half-lock position.

The sniper smiled. "You don't be fretting, my real skills'll come back."

Gut swallowed air right before Fuller turned sharply and fired at the train car two hundred yards down the narrow track, blowing a hole clean through the first O of COLORADO CENTRAL.

Hector whistled his admiration.

Fuller turned to Gut. "Start climbing."

Miles away, in a stone room cramped with lockers of weapons and ammunition, a telegraph operator was hunched over a Patrick and Bunnell set, listening to the code it was receiving. Somewhere, water was dripping. He wrote by the flicker of a candle, and when the metallic tapping stopped, he took Captain Creed's message and the candle with him, leaving the room in darkness.

"You all watch where I'm pointing at. I don't want to say this twice."

"Or Betsy'll bite?"

Chaney wasn't looking at Howard when he let the words slip, his head down, and hands deep in his pockets. They were all standing in the center of the Goodwill Mining Company making their battle plan, but Chaney was sick of the big man, and only looked up seconds before Howard charged at him, eyes wild-wide and giant fists tight.

Howard had taken a wild swing when the long-blade cleaver cut the air between him and Chaney before splitting the ice-hard ground at their feet. The handle wobbled as the blade sunk in.

"I could've taken off your foot, cut right through your boot." Beaudine stepped in front of Howard, grabbing the cleaver and turning to Chaney. "Or your ear."

He pulled the blade from the snow, and ran a finger tip lightly across it. "The edge should never touch the ground. You got this, Deadeye?"

Lem Wright's Colt in his right hand was a few inches from Chaney's temple, while the Smith and Wesson in his left was aimed directly at Howard's broad stomach. "Oh, I got them both."

Beaudine wiped down the blade. "This personal hash isn't why we're here. It's the mission you have to remember."

"What about his flannel mouth?"

Beaudine stepped close to Howard, holding the long cleaver with both hands like a medieval executioner. "That's all it is. He's playing you like you're in a poker game, keeping you riled, so you'll be a fool. That's right, isn't it Chaney?"

Lem brushed Chaney's neck with the barrel of the pistol. Chaney nodded, and let go of the Apache brass-knuckle pistol he had in his right front pocket. He pulled his hand out, and raised them both in mock surrender. "Right, right. Just playing."

"And why did you do this, boy? Cause this commotion?"

Chaney felt Lem's pistol brush his neck again. "Sorry. You've been handing me shit, and I got a bad habit of pushing back. Bad habit."

Lem said, "You've got to be real careful about that."

Chaney agreed with a nod, and then Beaudine said to the big man, "You a fool, Howard?"

"No, I ain't."

"Because I don't need fools in my squad."

"I said I ain't."

Howard kept his fists tight and eyes on the gambler. Beaudine's voice never rose: "Then think about everything that preacher taught you at Rawlins. You said his words changed you. Got rid of your ill temper. You left the penitentiary a different man, a man who thinks a thing through."

Howard said, "I was, damn it. I am."

"I haven't seen it."

"That's because you're making me forget

it all, going right out of my head."

Beaudine kept his voice level. "I know that confusion, but it'll pass. You're stronger than it is."

"I set the dynamite, and I shouldn't have done it." Howard's voice was frustrated shout. "This wasn't going to be my life no more! The gates of heaven were gonna open for me, and you're sending me down another road! Making me an outlaw again!"

"No, you're what you should be: a soldier in my army, and you got a mission." Beaudine kept turning the blade. "Treasure in gold. Just keep saying that, like a prayer, over and over. Treasure in gold." Then the cleaver was down at his side. "And you'll remember who you are. Not a paid-off deputy or a coffin builder making sixty cents a day, but a man with a mission. A solider."

"No. Not a soldier."

"A powder man."

"With a damn short fuse?"

That did it. Howard cracked, maybe half a smile at Lem's bad joke, called him a one-eyed son of a bitch, and shook off some of his anger. Some. Everyone took a breath, and Lem flashed Chaney a look, reminding him how close he'd come to being beaten to death.

Beaudine stepped back from between his

two men, wiping the smear of blood from the blade with his thumb. "You're calm now?"

Howard nodded. "Let's get to it."

"Hold. Boy?"

Beaudine turned and smashed Chaney's jaw with the long-handle, dropping him into the snow, his mouth spurting blood.

Beaudine took some deep breaths, his head jerking from side to side to order his thoughts: "Now, I don't want no more damn foolishness! We've got a hell of a battle in front of us. There's a plan here. A plan and you need to follow it, to follow me! Brothers in arms, understand? I want to hear you say it!"

Lem helped Chaney to his feet, and they all said, "Brothers in arms."

There were nods all around. Howard didn't look at Chaney as he started again. "We've got charges under the snow every twenty feet by my foot, so you best make it thirty. See how I got them in a circle? Them fuses are wrapped to stay dry, but you can see 'em. Each fuse sets off two bundles. The ones in them old sheds are bundled in threes, with short fuses, so light and run. That's what you wanted, right?"

Beaudine nodded. "There can't be a single place for anyone to hide."

Howard spit. "We set all this off, there won't be nothing left. The sticks on this other side of the pit are just sittin' under the snow, so you have to set them off with another stick, I saved ten, toss one, it'll set off them buried ones. But you got to hit it." Then, to Chaney: "No half-assed shots, no second chances."

Lem said, "That's enought to blow a hole straight through to Hell."

"I'm just doing what I'm told. That's what's going to get the gold, right?"

Beaudine was fixed on the mine shaft and its cross braces. "What about that?"

"You got two sticks on them four-by-fours."

"Just so long as my head's out of the way."

Beaudine turned to Lem as soon as he spoke. "That depends on where you're going to be, don't it?"

Lem pointed to the first small shack, one wall caved in. "Chaney'll be there. That's a good view of the trail in, and he'll be close if they open up. I'll be on top of the slag with a rifle, pick a few off, start some confusion before the first explosion."

"But you don't touch Bishop."

Lem spit, "I know Bishop's the money! But you don't know how many Creed's got with him. You said we could be facing an army. Well, let's get as many as we can, as fast as we can."

Chaney flicked his gold tooth with his finger, then said, "Yeah, even up the odds. Maybe."

Lem said, "Even if Bishop takes a slug, he can still tell us what we want to know. You got that all figured out, this time?"

Beaudine nodded, then smiled. "Two things we pay big money for: act out desires, and act out hates. I surely do."

Howard pissed in the snow. "Sounds like horseshit to me."

"This horseshit's going to make you the richest dynamiter in the country, so you better learn it like the gospel. He's got that girl?"

Chaney nodded, Beaudine continued: "After we wipe out Creed's misfits, you think Dr. Bishop won't strike a deal?" Beaudine chopped the air with the cleaver and grinned to himself. "To save her head, and get a chance at me? Hell yes, he will."

Lem said, "I've only seen Bishop twice in my life. The second time was in his house, and the first time I was in my cell, right after I'd had the living shit kicked out of me. Remember Smythe?"

Howard snorted. "Wanted to kill that bastard every day."

"He damn near killed me. Probably would have if Dr. Bishop hadn't forced him to put me in the prison hospital. Remember? He was standing at your cell, saying something to Dev, and you hung back. Dev gave him a letter, then he was walking out and saw me lying on my bunk, and said I needed to go to the hospital."

Beaudine turned from Lem. "You're saying you owe him?"

"Nope. Just getting our history straight."


White Fox jammed the knife through the side of the sleeve, cutting the cloth along its seam, then pulling it back to the shoulder. Bishop watched her while laying out the pistols and ammunition he'd gotten from Widow Kate's weapons cache. She cut the sleeve off at the elbow, tossed the rag into the small fire that warmed their campsite, before threading a needle to sew up the torn edges. The flames ate the cloth.

She sat on a blanket, the coat in her lap, and looked up to see Bishop looking, but not recognizing her. "Beaudine?"

Bishop loaded a Smith and Wesson .44. "You know the last time I saw his face?"

"I asked if you wanted this. You said yes."

"And I say it again. There's no doubt. *Tósée'e.*"

Bishop emphasized the final *e,* so Fox knew he was sure. She shrugged. "Then do your work."

Fox leaned closer to the fire, catching the light as she hemmed the jagged edge of the sleeve so the hammers of the shotgun wouldn't catch when Bishop raised his arm for a kill. The coat was special-made for an ammunition drummer who had secret pockets sewn into the lining for bullet samples, and he would never have left it behind except he had been shot by a drunken cowboy who'd thought one of Kate's China dolls was his personal property.

The drummer had been carried home naked with three holes in his chest, and his coat had gone into the closet, until Bishop and White Fox exchanged their bloody rags for what Kate had stashed. The widow opium-slurred, "It's purr-fect for your purr-poses."

Fox tugged on the tight denims she'd chosen, bringing them down to her hips so she could sit cross-legged, before drawing a last stitch on the coat sleeve, and biting through the heavy thread. She looked to Bishop, who was struggling to load the same pearl-handled Colt that Short Gun had tried to kill him with the day before.

Someone said, "Beaudine."

It was a distant echo in Bishop's mind, thick with a cigar smoker's hack and a Swedish accent. The name repeated itself, and Warden Allard became more and more anchored in memory: the voice, the cigar between his teeth, the wide moustache, and the wider belly that struggled not to burst the top button of his pinstriped trousers.

"Condemned men do get privileges for their last week. I insist on that. Good food, good drink."

Allard tried to stick out his sunken chest with pride at the declaration, even as he cigar-hacked again in his struggle to get out of his chair. John Bishop slipped his hands under Allard's arms, lifting the warden to his feet. "Your brother was given a chance to have a private cell these final days, but he refused. Wanted to stay with this crazy Beaudine."

"My brother can't write, sir. I think this prisoner's been his voice."

"He was being punished for an infraction, not his first."

"I'm sure."

"He chose to stay in the punishment cells with the other prisoners, rather than be moved." Allard spit his words out around his cigar. "Whatever the reason, I want it declared on record that I've offered him all possible comforts before his final day. And he's refused everything."

"It's on the record."

"With the family?"

"I'm all that's left, so yes."

"Then, you shall see him."

Allard took up almost half the width of the narrow stone hallway that connected his office to the cellblocks. Bishop walked alongside him, medical bag in hand, sometimes turning sideways to make room for the warden, as they maneuvered the corners. He listened dutifully, and the cigar never left Allard's mouth: "I've been given charge of the worst types this side of the Mississippi, and I do my best by them. That's not an easy task, if you think of what they've done."

"I'm sure it isn't."

Allard agreed with Bishop's agreement. "Every letter a prisoner mails, I read first. What your brother claims about his time here is slop for hogs."

Bishop nodded. "He's been a liar his whole life."

"But you're going to see for yourself? Fine. I am within the law, always. You treat all your patients the same, Doctor?"

"I try to."

"A killer comes to you with a bullet in his

stomach, and you treat him the same as an old woman dying from consumption? I don't think so, because what you do is between you and your conscience. But here, the law dictates that I see every man the same way."

"Since one of them's my brother, what way is that?"

They had reached the end of the hallway and stood before a large door made of riveted steel plates, with a drop bar braced across it. The stone floor was spatter-stained, rust mixing with blood.

Allard pulled wet tobacco from the end of his tongue. "These are the cells. Smythe."

A guard, his skin and hair the same apple color, stepped from an anteroom jangling a set of keys. He lifted the cross-brace, then unlocked the door. The tumblers cried of old metal as Smythe grunted them open. He was shiny with the brown sweat of last night's whiskey, and wiped his face with a stained handkerchief he kept balled in one of his enormous hands. He looked to Allard, then to Bishop. "Well?"

"Take the good doctor to Devlin Bishop's cell, then escort him safely off the premises. And answer any questions he might have about our policies, my policies."

Bishop said, "What has you worried? I'm

not here for an inspection."

"You're here for family, but you will talk about your experience, I'm sure. We don't have statehood yet, but this institution operates within the letter of territorial law. I insist on that."

"You've made that clear, Warden."

Allard said, "Letter of the law," again, pushing each word for emphasis, then added, "No favorites, no compromises. And that includes your brother's execution."

Allard extended his hand, and Bishop started to shake it.

"Your medical bag."

"I have no intention of cheating the hangman. Believe me."

"For your own protection, Doctor. These are desperate men — why tempt them? You'll get it on your way out."

Bishop handed over the bag, then stepped around Smythe into the shadowed corridor that led to the cellblock. The guard snickered at the formality, before pulling the huge steel door closed behind them.

The only light coming into the corridor was from the end that opened into the prison's common area. A heavy chain strung along the wall guided the way. Bishop regarded Smythe's near-blue knuckles that had been skinned almost to the bone. "Must have been a hell of a fight."

"Haven't met me match yet."

"Looks like a few knuckles are broken."

"After ten years on the job, I don't feel nothing."

A din of shouted curses, laughter, and crying rose as they got closer to the common. Incoherent, hysterical screaming hit Bishop between the eyes.

Smythe plugged his ears with thick fingers. "He sounds happy, don't he?"

Grinning, the guard fell back a step, letting Bishop into the common area first. This was the heart of the prison: a large structure that seemed chiseled from a single piece of rock, with curved, arena-like walls that supported a high, domed ceiling. There were no windows, and there was only a single stovepipe for ventilation.

The pitched screaming came from one of the community cells that were on all sides of the ground level: six prisoners together, with a piss bucket and a straw mattress for comfort. The air was choked by noise, stench, and the smoke from the torches mounted on the walls.

The middle of the commons was taken up by rude tables for meals, and a pair of whipping posts, while guards with Winchesters took position around the area like the points on a compass, kerchiefs shielding their faces.

Bishop said to no one, "The letter of the law. God almighty."

"Don't be getting yourself in a twist, Doc. It stinks worse than it is. Ain't nobody been on them posts since the war, and most of this bunch drew short stretches. Get caught with something that ain't yours, settle here for six months, and you'll never steal again."

"I sure as hell wouldn't."

"Hell's the word all right, but they eat pretty good. The circuit judge favors our example right well."

The scream ripped again, then became a laugh, then a sob. Bishop edged toward the catwalk that led to the cells, but Smythe's busted hand was instantly on his shoulder. "Bastard's all yelled out."

"Sounds possible, but he might need medical attention."

"But you don't have your little black bag. Want to see that brother of yours or not?"

Smythe took a step closer. Bishop said, "Where is he?"

"That way."

On the other side of the whipping posts, a bone-thin guard hooked one end of the crow bar through the metal ring on a trap door, and pulled, straining like hell and swearing through his kerchief. Smythe lent an arm. The door lifted up from the stone floor, revealing a set of iron stairs that descended into pitch-dark.

Bishop looked down into the opening. The skinny guard said, "Want your brother?"

The din around them was now the roar of prisoners banging tin plates and cups on their cage doors, slopped with a thousand obscenities in ten languages. Some chanted, "Smytheee!"

An old guard with a Spencer rifle fired a shot into the ceiling, a blast of thunder that stun-silenced them.

Then, in the last cell, Chester Pardee hurled his piss through the bars, trying for Smythe. "You're goin' to the Tombs, give my regards to Major Beaudine! Hope he guts ya like a deer, you son of a bitch!"

Pardee's gift didn't come close enough to splash. Bishop started down the stairs, with Smythe right behind, and the trap door closed above their heads, leaving them in total darkness. Smythe lit a small candle, a yellow flicker barely showing Bishop the way down the broken, wet stairs, and the squealing swarm of rats darting from the shadows.

The guard nudged Bishop down. "Rats. That's all what's down here."

"I thought it was prisoners who're being punished."

"Ain't that what I said?"

Devlin Bishop leaned back against the cell wall, almost totally lost in the complete dark that swallowed it. Even though he was just feet away in the same cell, all Dev could see of Beaudine was the shape of a man, sitting on the floor, with something resting on his knees. Not that Dev cared. He knew what his cellmate looked like, and more importantly, what he was worth.

Beaudine hunched over the student's tablet using the nub of a pencil to write on cream laid stationery. "We're truly suffering without a pen."

Dev half-smiled. "We're suffering anyway," he said and then, quietly: "And me, for not much longer."

"I meant this letter is your will and testament, Dev. It should have permanence."

"I don't get a real funeral. So if that can be read when I'm gone, it's enough."

"No need to fret, it'll be read."

"Just what I said?"

Beaudine continued writing. "Exactly your words."

Dev traced the edges of his moustache with his fingers, neatening its edges. "Maybe you could write something out for the hangman. Make sure things go just right."

"I don't think you've got much choice in that."

Dev shut his eyes for just a moment. "Just thinking out loud," he said, and then he snapped his eyes open at the sound of footsteps coming toward the cell, accompanied by the ghost of a yellow light.

One of the prisoners yelled from another cell, "Is that chow comin'?"

Dev Bishop sat up, wiping the stink of the Tomb from his eyes, as he focused on the man now standing by his cell door. Dev answered back, "It ain't chow! I'll be damned if it ain't my baby brother."

John Bishop stood near the bars, but not too close, with Smythe holding the candle just over his shoulder. Beaudine was on the edge of the tiny circle of candlelight.

"It's a fine thing to see you at last."

Dev took the five steps to the door. "You should introduce yourself, Major. It's been so long, my brother may think you're me."

"I recognize you, Dev."

"Don't see how. I never favored Ma or Pa, except her temper. And we sure don't look alike, but you haven't changed. Even as a kid, polished and respectable. But I guess brothers always know each other." Dev gestured toward Beaudine, who kept on writing. "The invitation to come was the

216

major's. He's the reason you're here, Johnny. He puts down my thoughts better than I ever could."

"I'm here because of you. No offense, sir."

Beaudine didn't look up. "None offered, none taken."

"I'd want to see you, whether you wrote or not."

Smythe yawned. "And when are you bein' hung, boy-o?"

Dev paused as if he was figuring his answer. "Four days."

"Good. I've got duty that Wednesday. Wouldn't want to miss it."

Bishop said, "Can I talk to my brother?"

"I ain't stopping you."

Dev extended his hand through the narrow opening between the bars. "I wish we could have met at the Metropolitan House instead, but fate stepped in. They call this part of the prison the Tomb, 'cause it feels like you're buried. Gets you used to the idea."

Smythe low-whistled a little tune. "Better to be dead-alive, than dead-dead. And you're gonna find out the difference, boy-o."

Bishop shook his brother's hand. "Warden said you had a chance to get out, and wouldn't take it."

Someone in the dark snorted a laugh. Dev said, "I have business to tend to, and the major's been my —"

Beaudine threw in, "Representative. You wouldn't assume it, but during my time in the army, I became a top-level assistant to a number of generals and I've put those learned skills to use. Even here."

Bishop said, "I appreciate your writing letters for my brother."

"He's finishing one now. Something to remember me by."

"Dev, we haven't seen each other since before Mama and Pa died. I'm glad I'm here, but don't know what I can do to help. Tell me."

"That's your Christian side coming up. There's nothin'. You're the only family I've got, and I figured we should be together one last time before Wednesday morning." Dev took a step back, calling out to the Tomb, "My baby brother, the doctor! Who got the chances I never did! I know you've got a fine, fine life, with a wife, son, folks who respect you. You ever tell anybody about *your* brother, the outlaw? I'd bet Union money you don't."

"It never really comes up."

"Oh, I'm sure, I'm sure. Nobody wants a doc with mud on his boots, or blood on his family name."

"I don't think that way."

"My own fault. I'm the law-breaker, and you're the one everyone ass-kisses."

Smythe said, "This here candle's almost burned down."

Bishop turned away from the cell. "It's all right, I think my visit's done. Good luck, Dev."

Dev laughed. "You can't go yet. This is a special treat for us. They only bring candles when we eat. The rest of the time, we're in the dark."

Beaudine handed Dev the finished letter. "And I have learned to write that way, with a decent hand."

Dev folded the letter into neat threes, before holding it out to his brother. "I hope this will clear things up between us. I shouldn't have shot my mouth off, because I'm proud of what you've become."

Bishop slipped the letter into his coat. "Forget it. But, I haven't done anything, and I wish I had."

"I'm talking about our partnership, brother."

Beaudine stood, his eyes narrowed on Bishop's puzzled reaction: "We've never been partners, Dev. . . ."

"You don't have to say more, Johnny. Just

know that I'm grateful. For everything you did, and helped with. And after Wednesday, I'll be eternally grateful."

The rest of the Tomb busted into laughter fits, filling the tiny space. Dev Bishop dropped back on his iron bunk. "I'll see you on the other side, brother! Now get out of here so that mule's ass can fetch us our dinner!"

Smythe roared, "You want me to put somethin' special in it?"

Bishop gave Dev a puzzled nod. "God have mercy, Dev," he said and started away. He stopped, using the last bit of yellow light to peer into the next cell. Lem Wright's body was twisted on the filth-thick floor, almost folded over, lying on his side. His face was a mush of purple folds, with dried blood outlining his mouth, nose, and ears. His cellmate, a massive, dark shape taking up most of the cage, snored in the corner.

"What the hell happened to this man?"

Smythe's breath was corpse-fresh. "Your visit's done!"

"Get him out of here, or he'll die. And I'll bring a murder charge!"

Dev said, "Better listen up, screw. My baby brother takes his doctoring very, very seriously."

Smythe placed his heel on Bishop's foot,

shifting his enormous weight. Something cracked. "The thing about the Tomb is, you can get forgotten down here."

Bishop didn't flinch. "That could be true for you as well. The best thing to do is help that man, and I'll have no reason to say anything to the warden, or the territorial authorities."

The keys rattled in Smythe's hands. "I don't give two shits about family. No more visitors!"

Smythe yanked the cell door open, and Bishop helped Lem to his feet, throwing his arm over his shoulder. Lem tried to speak, but nothing happened, his head dropping to his chest. Bishop made his way back to the trapdoor stairs, dragging Lem with him. Smythe kept his pistol on them both.

The candle flickered, before finally burning down to nothing, leaving the Tomb in pitch. One of the prisoners started to scream.

Lem's weight seemed to double as Bishop took each step, his arms under his shoulders for support, hefting him up the stairs inches at a time. Bishop grunted, asked for help. Smythe offered his gun on their backs.

There was a quiet laugh, but Bishop couldn't tell who it was, because the rats were scurrying again, squeals and toenails against the wet stone.

Beaudine called out from his cell, "It's been a sure pleasure to finally make your acquaintance, Dr. Bishop! Give my best to your wife and son!"

Bishop didn't answer as he struggled up another step.

A different voice in the dark, said, "Beaudine."

It was White Fox, pulling a heavy blanket around Bishop's shoulders, as he came back from somewhere lost in his sleep. "You don't need that dream."

He felt the warmth of the campfire, and opened his eyes to see weapons laid out, the saddlebags packed, the bay and the painted quietly grazing. Bishop started to sit up, but she stopped him. "You know what tomorrow brings. Clear your mind, build your strength."

She was right, and Bishop didn't fight the wave that was carrying him away. He heard her voice again, telling him what he needed. *"He'kotâhestôtse."*

Bishop whispered the word, as he knew it. "Peace."

# CHAPTER EIGHTEEN: THE STRENGTH OF MY ENEMIES

Chaney was the first to hear the eight riders as they approached the mouth of the small canyon that shielded the Goodwill silver strike. They didn't speak, and their horses moved gingerly over the thin crust of ice that sheeted the ground during the night, but something bolted Chaney awake, and he was standing with his Colt 45 drawn when they pulled to a mutual stop.

The animals snorted, but the riders stayed silent.

The sun was struggling, and the sky was more the grey-blue of night, instead of red morning, which made making out the faces of the men near impossible. They were dull, broken shadows, with weapons resting across their laps.

One of them said, "It's too damn early to be dealin' with a fool."

Chaney didn't take a step. "I bet I can kill at least two of you before you take me."

The same rider said, "No need for that. We was told there was work here."

Chaney didn't flinch. "The mine's played out."

The other riders aimed their guns so all shots would pound into Chaney's chest in the same spot. "We didn't come here to dig no silver."

"Then what the hell are you doing here?"

Lem Wright stepped from behind the caved-in shack, a Winchester on his shoulder, and threw a smirk at Chaney. "Who'd you borrow your iron balls from, son?"

The riders gut-laughed as Lem shook their hands before turning to Chaney, who had holstered his gun. "These are the extra boys Beaudine said he needed." Lem shook hands with his old buddy in front. "Who passed you the word?"

Lem's buddy said, "Old Kirby. Had a wagonload of stolen dynamite, said you got some of it and could cut us in on something big."

"Did you leave him under the grass?"

"Nope. And didn't rob him neither, to thank him for the tip. He'll be easy to find if this don't work out."

Chaney barked, "Well, how are we knowing they're not the law?"

Lem turned and threw his dead eye at

Chaney. "What?"

Howard and Beaudine were standing by the mine's old cross braces, Howard holding Betsy and Beaudine with a rifle aimed from the hip. He punched his words with the sound of the repeater being cocked. "The boy asked a question, and it was a good one."

Lem pointed to his friend. "I did a hard-labor stretch in Arkansas with this jaybird, and I damn well know he didn't go straight."

Lem's buddy flashed yellow 'n' green teeth. "I think I've killed three or four since I saw you last, Lem. And these boys, well, they ain't got nothing to lose."

"That's a meaningful endorsement." Beaudine let the repeater drop. "Coffee's on the boil. I'll let you in on the plan of battle, and what's expected of each of you."

One of the new boys said, "We expect pay, brother."

"Not your brother, and there's money to be had."

The riders stepped down from their horses, chortling as they passed Chaney.

Beaudine said, "There will be a man with one arm, and a little Cheyenne girl with him."

Lem's buddy said, "What are we gonna do for the rest of the day?"

Chaney wasn't impressed. "This ain't going to be a hog killin'."

"Go boil your shirt."

Howard let go with a whistle-snort, then blew his nose on his sleeve. Lem handed Chaney a set of reins. "Don't get worked up again. These ponies have to get out of sight."

Chaney grabbed another mount when Lem prodded, "Now, where'd you say your new balls came from?"

Chaney flicked his gold tooth. "Guess I'm finally tasting the gold."

"And you're not keen on shares."

Chaney didn't add another word.

The trail White Fox and Bishop followed had been hard-beaten into the earth by the weight of wagons loaded with miners and silver, pulled through the rough by a convoy of steam tractors. The man and machine traffic that had travelled here, before the Goodwill was pronounced dead, had left deep scars the Rockies could never heal. A constant, bitter cold and whip-harsh wind, strangled any hope of plants reclaiming the place, and what trees there were had been cut and left to rot into grey nothing.

Snow dusted the blank morning sky.

*"Naévêháne."*

White Fox nodded. "You're learning. Yes, it feels like death. And you?"

Bishop absently placed his left hand on the shotgun rig, his fingers sticking to the weapon's cold metal before answering. "We're riding into a massacre. This is how it should be."

"And death rides, with us."

"Creed used to say the same thing every time we went into battle. Win or lose, he was right."

The words settled. Bishop looked at her, waiting to see if Fox's eyes would meet his to offer reassurance of their survival, but they didn't. Fox wasn't going to give a false promise, and that was right fine with Bishop, who watched her ride a few paces ahead, saddle heavy with bow, arrows, and blades.

He kept the bay steady, his thoughts about what needed to be done for the memory of his wife and son; that was the bloody mission, though he knew well that Amaryllis would hate what he was doing. She had loved the doctor, not this assassin, and even though they both lived inside the same man, Amaryllis had never seen the latter. Only the good, only charity, found her eyes. That was her special gift.

Bishop almost slipped back to those

memories, the light notes of her voice even when she was being strong; a joke that she always told wrong, but that he loved. He forced those thoughts down, killing them. He had to.

Bishop let the rig rest in its saddle sling, allowing him to relax his shoulder. His body was now serving the shotgun; the weapon had taken over, telling the healer what to do. And he wasn't fighting the change.

He and Fox rode farther, no words between them, before approaching the edge of the canyon that broke this side of the mountains in half. Fox eased the painted to a stop about twenty feet from the rough drop into the man-made opening, where she could see the bits of the braces and crumbling rooftops the Goodwill Company had built close to the edge.

Bishop took a brass field telescope from his coat as he light-footed to a place where he could spy the area below. Fox was suddenly next to him, pointing to the tiny figures huddled around the damaged buildings, their low voices garbled into a common echo. Bishop held one end of the scope between his teeth, pulled it to its length, and brought the glass to his eye. Fox leaned over his shoulder, twisting the focus ring so he could make out the face of the man standing apart from the others, making sweeping motions with his arms.

Through the lens, he watched as Beaudine gave orders to Chaney and other outlaws Bishop didn't recognize. Howard, holding bundles of dynamite, barked silent instructions, walking around the perimeter of the mining camp, before tying charges off on an old mine support. Howard adjusted the charge, and nudged Lem, who looked up, facing Bishop directly, his good eye maybe catching a glint of light off the scope. Bishop pulled back, snapping the telescope shut.

"He saw?"

"Not sure. They're not expecting us from here. They think we'll be coming from the canyon entrance, as Creed's prisoners. If they saw something, they don't know what it is."

"Too many. *Heómesto.*"

"Kate said it was a massacre. Creed thought he was getting paid, but they're going to slaughter him, and then Beaudine planned to do God knows what with us."

Fox's eyes met Bishop's this time. "There is no Creed."

Before Bishop could even agree, Fox put her hand up for silence, cocking her head toward a sound that was distant, but rising.

The first shreds were low and vague; the echo of a thousand trees falling together, miles away.

Fox stood, turning toward an ice-scattered ridge that had a small pass worn into it. Bishop turned also, with the sound growing louder from the ridge, like a constant beating of huge drums, and then, there was the stretch of moving red.

Men on horseback poured through the pass, nearly keeping shoulder to shoulder, their scarlet hoods and tunics forming a solid field of color that blew apart as they rode off in different directions. The thunder of running mounts pounded the air, becoming a roar as rider after rider followed, charging like a cavalry.

Bishop and White Fox leapt onto the bay and painted.

The Fire Riders circled wide, blocking the trail that led to the other side of the mountain. Others ran to flank the top of the canyon, drawing Prussian needle rifles from saddle scabbards and Colts from holsters. The guns were new, polished. Others swung knives, clubs, and axes. Strips of red cloth had been braided into their horses' tails and manes, so it looked as if flames were bursting from their bodies, while their heads had been painted silver-white, like bleached skulls.

Even in the light of morning, they were demonic.

Bishop and Fox pushed their horses fast along the broken rim of the drop-off, the rocky edge turning to gravel under their hoofs, as they angled toward a small grade leading to the canyon's mouth.

A patrol of Riders gave chase, shooting wild.

Their first shots were a miss, but another ricocheted off the barrel of the shotgun rig, sparking hot, nearly throwing Bishop from his saddle. Bishop swung the bay around and drew his Peacemaker, firing four times with his left and hitting two of the Riders chest-center. Red sprayed beyond their crimson tunics.

Fox kept parallel to Bishop, running close. She drew an arrow, then swung around on her horse's back, facing the Fire Rider closing in. She raised the bow, her muscled body compensating for the horse's every motion, absorbing its rhythm, making her aim rocksteady.

The Rider brought up a breach-loading Prussian rifle. She made her shot. It was clean, into the throat, pinning his hood to him. His scream was a muffled choke as he tumbled over his horse's neck, the arrow snapping in two, before he dead-rolled off the edge of the canyon wall, smashing onto the roof of a Goodwill mine shack below; shattered wood, glass, and bone.

The breach-loader never fired.

Beaudine stepped from a cut in the canyon wall, the repeater in one hand, long cleaver in the other. "Everybody hold!"

They all kept their positions, swearing.

Lem jabbed a thumb toward the Fire Rider corpse sprawled in front of them. "That ain't a Creed man! Look at him! What the hell do you call that getup? Beaudine!"

"It's what I said, what I told you." Beaudine rubbed his temple, as if pushing his thoughts together, before barking, "War!"

"With who? He's got an arrow in him, for God's sake!"

Lem's buddy perched low among the miner's graves, with two of his gang, one of them just a kid. He shook his head, lit a cigarette. "Them two sound worse than my wife and her sister. One dead ain't nothing. Let's do this, get paid, go home."

Beaudine stepped back. "You've got — you've got your orders! I'll tell you when to fire!"

Lem's buddy said, "Bullll-shit."

232

On the canyon rim, the Fire Riders called out commands, fragments of their voices echoing down to Beaudine's men. Lem shielded his eyes, to see the troop of red-clad demons staking the edge, targeting the mine area, weapons ready.

Lem said, "Sweet Mary, mother of us all," to no one, and stood beside the silver shaft's old cross braces, Peacemaker aimed, pockets filled with ammo, and a rifle beside him. He moved the rifle six inches closer, and said, "Seen that bunch? Still got your new balls?"

Chaney heard Lem and threw back "Hell's fire, yes," while pressed against a broken-in door of the collapsed mine shed, his Colt at his side and another tucked in his waist-band. Howard was the closest to the canyon entrance, protected by a huge slag heap opposite the shed. He had Betsy out of her leather, but was damn ready to throw the dynamite stacked at his elbow.

Waiting. Ready.

Above the canyon, Fox and Bishop pounded the trail to the sloping grade that led to the Goodwill road and the mine. They were running, keeping a lead in front of the Fire Riders, but the Riders were closing. One broke ahead, pushing a tall stallion, getting close to Fox, his horse and her painted almost colliding.

The Rider fury-slashed with a cavalry saber. Fox dodged, but he cut, the blade slicing her shoulder, creating a bloody opening in her jacket and skin. She heel-kicked the Rider, cracking his knee. He howled through his red hood, twisting in agony. Fox pulled back on her painted, jerking the horse to slow his run, and getting out of the way of Bishop's aim.

Bishop's shot was now clear.

The Rider's eyes panicked wide as the shotgun rig swung toward him. Rider slashed again, the saber bouncing off of Bishop's saddle. One barrel of buckshot caught him solid in the side, tearing a good bit of him away. He hit the ground as a lifeless bag, his stallion still running.

The other Riders, in formation, reacted and charged faster.

Bishop and Fox broke hard down a small trail, the grade from the top of the canyon to the mine's entrance road only yards away. Fox glanced over her wounded shoulder to see red demons taking positions with rifles and pistols.

Bishop and Fox jumped a fallen log. The Riders leveled, shooting at them as a practiced one, a firing squad. Their guns flamed, the joined sound thundering across the flats, and bouncing against the canyon walls.

The log blew apart, but the targets kept moving.

A slug creased the side of Bishop's neck. He ignored the burn, and angled the bay for the road. Fox got off an arrow, tearing a lead Rider through the gut. He stayed his horse, soaking red, while signaling the others to ride on.

A battle cry erupted from the Riders.

Fox called above them, *"Mâhenot!"*


At the mine, Chaney cleared his head of all but the "gold reasons," before stepping away from the cover of the shed, and shooting at the Fire Riders along the ridge above, aiming at everything. And nothing.

Beaudine yelled, "I didn't give the command!"

Chaney emptied both pistols. "They're gonna wipe us out!"

The Riders returned fire, blasting calibers of all types from the backs of their running horses. Near impossible to hit, as they swept the mine with bullets. The dead buildings and dead ground ate the slugs, while Beaudine's men leapt from their cover, firing back at what they could see. Quick shots, then ducking back.

Beaudine cracked his repeater until it was empty.

One of the new boys yelled to Lem, "Sweet Jesus on Sunday, what did you get us into?" before a .44 slug blew out his back, spinning him onto a slag heap. Smaller slugs tore him up as he lay still.

The Fire Riders retreated from the canyon edge, reloaded, and started Hell again. Lem let it happen around him, bullets chewing the wall of the building where he was taking cover. He aimed carefully at them with his one eye, showing his hand, and killed three.

Smoke and sound thickened the air, as Bishop and Fox reached the road to the mine, their horses plowing gravel. A single Fire Rider stood as sentry, blocking the road in the opposite direction — an easy kill to get off the mountain, and ride away.

But that wasn't their mission.

The sentry moved to the middle of the road, but didn't advance, his horse pawing at the ground. He watched them, a new Smith and Wesson .38 hidden in the sleeve of his red tunic.

He saw Bishop breaching the shotgun rig, shuck the spent shells, and reload. He kept his hands tight on his gun, while Fox shouldered her bow and a sling of arrows, then took an ax from her belt and slipped her wrist through the leather thong on the end of its handle. Ready to throw.

Fire Riders were charging down hard from the top of the canyon, raising more dust and noise, but Fox and Bishop didn't bolt. Instead, they ignored their own wounds and shared a water bag with their horses. They did what they needed to do, never looking back at the Riders, or anything else.

The red-hooded sentry said, "You're damned to hell, Dr. Bishop," lifted his hood, and spit.

But they didn't hear or see him. Fox and Bishop only regarded each other for a moment, hands just brushing, before they urged the bay and the painted into full runs, galloping for the Goodwill Mine, and Beaudine.

Beaudine's hands were clamped around his skull, pain bursting through him. He murdered his own scream by locking his jaws tight, so nothing could escape. His back was shielded by the canyon wall, and he was in a good position, still ready to fight Creed's men, and take John Bishop as his prisoner. Still ready, but boiling inside his head. Boiling.

He dropped to one knee, water from his canteen washing over him. Cooling down, letting him find his thoughts. This wasn't the time to be lost, to be unsure. He drew a deep breath, neatened his hair as an officer should, before standing again. He stepped around a decaying mine support, noting the placement of his men: behind the old mining office and land shack to the right, and the slag heap on the left.

The pain behind his eyes eased, like a fever breaking.

He'd ordered the Goodwill ringed with explosives, and it was. He'd reunited his company, and even though there had been a burst of insubordination, his men were up to the skirmishes ahead. He knew that, and that calmed him. The pain continued to subside.

Beaudine knew he'd made a good plan, and could lead his men to victory, and allowed himself that satisfaction.

His mind was clearing. Calm before battle.

Beaudine saw Howard, his massive hand on Betsy, staring directly at him. Howard distinctly mouthed, *Loco,* with a twisted face and crossed eyes. Beaudine didn't flare. He steadied his rifle at Howard, and held the long cleaver like a battle ax, but the coffin maker was already looking away, shaking his head.

Beaudine reminded all, "We're doing this

for gold!"

Howard gut-hollered, "Then where the hell is it?"

"You're forgetting yourself, soldier! I give the orders!"

Howard lit a cheap cigar, inhaled deeply. "I should've stayed where I was. Hell —"

Howard's words were shot dead by a .44 slug ripping the slag heap, pieces of rock flying jagged. He ducked, as more bullets struck around him. He rolled to one side, and Betsy exploded in his hand toward the red shapes riding along the canyon rim, her voice .44 thunder.

From his spot, Beaudine opened up with the repeater, laying fire on the enemy's position above, covering for his men. Beaudine got off as many rounds as his hands allowed, taking down two Riders, screaming, "You're outmanned! Come on down, and talk your surrender!"

He fell back just as the enemy returned maximum fire, blowing away huge chunks of the support braces. Beaudine kept low, fitting more ammo into the rifle, singing, "Roll out the drums of war, let's speak of things worth fighting for! Roll out the drums of war!"

The battle was erupting just as he'd always dreamed it.

Chaney kept close to the falling-in wall of the old shed, even as sniper shots blew out the window next to him. He fired back everything he had, tried to reload again, but the gun was too damn hot. More rounds pounded the Goodwill, ricochets screeching off rusty metal and powdering the rotting wood.

Two of the new boys were blasted from their place atop the four-by-four braces, and they fell without screams.

Lem's buddy cracked off rounds for cover, yelling from beside a grave, "They're going to bring out a damn Howitzer next!"

Chaney wiped dust and smoke from his eyes. "Beaudine said we'd have to take him!"

"From five men, not fifty!"

Lem Wright steady-aimed from the other side of the shed, firing twice and hitting two more of the Red Hoods, one in the face and another in the chest. Target practice. He lowered his gun, watched them fall back twitching, and their horses scatter along the top of the canyon. He refused to be rattled.

Lem cocked his own smile. "Dead or alive, we're in it now!"

# CHAPTER NINETEEN:
## TASTE OF HELL

The sounds of the firefight surrounded John Bishop minutes before he passed through the split in the mountain that opened into Goodwill Canyon. It was a barrage he hadn't heard since the bloody fields of the war: all manner of gunfire, the shots crashing into each other, punched with the cries of men.

His reaction now was different from how it had been during the "conflicts." The shootings didn't matter, and the screams weren't reaching him. Bishop wasn't there to save anyone's life; his mission was his own. He lifted the rig from its saddle sling, keeping his arm extended, ready with double barrels as soon as Beaudine was in range.

Fox saw the dead look behind his eyes, and slowed the painted, giving Bishop the point, while covering his back. She knew he was riding alone, even if he wasn't. Her

hand was tight around the throwing ax
tethered to her wrist, and the bow was slung
across her shoulder, rubbing her wound raw.
Her breathing began to shallow, but she
fought it. She had her mission, too, so pain
had to wait.

Guns bellowed from the canyon, and
Bishop raced to meet them, Fox riding close
behind. He rode faster, determined, the rig
hoisted like a battle standard.

At the Goodwill, Lem Wright watched the
Red Hoods regroup after he'd shot two. He
moved around the side of the old shed,
where Chaney was pressing close to its shattered walls. An outlaw they hadn't even seen
get shot was lying dead in the weeds, one of
his boots blasted open.

Lem said, "Must've had his pistol pointed
down at his foot when he took the bullet.
That's a lesson."

Chaney could only nod.

Lem threw a smile to his buddy and the
kid who'd taken cover in the miner's cemetery just beyond the shed's porch. They
were hunkered by the graves, cracking off
shots toward the canyon rim when it was
clear. The kid was wiping away tears and
sweat.

Lem called out, "Dead or alive, we're in it
now!"

The kid froze, his gun hand shaking. Lem pushed it, as he brought up his Colt. "Boy, if you don't shoot, they'll shoot you. It's the way of the world."

Lem fired three times, delighting in his own marksmanship.

The kid shot toward the rim, forcing some Red Hoods back, but hitting nothing. You could almost hear the laughter, as they loaded up again, and the kid scrambled from the cemetery, toe-tripping over a marker.

Lem's buddy grabbed him by the arm. "I brought you in on this deal, your gun's mine!"

"You said it'd be a holdup! I did this when I was an infantry drummer, I ain't doing it again!"

"You're forgetting the gold."

"No, I ain't."

The kid blew a hole in his buddy's elbow, and made a panicked try for his horse. Running blind. That's when White Fox saw him. She and Bishop were still a distance out. The Goodwill was in front of them, and the kid was dead set between the old mine buildings and the canyon wall, fear-struck, his feet refusing to move, with Red Hood gunfire pocking around him.

Lem's buddy fired the shot that mule-kicked the kid sideways. Somehow the kid couldn't believe he'd been hit. "I never been in no real gunfight before," he said as he collapsed, his own dead weight pinning him down.

Bishop and White Fox rode hell-bent into the canyon.

The Fire Riders watched it all from the rim, and opened up, their muzzle flashes streaks of heat lightning. Bullets cut the air like hard rain, as Fox and Bishop split, each running full-out on opposite sides of the Goodwill, trying for cover.

Another new boy shot at the Red Hoods from behind the old mining office, and got ventilated three times.

The kid struggled in the middle of the road: pushing himself off the frozen mud, trying to stand, his life pouring out. Not making it. Bishop rode to him, the bay rearing.

Bishop demanded "Beaudine!"

Above them, Red Hoods were refocusing their aim.

The kid tried to speak, his blood-slick hands a flag he was waving, but his voice had strangled to nothing. The kid pointed toward the mine entrance. Two shots from the rim dead-danced him a few feet, before letting him drop.

Enemy snipers had strafed Bishop before, and that instinct took him over. He gaffed his horse, breaking left, and then running right, to the old mine entrance.

The next shot hit the bay.

The horse screamed, bucking wild as a slug tore her rump. Bishop lurched from his saddle, landing hard on the rig, the double barrel bashing his ribs.

Chaney and Lem stepped from the cover of the old mine shack, crouching low, popping shots at the Red Hoods above, then turning their guns on Bishop. Their buddy was holding his arm, gritting through the fire.

Chaney, the gambler, yelled, "And there's our goddamn gold!"

In a few simultaneous heartbeats: Fox's throwing ax hit Lem's leg above the knee, cutting muscle. He went down, trying to yank it free. Fox dropped from her horse, ran to Bishop, took the reins of both animals. Chaney followed her moves, thumb on the hammer of his Colt.

Bishop caught Chaney's action from the corner of his eye, got a sense of it, and protected her, shoulder-firing both barrels. The shotgun blew another hole in Chaney's hiding place, while he mostly dodged the blast. But it was a maneuver that worked, giving Fox time.

Bishop took cover in a small drainage ditch, slamming home two more shells.

Fox ran the horses toward a large stack of rail ties, bound with metal bands. The shots from above were random, targeting anything, chewing the ground around her. Fox kept the animals steady.

The bay snorted, as Fox worked to pull her down behind the barricade: getting her settled, on her knees, and then lying flat, so Fox could lie across her belly.

On the canyon rim, the Red Hoods opened ammo boxes, got set.

The bay was twisting, and Fox spoke, just letting the horse hear her voice. After some moments, there was no resistance as Fox pressed against her, the horse feeling the warmth of her body, calm in the chaos.

A new volley pounded every bit of the Goodwill, shooting the buildings and surrounding area to death: chewing the rail ties, ricochets screeching off the old iron, shattering already shattered glass.

The painted reacted to the gunfire, throwing his head back, biting at the air. Fox brought him down on his knees too, then to his side; finally, he did what she wanted. Straining, Fox kept both horses lying flat on the ground.

Bishop threw a shotgun blast at the old mine shed, turned and threw another at the slag heap where Howard was ducking low.

Lem screamed as he worked the throwing ax from his leg, pulling the blade free, red washing him. His buddy grabbed it, noting its feathers and markings, and yelled, "You're a coward, Bishop! Hidin' behind that Cheyenne bang-tail!"

Bishop lowered the empty rig, drew the Colt Peacemaker with his left, and shot Lem's buddy square in the chest. He turned, not returning fire, and staggered off the porch, and through the cemetery before crushing an old wooden cross that had DIED BROKE scrawled on it. The joke didn't escape him, and he death-laughed.

The Red Hoods, and the rim-fire, exploded again.

Bishop ran low across the field of battle, holding up the double barrels for protection, shots tearing at everything around him. He jumped behind the stacked rail ties as if tumbling into a shell hole. The bay reacted by sitting up, her muscles rolling, but didn't stand. Spasms racked her back flank.

The front of Fox's jacket was a wide smear of the bay's blood, but she calmed both animals as the shooting continued. She used her hands, voice, and body to keep them lying on their sides, out of the gun sights. Her touch was soothing and her quiet words somehow cut through the gunfire. The horses stayed down.

But Bishop's eyes were on the blasted-apart remains of the Goodwill and the scattered dead, as he tried to figure who was hiding where. "I couldn't find him, but Beaudine's here. He's got to be!"

"Then he is."

Bishop's voice was skidding. "Two of these men were there that night, I know it, as sure as anything."

"*Oóoxo'eéstómáne.*"

The Cheyenne word for revenge had just been evenly spoken when more bullets tore into the rail ties, wood chips flying. Bishop and Fox kept the animals lying down. The horses didn't struggle.

The bay's head lolled, and Bishop said, "We can't lose these horses!" He pulled his medical kit from the saddlebag with his left hand, frantically going through it, finally dumping half of it. "Did you check the wound? Completely?"

"I was saving her."

"Not if she dies of blood poisoning! What about the slug?"

Bishop's words were sharp, impatient, as he cleaned the blood away from the bullet strike on the bay's rump. The wound was a crease in her flesh, the hair around it scorched.

Bishop absently touched the bullet trench on his own neck. "It's all right. There's no slug, no lead."

Bishop looked to Fox, took a breath. She nodded. He massaged the bay's neck, as he always had, before dabbing the wound with water and iodine. The horse half-kicked at his touch, straightening her leg and whinnying, but letting the doc finish. Trusting him.

Bishop dried the wound, then ran his left hand over the bay, patting her gently. White Fox watched him struggling to put the supplies back in the kit and snap it closed. She reached over and did it for him.

Fox said, *"Otahe."*

Bishop listened.

There followed a few moments of rumbled-echo gunfire, and then nothing. Not even the metallic cocking of weapons for the next barrage, or orders being barked.

Nothing.

No one spoke, or seemed to move. The shooting had actually stopped; the canyon was still. The steady wind disturbed pieces of broken glass and wood, jarring them to the ground, and then there was nothing. Again.

At the mining shed, Chaney stayed crouched, peeking his head around a corner to eye the movement along the top of the ridge. From what he could see, the Fire Riders had pulled back.

He stayed in place and checked his guns. Fully loaded.

A few of Beaudine's new boys emerged from their places behind the old shacks or piles of lumber, in bloody shock after the battle. One of them walked to the body of Lem's buddy, still sprawled in the miner's bone orchard, and kicked him over to make sure he was gone. Then he grabbed his wallet.

Behind the slag heap, Howard pressed himself against the rocky trash, holding his lit cigar half an inch from the fuse on a dynamite bundle. Listening. Waiting.

He got through half a prayer, but couldn't remember the rest. The smoke was tickling his nose, and he sneezed, giving himself away. Howard ducked for cover from the bullet rain he expected, but it never happened.

Bishop heard Lem Wright moaning in pain by the old shed, but there were no other voices. Not even whispers. He and Fox stayed low behind the stack of rail ties, their horses flat against the ground, starting to stir, snorting.

Bishop reloaded the shotgun rig, eased it shut, smothering the sound of the barrel locking with the palm of his left hand. Fox drew an arrow for her bow, and fitted it tight, but didn't draw back. Not yet.

They watched as Howard stood up from the cover of the slag heap, his fist around some dynamite, the cigar clenched in busted teeth. Betsy was holstered. He drew on the cigar, and sneezed again, his eyes watering at the awful smell. He was a huge target, but no one took a shot.

"See? You had no confidence, but I knew you were a good soldier. We shouldn't have revealed our positions all at once, but I suspect Dr. Bishop knows us by now."

The familiar voice spoke from behind the cross braces that supported the collapsing entrance to the silver mine on the far side of the canyon. Bishop lifted the rig toward the voice, his body tensing as it continued: "I would say our common enemy has decided to let us settle our differences without them."

Beaudine stepped from his place between the large support timbers and the canyon wall, carrying his rifle and the long cleaver. He was over fifty yards away from where Bishop and White Fox had taken cover, and out of their range. They could only watch as he walked around the bodies of the Red Hoods and their horses, their blood mixing with the icy slush and mud, long gone.

He poked at each with the cleaver blade, as a triumphant warrior would use his broadsword. His tone was pure victory: "I brought this one down, and those other two, and more I suspect. But you all did your part, so earned your share. I'm proud of you, men."

Chaney barked, "Yeah, fine. When the hell do we get it?"

Beaudine took a few steps closer to Bishop and Fox, but kept his body angled, still at too far a distance for the shotgun's spread. Fox sat up on her knees, drawing her bow and aiming to shoot just over the top of their wooden protection, hitting Beaudine in the upper chest or throat.

He shielded himself with the cleaver blade, taunting. "That's up to Dr. Bishop, now that he's our prisoner."

Fox adjusted her shot, not taking her eyes off her target and reminding Bishop: *"He'kotóomoehá."*

*Calm in words, fierce in action.*

Bishop then called out, "You made your deal with Captain Creed, not me."

"All that matters is you understand that

you and your gold are now spoils of war."

Bishop squeezed Fox's shoulder, letting Beaudine's declaration bounce off the canyon walls and vanish before he stood up from behind the rail ties. The bay and the painted both got to their feet, flanking him.

Fox, and her aim, stayed low and fixed.

Bishop held the rig, taking in the damaged and dead of the Goodwill. Chaney, Howard, and Lem stayed on the ragged edge of their positions, holding weapons and the few new guns. Waiting to make a move, they stood bloody and tired.

Bishop measured his words. "Does this bunch understand that killing me gets you no gold?"

"They follow my orders."

"I'm barely holding back; a few of those dead are my doing, and I've left more behind." Bishop turned, pointing to Howard, Chaney, and Lem with the shotgun. "So, you might want to hear me out, Major."

Beaudine tossed an order, "You all stand at ease." Then he faced Bishop, "I appreciate the military courtesy."

"Did you forget that I used to be a doctor?"

Beaudine nodded. "No, I have not." Then he grandly pointed to the shotgun rig with the cleaver. "And that addition you've made for yourself is ample testament."

Bishop raised the shotgun level with Beaudine's stomach. "What I mean is, you think I don't recognize a man with a mental disorder?"

Chaney spit, "Jesus, another losing game."

Beaudine's words tumbled. "You're not in a position to be saying these things — things like this. Testing me is foolish. You, of all people, should know that! Howard, do you want your share? Ready to take it?"

Howard held up the dynamite bundle in one hand and the lit cigar in the other. "How many times you gonna ask?"

"That dynamite? Every shack. You're surrounded by it. Mr. Howard has made sure this entire place could be blown straight to Heaven." Beaudine turned the long cleaver in his palms, as he had that winter night. "We're all prepared to do what we need to do, so I'd think you'd stop flapjacking, and start cooperating!"

Bishop used his old bedside manner: "You need to stay calm, think, think of your officer's training. Get yourself clear." He adjusted his shoulders, tightening the line to the triggers. "Look around you. This didn't go as planned. These aren't Creed's men, so you tell me — vigilantes? Someone sent a damn army after you, Major."

Beaudine's voice jumped. "And we're victorious! We walked through the gates of hell for that gold, and it's ours! Are you saying you're not going to surrender it? Play that game again?"

"The gold's not here."

Chaney called out, "Then you take us to where you got it buried, or whatever. What's this stall for?"

"These aren't the only Red Hoods! They were riding down on us when we came into this canyon." Bishop yelled out to Lem, who had tied a belt above his knee to slow his bleeding, "You think this is over?"

Lem strained, "Going to help me, Doc?"

"Tell Beaudine what you think."

Lem threw it out, "We've got to get the hell out of here."

Beaudine shook his head, thoughts breaking. "No, no. We won this battle, and you're my prisoner, and you better damn well start acting like it!"

Bishop hit hard: "In truth, you're the prisoner. You believe I have this gold? If you don't follow my orders, you'll never see a bit of it."

Beaudine closed his eyes, sorting thoughts. Chaney stepped from behind the shed, arms outstretched. "What the hell do you want, then? This standoff isn't taking us no place."

"Beaudine, the bastard with the blind eye, and the big one. I don't know the rest of you, I don't care. Ride on."

Chaney said, "We're here for gold."

"We can talk about that, after I've settled my business."

Beaudine raised the cleaver, throwing away a laugh. "You are a man who refuses to accept his circumstances, and we will get that gold, one way or t'other."

White Fox stood, the bow drawn tight, the string slicing her fingers. A hint of sun highlighted the jagged edge of the arrowhead.

Bishop said, "The offer stands. The rest of you can ride out. Now. Maybe have a chance at that gold, but as long as this man's alive, you get nothing."

Lem quieted his moans, and Chaney was gun-ready. The last of the new boys looked to each other, not sure about their next move. One of them shifted on his feet, about to bolt.

Bishop didn't even blink, staying steady on Beaudine: "Just so we're clear: I came here to kill you. How many other enemies you have doesn't matter, because it's going to be *my* privilege to end your life."

Beaudine cleared his throat, and his mind: "Quite a declaration, Dr. Bishop. Not quite the Hippocratic oath, is it?"

Howard topped everyone: "What about our goddamn money! You're gonna come across this time!"

That's when the hammer dropped.

The black powder flamed on the Prussian needle rifle, sending the acorn-shaped bullet to find its target.

Time slowed on impact; the first shot hit one of the new boys in the neck, and traveled through to his partner standing next to him. The bodies were falling to the ground, pistols out of their leather and arms flailing, as all eyes turned toward the shots.

The Fire Riders ripped into the canyon pass at full thunder on white-skulled horses. There were about twenty Red Hoods in the wave, attacking the Goodwill with rifles blazing.

White Fox let fly the first arrow, tearing into a Red Hood as he rode by shooting at Bishop with a pair of barking Colts. The arrow cut through the Hood's leg, his horse wailing back, as he fired. Bishop blasted him out of the saddle with a single barrel, turned around, and used the second on a Hood who was swinging an ax.

Bishop snapped the rig, loaded fresh shells, as the first stick of Howard's dynamite spun through the air over his head, fuse burning down. It landed between the Riders, the explosion erupting beneath Hoods and horses, catching them running, tossing them, slamming them down.

Fox whipped arrows in quick succession, hitting two more Red Hoods, as Bishop jumped over the barricade, and ran for Beaudine. Howard threw more dynamite, the explosion pushing Bishop to the ground, raining ice and bloody mud.

The Red Hoods rode in a wide circle around the small canyon, closing off the Goodwill, wiping out Beaudine's new men with rifle fire. They were knocked off their feet, sent spinning, landing dead.

Two of Beaudine's outlaws ran for White Fox, laying cover fire, diving for the barricade. Her war club shattered one in the temple, then she spun with a battle knife in her hand, opening the other one's throat. One tried to ask something before he dropped. She kicked both bodies against the rail ties, adding to her shield.

Bishop pulled himself up from the ground to see Beaudine through a veil of blowing smoke: slashing at the masked riders with the cleaver, laying open their chests or knees, whatever he could catch with the blade, as they rode down on him. His screams were louder than theirs, hysterical rage, as he battled his way past them.

One of the Red Hoods put a pistol to the back of Beaudine's head. Beaudine turned, with his blade, facing the gun. Another explosion tore the ground around them.

Howard lit one, then another, stick of dynamite, throwing each to opposite ends of the canyon. The blasts sent old lumber, hooded men, and horses scattering wild. Bishop rolled out of the way of two skull-headed stallions, their hooves just missing him.

Bishop stood and shot one Fire Rider off his horse, and he went down, firing back. He missed. Slugs from somewhere else finished the Rider off.

Lem Wright yelled to Bishop, "Think that came from one of us! Maybe you don't know who your enemies are, Doc!"

Bishop moved to Lem, still with one shell in the rig, and pointed directly at his head. "I know."

Lem cocked his dead eye. "If one of us just saved your bacon, then you'd be obliged. You see Beaudine?"

The smoke of the fires and dynamite blasts was blown aside by a whip-snap of cold wind, revealing hooded riders still tearing wild, guns roaring, a few men crawling before dying, but Major Beaudine was nowhere to be seen. There were just more casualties of battle, more bodies.

"He isn't hiding out here, if that's what you're thinking. You really want Beaudine or not?"

They both ducked Red Hood gunfire, before Chaney stopped it with five shots from behind the old shack. They heard a body crash.

Lem called out, "Good work, gambler!" Then, back to Bishop, "See? It just takes one, and you'll never get what you want."

"Where is he?"

Lem's pain was a whispered, "Help me, damn it."

Bishop was next to Lem, and used his left to unhook the belt around the damaged leg, with Lem watching through his good eye and gritted teeth. "That little Cheyenne can do some real cutting. I'd watch my back."

Bishop rewrapped the belt inches from the wound, and pulled it tight with his one arm, stopping the bleeding. "You had this in the wrong place, lost a lot of blood."

"Tell me I'm going to make it, at least to ride out of here."

Bishop didn't say a word; all around them was the sound of a new attack and retreat. Lem took a deep breath, and ran his hands over his leg, rubbing some feeling back into it. "Son of a bitch, that pains!"

"The nerves are getting blood again. You might pass out."

"But I be alive. We're in the middle of a battle, and you can't help being a doc. You want Beaudine? He had his escape all planned out, just in case. He's loco, but he knew."

"Help you, and let you go?"

"Then, I'm staying alive?"

"You need that leg sewn up right away, and my med kit's in my saddlebags."

"So I'll be fine? You haven't said it yet!"

By the canyon entrance, Howard puffed his cigar before lighting another bundle, and hurling it toward one of the buried charges. The ground blew apart, driving a posse of Fire Riders away from the old mine, their horses tossed off balance. The sound of the blast was trapped against the walls, and pounded back, over and over. One explosion became an echoed dozen.

Howard tossed the dynamite as grenades, every blast tearing through the Fire Riders.

A few Riders opened up on the slag heap, punching it with bullets. Howard shot back with Betsy, but stayed low after every trigger pull, their return fire slicing damn close. He drew deeply on the green cigar, eyes watering, before leaning close to the exposed end of the fuse to the dynamite bundles planted around the mine perimeter.

Howard sneezed out half his nose with the green smoke, then lit the fuse.

Lem Wright angled over in pain. "I can't sit a horse like this. You've got to do more."

"Where's Beaudine?"

Behind them, Chaney was belly-crawling from the old shack, stray slugs ripping around him.

Lem cried, "Think about that night! You know I didn't raise a hand to hurt your wife or son."

Bishop drew the trigger line tight. "Where?"

"This is worse than it was before!"

Bishop pressed the double-barrel rig against Lem's chest, boiling. "Where'd he escape to?"

"I'll show you, but — but you've got to fix me!"

Lem continued his begging, but Bishop wasn't hearing it. The outlaw's voice had been replaced by the screams of his wife and son. No words, just their sound, filling his head. Bishop felt his own blood pulsing, boiling through, as their painful cries grew louder and louder in his mind.

He leaned harder on the rig, busting one of Lem's ribs.

The bullet from Chaney's gun exited out of Lem's dead eye.

Bishop fell back, as Chaney moved on him, a Wesson two-shot Blade Derringer in his hand. "They call it the Gambler's Gun, and wasn't Deadeye surprised? Now, you're *my* prisoner, and going to take me to that goddamn gold."

The blast of a dynamite bundle shook the ground with cannonball force, tossing more Riders, setting one of them aflame. Their skull horses ran from the canyon, dead men dragging in their stirrups.

Bishop and Chaney faced each other's guns and eyes, the battle around them raging someplace else. Bishop said, "I've got no interest in you. You weren't with Beaudine the night this all happened."

Chaney flicked his gold tooth. "I ain't with him now. This is strictly a two-person game, and no one's sitting in."

Bishop eyed the palm-fit gun. "Give yourself a chance, son. Ride out. I'm on my own mission."

Chaney held out the Derringer. "You forget, I seen that thing in action," he said before plugging the shotgun barrel with the gun, and pulling the trigger. The small caliber bullet screamed up the barrel, before ripping into the black powder shell in the chamber, blowing the weapon apart at the breach.

Bishop spun off his feet as if he'd been hit with a sniper's bullet, his jacket and the rig's leather harness in shredded pieces. Blood began soaking the sleeve of his half-arm. Bishop tried standing, fighting against the numb feeling that was blanketing him, that he knew was shock.

Chaney said, "You don't even have an arm, and right now it hurts like hell."

The echo of the shotgun's bursting apart hid the sound of the arrow as it struck Chaney between the fourth and fifth ribs. He lurched in surprise before collapsing, the gun snug in his hand.

White Fox leapt the painted over Chaney, the reins to the bay in her teeth. She dropped from her own horse as Bishop tied off his bloody sleeve, the destroyed rig hanging loose from his elbow joint. He stumbled. She put her arms under him, giving him a boost onto the bay. Both horses snorted, ready to run.

Bishop had settled onto his saddle when the first set of mine supports along the canyon wall exploded, the force of the blast a sledgehammer blow to anyone standing.

The buried fuse burned from bundle to bundle, each support shattering with their detonation, sending burning wood, and metal in a wild burst across the mine, the four-by-fours becoming flying battering rams. Riders in red dove for cover, their horses cutting loose.

The old shed was next, the roof thrown into the air, then coming down on two Fire Riders, shards ripping them as jagged darts, a flaming cave-in from the sky.

Another blast tore the mine walkway from the canyon wall, huge sections tumbling, crashing to the ground, bringing tons of stone and gravel with it, blowing a hole in the earth.

White Fox and Bishop galloped through a thick curtain of violent dust, dodging the fallen and the debris, riding blind for the canyon entrance.

Howard took a draw on his cigar, and lit the fuses on two sticks of dynamite, before thumb-stubbing it out. He held the sticks as they burned down, watching the red glow eating the fuse, when a cry erupted from his massive chest; first it was a laugh, then a scream for "goddamn gold!" that became a wild animal howl that was beyond words.

He leapt from behind the slag heap and tossed the two sticks, holding back the Fire Riders with their explosions, as he ran for the open shaft of the old silver mine. He dove away from their rifle fire, scrambling on his feet, always moving.

Chaney managed his knees, breaking part of the arrow from his side, the pain eating him. He yelled, "You going to leave me in this Hell? I'm your partner!"

Howard's broken-by-laughter howl continued.

On the road to the canyon, the howl was just another distant note, followed by more explosions and cries. Bishop and White Fox broke clear of the Goodwill, those damned sounds fading, before another huge blast rocked the ground.

The dynamite quake shook boulders from the top of the canyon until they slid down the walls, breaking apart into huge chunks, blocking the entrance in a dust and gravel eruption.

The sound was louder than the hundred blasts that had come before it.

Bishop and Fox looked back at the Goodwill, half buried, as their horses ran hard toward the downsloped trail off the mountain. The Fire Rider sentry, guarding the way out, charged them, firing warning shots. Fox drew, and hit him with a warning shot of her own, the arrow puncturing the meat of his shoulder. It was pure whip-fast movement, and perfectly accurate.

The Fire Rider's red hood garbled his howling as he pulled back on his horse too hard, tangling his footing. They tumbled hard into the ditch alongside the canyon road.

The Rider kept swearing at Bishop and Fox as they leapt down an ice-slick hill, to a small cut in the trail. Not more than a break between rocks and dead trees, but it was a door to the other side of the frozen Colorado.

He pulled off his hood, and watched the last burst of flames and black smoke erupting from the Goodwill, feeling the sound of those final explosions, then shook his head. "God Almighty."

He bit off a plug of hard tobacco, ignoring the arrow protruding from his shoulder. He wasn't entreating the Lord, or seeing the Goodwill as a Biblical pit of sulfur, or doing any damn thing, but just sitting.

Having a quiet chew at the end of the day, a hundred yards from an open grave stacked with corpses.

The opium smoke was gossamer, a light fog that hovered close to the ceiling of Widow Kate's office. The dragon pipe next to her was lit, but she didn't draw from it, just took deep breaths of the air, working at her desk.

She carefully wrote half of the last zero of "100,000," then urged the ink into the tip of her new Waterman with a quick shake, to complete it.

The columns of figures in the ledger were neatly entered, and their total was her testament. Kate took satisfaction from just looking at the numbers, not thinking about the money, only seeing that each total was greater than the last entry. She could lose herself in numerals.

The knock on her office door was precisely three times, and there was a wait until Kate called, "Enter!"

Soiled Dove slid the doors open, and closed them behind her before saying a word. She placed five stacks of bills, each with a name written on a small slip of paper on top, on Kate's leather desk blotter.

"I double-checked every girl, makin' sure they wasn't holding out nothing. That's everything, to the dollar."

"Any gold? Silver?"

"No, ma'am, this was strictly a paper day."

Kate smiled as she gathered the cash, counting it for herself. "You're doing very well, girl. This place is running like clockwork, and I'm obliged, since I still can't get up and down those stairs."

Soiled Dove nodded. "I just want to be of

help. Here." She held out White Fox's torn skirt and top that had been wrapped and tied around something small.

Kate took the bundle. "I was just thinking about those two, wondering if they did what they set out to do. Or maybe got killed. That would be a shame. You should burn these."

"Yes ma'am. There's something inside."

Kate unfolded the bloody clothes, revealing an earthen jar of salve with something written on its side: *For your scars.*

Kate stroked the bandage protecting the stitches along her massive side, luxuriating in the opiate fog, and said, "Now, I'm obliged to the Cheyenne."

# CHAPTER TWENTY:
## ESCAPES

The explosion gut-punched Howard, Chaney, and Beaudine against the mine wall, pieces of the rotting ceiling beams falling around them, followed by broken chunks of rock and tarry mud. They kept their heads down as the force pushed past them, grit raining into their eyes. The grit shimmered, with a taste of silver fog.

"Was that the last?"

Howard didn't hear Beaudine. He was holding his nose and blowing, to clear out his ears. Beaudine asked again, and Howard said, "I ain't sure. Should be though."

"Let me put it this way, are there any more charges that are closer?"

"You saw where I put 'em."

"I'm saving your life bringing you here. Want to answer me straight?"

Howard blew his nose again. "There aren't no more that are closer."

The three looked back down the shaft to

the opening of the Goodwill silver mine, which was now blocked by collapsed timbers, and fallen-in walls. Chaney inched his way to his feet, holding his bleeding side. "It don't make no difference. We're trapped. My thanks for saving us, though."

Beaudine didn't respond. Chaney cleared his eyes with his fingers, looked at the flecks of silver on their edge. "But at least I'll die a rich man."

Beaudine, holding the long cleaver and one of the Fire Riders' red hoods, said, "Rich is what we're all working for, but your death will not be today. We've escaped prisoners to find, and we're wasting time. There's an air duct tunnel right up ahead, opens above the river."

Chaney and Howard looked to each other, bloody and tired. Beaudine said, "See for yourself."

Chaney and Howard hauled themselves up and followed Beaudine farther into the mine, the dark of it becoming even darker, as they felt their way along the narrowing walls.

"Don't get ideas about picking up nuggets. This was played out years ago, if it played at all. And that stuff on your hands is residue from the mucking. Worthless."

Howard said, "Forget the silver, I'd just

a-soon get the hell out of here."

"We will."

Chaney wiped off the worthless. "How'd you know about an airway? I thought Creed picked this place."

Beaudine said, "My brother told me. He's buried in that miner's bone orchard that you blew to smithereens, Mr. Howard. When Creed suggested the Goodwill, I did what a good soldier does in the face of the enemy, and revealed nothing."

Beaudine stopped, with Howard and Chaney next to him, their eyes hit with a narrow slice of sunlight coming from the end of a small tunnel cut in a sidewall.

Chaney started around Beaudine. "Let's go!"

"Hold on. Mr. Howard, you first. There are planks at the end that need to be broken through to the outside, and your strength is mandatory. But before you do, Mr. Chaney?"

Beaudine handed Chaney the red hood. He held it for just a moment, feeling its curious weight. Chaney's eyes adjusted, focusing first on the blood soaking one side of the hood, then on the Rider's head still inside it, lopped cleanly at the neck with the cleaver blade.

Chaney dropped the hood, choking air.

Beaudine kicked it aside. "This was a difficult day, gentlemen. We fought hard and let the savage loose, but now we're an army of three. If we're going to find our way to Bishop's gold, there can be no mutiny, no disloyalties. If your heart is traveling in that direction, now would be the time to tell me."

Chaney held his wounded side with red-wet fingers. "I'll do what's needed."

"Mr. Howard?"

Howard regarded the head at his feet, then said, "You keep asking like I don't want that gold no more. I want it."

The ceiling shifted with a low rumble, a crack above them widening. Chaney half-crouched as Beaudine stepped to one side, pointing to the air way with the cleaver blade.

Howard worked his way through the stone cut, to the opening fifty feet in. The passage was too small for him to raise his arms, so he smashed through the boards with a single head butt, flooding the mine with sunlight and the fresh sound of the river below.

The finger of water coming off this side of the Colorado didn't have a name, but ran cold and fast down the mountain, before splitting into a dozen streams cutting through winter-bare woods. White Fox and

Bishop stood on one of those stream banks, frosted with snow to the water's edge, tending themselves.

Caked with black gunpowder, dust from the Goodwill, and blood, they washed as best they could, with handfuls of icy water splashing across their wounds. Fox pulled the shotgun rig from Bishop's arm, the blasted-jagged section of the breach slicing her hand.

She sucked on the cut, started to unhook the leather straps across his back, pain eating at them both. Bishop kept his voice flat: "The gambler was going to give us Beaudine. Give us. You didn't have to shoot."

Fox pulled the leather free. "We don't have the word. You'd say it was 'a choice.' " Then she stuffed the broken rig into Bishop's saddlebag.

Fox took a deep breath and held it, feeling the mountain cool, before she said, *"Ametané'ôsené."*

"You think you gifted me life?"

She smeared the blood from her hand onto the blood on her clothes. "We wouldn't have survived. Now, you can go on with the hunt."

She knelt by the water, pulling her shirt down over her shoulders, so he could clean the deep sore there, rubbed to the muscle by her bowstring.

Bishop looked through the medical kit. "Your salve would be good for that."

"I gave the last away."

"Another choice?"

The tiny voice from behind the trees chirped: "Mister, if you've got money hid, you need to give it over. Really slow."

The little girl was about four feet tall, with a flat nose that seemed to run directly from her mouth with no break, and blue eyes that were too far apart. Her hair was straight, cornstalk yellow, and in desperate need of a ribbon or a comb that would have helped it hide her enormous ears. She held a rusting squirrel rifle crimped against her, and she moved it around every time she spoke in a way that was oddly musical. Tuneful, even when she mangled her words.

"That there the money? I'll be wanting it."

Bishop's arm went into firing position, without his thinking, and without a weapon. His eyes met Fox, and his instincts cooled. "Really don't think you need a gun."

Bishop tried to follow the end of the rifle as it moved in circles while the little girl bobbed her head about, almost singing. "I do need it, to make you give over money. Or I'll shoot. You. And her. And then, maybe, you again."

"It'll probably hurt some, but that's not going to kill either one of us. Or even a squirrel for supper. Is that what you're doing out here?"

"Ask you the same question!"

"We're just riding through. Is this your land? Is that it?"

"No, it ain't."

"Then why are you pointing that? Are you a robber?"

The rifle started moving again, and so did the "voice music": "My sister's ailing bad, and we can't fix our wagon, and my pa don't know which end is up, so I'm taking charge. And you all are the first things I'm taking charge of."

Fox said, "Where is your father?"

"No business of yours! Show me your hands!"

Bishop raised his left hand, and half a right arm skyward. The little girl said, "Was you born that way, or did somebody take after you?"

"Somebody took after me. We can help you, and your sister."

"She's been dyin' for as long as I can remember."

White Fox said, "He is a doctor."

"You're like somethin' the devil coughed

up! I seen doctors afore, and they didn't look nothing like you. Or her!"

Bishop smiled. "You're surely right, most don't look like me, but I am a doctor. Let me try helping your sister, and if you don't like it, you can still shoot me."

Nodding, the little girl lowered her rifle, blurting, "Don't think I won't!" She repeated it as if it were a chorus.

The Conestoga was propped on a tree stump, leaving the back axle to freely turn, without the weight of its shattered wheel. At first glance, it looked to be the wagon of a broken-down circus: the canvas top had seen too many repairs, with patches of all colors, as had the too-large wagon bed, which was pieced together from half a dozen freight schooners by a carpenter with no skills.

The campsite could have dropped out of the sky to land in this most unlikely place: there was a small fire with a fine, polished steel cook pot and implements hanging over it, surrounded by two upholstered rocking chairs, a mahogany dresser with bottles of perfume scattered across the top, most of which had spilled down its side, and a large vanity mirror mounted in a standing frame.

Albert Tomlinson stepped from the back of the Conestoga, wringing out a washcloth, when he saw his daughter rifle-marching between Bishop and White Fox, as they rode from the woods to the campsite. Albert, whose body could barely support the clothes he was wearing, waved to his little girl with a tired, grey smile.

"Well, how're you folks doing today?"

The girl started running to Albert, turned midway to keep her bent rifle on her new prisoners, then back-stepped the rest of the way to his side. Her voice was all highs and lows. "Look what I found in the woods, Papa! Caught 'em on my own, brung 'em in on my own. And you know they got money!"

Albert patted the top of her head. "Now, May Flowers, I think you were supposed to get us some dinner."

"But they're better!"

Bishop and Fox got down from their horses as Albert extended a bony hand. "Albert Tomlinson, over to Arkansas. Surely am sorry about this. Hope you didn't feel too threatened." Then he whispered, "My May Flowers wouldn't really shoot nobody."

Bishop shook with his left. "She's a good protector. How long have you been here, Mr. Tomlinson?"

"Nigh on three days."

"And we're the first to find you?"

"This is a pretty lonesome spot, I guess. There was a Shoshoni scout party one night, but they didn't come in."

"What happened to your outfit?"

May Flowers said, "Have 'em empty up their pockets!"

Albert took the rifle from his daughter as he scarecrowed back to the wagon, settling by the empty axle. May Flowers jammed her tongue stubbornly behind her lower lip as her father spoke: "The axle started turning funny coming down the trail out of that low range, and then we lost the wheel."

White Fox looked underneath the wagon, pointing to the loose iron above the axle braces. "The brake rocker is broken."

Albert said, "Yes, ma'am. We couldn't control nothing the last bit, and crossed the water too fast. Darn near toppled over completely. That's when we lost the wheel, and I had to fish it out. But I was surely glad to get to this side, with the girls and all."

Fox moved to the wheel, which was leaning against the mahogany dresser. She rolled it in the grass, to the place where the iron flatting had peeled back, splintering the wood.

"The felly is split. This can't be fixed."

May Flowers singsonged, "She knows

about all of this?"

Bishop said, "She knows. If you don't pull out of this mud soon, this wagon's staying put."

Albert said, "We're worse than the church mouse right now, can't afford a darn thing."

"You've got some fine furniture, Mr. Tomlinson."

"My wife's things. She's gone."

"Why don't you sell a piece, get a new wheel?"

May Flowers grabbed one of the bottles of perfume and began dousing herself. "That's how come I was getting us money." Then she stuck out her tongue at White Fox.

Albert said, "I got me another daughter who's with bronchitis. That's the baby, and I can't leave her to go to town, to do business."

"May told us. I'm a doctor."

Albert took a long look at Bishop, in tatters, before finally saying, "Really?"

Little May Showers had a Chinese abacas lying on her tummy, and she pushed the beads around trying to match the colors in a row. If she managed it, she allowed herself a thin smile between fits of harsh coughing. A slip of a girl, tucked up tight in a hammock strung across the back of the freight schooner, she rocked it defiantly when her father came close.

She looked a great deal like her sister, but her face was smaller, and meaner, with coarse black hair instead of blond. She shared the same blue eyes, but they didn't soften her features, or invite anyone closer.

Albert entered the wagon, which was filled with more furniture, including a spinning wheel, and moved carefully to his daughter. May Showers huddled in her hammock, racking the beads on the abacas, back and forth, clicking them together with every step Albert took, as if he were approaching a rattler about to strike.

"May Showers, this here's a doctor, honey. He's going to help you, so you behave and let him."

The little girl thrashed violently, as Albert pried the abacas from her fingers. She didn't yell, but burst into a fit of deep, raw coughing. Albert tried more water, which she couldn't swallow, the spittle running down her chin. Her chest finally relaxed, and she settled back into her sweat-dirty pillow. She never said a word, but thrust her hands out for the abacas.

Albert put it aside. "I'm a bookkeeper by trade, and I find this exotic device very useful. The girls think it's a plaything. They don't like no dolls or nothing."

White Fox opened the medical kit, as Bishop reached inside for a small mirror. "How long has it been since she's washed?"

"I try my best. We got a bathtub, but it's packed away."

"Part of getting her well is keeping her clean."

Bishop handed the mirror to Fox, who angled it to catch a ball of sunlight, which she focused on May Showers' chin. May hit her father with furious eyes, clutched the sides of the hammock, and was about to twist.

Albert stammered something about behaving, but Bishop cut into it: "May, I don't look like a doctor, but I am, and I know how to make folks feel better. All I want you to do is open your mouth just a little bit, so I can look inside with this glass. I promise not to sneak in any nasty medicine. And, I do anything you don't like your sister's going to shoot me with her squirrel gun. Okay?"

The girl's jaw was clenched angry-tight. White Fox ran her hand across her forehead, brushing her unwashed hair out of her eyes, and letting it rest there. May sagged her mouth open. Bishop adjusted an examining lens to see into her throat, illuminated by the sunlight reflected in the hand mirror.

"There's no infection."

"The Little Rock docs said it was the bronchitis."

"Her airway's blocked. That's different."

Bishop held out his hand, and Fox automatically gave him his monaural stethoscope. He placed it on May's chest, and listened, looked to Fox and said, "She sounds like you."

White Fox reached into the medical kit.

The reservoir of the oxygen pump filled instantly with running water from the stream. White Fox picked out slivers of ice, while May Flowers peered over her shoulder.

"What's that thing? It worth any money?"

"For your sister."

"What's it worth?"

Fox stood, checking the rubber tubes. "It will save her life."

May Flowers stayed on Fox's heels as they walked back to the wagon. "But what's it worth?"

May Showers' hands fought the celluloid oxygen mask, clawing at it until Bishop pulled it back. "May, this is what you need. You don't have to do anything but breathe. Won't that feel good? No more coughing?"

The little girl screamed, throwing a tiny,

balled fist, before doubling over, her chest racking. Fox held her hands as Bishop fitted the mask over her mouth and nose, tightening the strap around her head.

"Turn it!"

Albert jumped at Bishop's voice, and started to crank the device, bringing the oxygen from the water through the tube to the mask. May Showers took the new air in, but her hands went to the mask again, her fingers clawing.

Albert said, "Daughter May Flowers? Mr. Foster's song, now."

May Flowers stood behind her sister, her downturned face sullen and dark, but she began to sing, "Slumber, my darling, thy mother is near, / Guarding thy dreams, from all terror and fear," bringing her voice up from someplace beyond her, filling the wagon.

May Showers settled in her hammock, breathing quietly, her sister's voice wrapping around her.

May Flowers carried Stephen Foster's lullaby out of the wagon on wings, to the edge of the stream and the horses, where Bishop and Fox were checking their saddles. They listened to that perfect voice, clear as mountain air, and a smile traveled between them. Albert shrugged at his daughter's talent.

Bishop said, "That's an amazing gift she's got."

"Like their mama. Not much to look at, but they do have those voices. Both of 'em."

"I didn't presume, Albert. Did your wife pass?"

"No, sir, she run off. So guess I'm divorced, but without papers. Uglier than a two-snout pig, but she found another fella."

The song hid White Fox's reaction, and she sneezed her laugh, as Bishop nodded toward the dresser. "Then, I suppose if it doesn't pain too much, sell one of her pieces, get that wheel? You can go to town now, your girls will be all right."

"Now." Albert dug his hands in his pockets. "That's just what I'm going to do, get fixed up, and to my new job. But I don't have no money to pay you, Doc. You want to take a chair? They're nice sitters. Frenchie imports from New Orleans."

Bishop secured his med kit in the saddlebag. "Your daughter's sleeping easy because of this young woman. That breather belongs to her."

"Then I thank you greatly, ma'am. Maybe you'd like to take something with you?"

White Fox got on her horse. "I am."

■ ■ ■ ■

"There are a lot of good reasons to kill a man, but target practice ain't one of 'em," Fuller said.

"Is he being ironic? Is there a smile there?" Creed asked.

Hector gently gaffed Creed's Pride to quicken his pace, so that he was now riding parallel with Fuller. The sniper glanced at the boy and Captain Creed, who were saddled together. There wasn't a hint of a smile on Fuller's face, or anything to read in his eyes, except the burning from the bullet in him.

"Satisfied?"

Hector nodded his approval of Fuller's expression and response, a kid pretending to be an officer in a mirror.

Fuller returned his eyes to the horizon, and the storm roiling there, its light presnow just starting to reach them.

"Report?"

Hector spoke over his shoulder. "Sir, I'm looking at Mr. Fuller, and I think he's saying exactly what he means."

"I won't make it a direct order, but you'd be doing the company right, getting rid of that useless sack."

Fuller kept riding, his hands almost going to his sniper's rifle. Almost.

Creed's Pride whinnied. The captain leaned in, squeezing Hector's shoulders to the bone. "You're holding Pride back. Appreciate the honor of where you are; let him have his way."

Hector loosened his pull, trying to fall into the rhythm of Pride's gait, but was still a plowboy on a thoroughbred. The boy's awkward movements, sputtering and gangly, got a half smile from Fuller, but he stayed fixed on the flattening land, and the mountains that were changing shape and color the farther they rode into Wyoming.

Behind them, a ways back, Fat Gut was running his nag hard across the flats, trying to catch up. He yelled to everyone at the top of his lungs, but there was no attention paid to his mush.

Fat Gut tried calling again, and Creed said to Fuller, "You still favoring that shoulder?"

"I expect to for some time."

Creed considered the sniper's response by adjusting his sunglasses, new snow collecting on the lenses. "We still have a mission, and I expect every man to do his part."

"I will, sir." Fuller let that stand, and then: "I already have, as best I could."

"Thinking of your failure in the woods?"

"I'm thinking about my wife and son."

Creed's voice rose. "Want to do right by them? Then you need to know just how much your skills have been compromised, to make sure you can claim your fair share of that money. There's a target running up on us, and I'm giving you a direct order to fire at it."

"I'll get myself back up. You'll see."

Creed said, "Actually, I won't. But I'll know."

Hector yanked Pride to a sudden stop, jolting the saddle. Creed slammed the boy hard with a double-fist against his side, knocking him clean out of his stirrups, and landing him hard.

"What are you doing, boy? You don't treat this animal with disrespect!"

Hector stood, rubbing the feeling back into his elbow, his eyes trying to focus on a rider in the distance. "Truly sorry, sir. It's that, ahead. I-I never seen nothing like it."

He took a rosewood and dragon's blood rosary from his pocket, and held the simple wooden cross close to his lips. "My mama, she swore me a Catholic. Don't know why."

The horse was a living skeleton, skull head mounted on bleached bones, with fire pouring from its sides. A red, faceless demon, was running the animal straight out of hell,

288

cutting through the grey of the horizon, to come for Creed, Fuller, and Hector.

"Report! What is it you're seeing?"

Fuller put his arm through his rifle sling, and brought up the weapon. "Man in a hood, sir."

"Sniper, I imagine you've already got your finger on the trigger." Creed patted his horse's neck. "It's not needed."

Fuller steadied the butt of the Morgan-James against his still, blood-wet shoulder, shutting one eye to site this new target. "We'll see."

Fat Gut short-pulled on his horse, bringing it to a stumbling halt beside Creed's Pride. Gut and the nag were both sweat-winded, and his words still beaten by broken teeth: "It'th about timeth you thtopped! Dinn't you hear me, cousin?"

Creed said, "We heard."

Gut squinted in the direction everyone was looking, at the Fire Rider getting closer. "Who the thell is dat?"

"Exactly."

The skeletal horse eased its run, the flames in its mane and tail relaxing, as it slowed to a perfect stop before Creed. Fuller kept his rifle steady, aiming at the place directly between the eyeholes of the crimson hood.

The Fire Rider waved. "Captain, you're fighting light."

Creed said, "These men are my hand-picked best."

"Not all of them."

Smythe pulled off his hood, smoothing his wiry red hair with one hand, while keeping the other resting in his lap. He looked to Fuller, bit off a chaw, then rubbed his shoulder where White Fox had left her arrow.

"You look to have the same problem I do, boy-o. That shoulder? Little whore stick you with an arrow, too?"

Fat Gut got out between laughs, "Nopeth! A bulleth!"

Smythe looked directly at the inescapable barrel of the long-range rifle. "That's a beef-headed way of doing things, ain't it? You loaded? Capped?"

Fuller nodded, and Smythe said, "Then lower it. You've all made too many damn mistakes. Don't make another. I'm taking you in, so you can alibi yourselves."

"Stand down, sniper Fuller." Fuller let a few heartbeats pass, then followed Creed's order, pulling the rifle up, resting it on his hip, arm still through the sling.

Creed said, "Did you get the prisoners?"

"No, Captain, we ain't."

"We sent a message, and you had a lot more men than I did."

"Beaudine brought the whole Goodwill down on their damn heads."

"I'm a military officer —"

"A blind man."

Creed continued as if Smythe hadn't uttered a thing. "— who captured Bishop, and held on to him. Most of my volunteers are left frozen in those mountains, but we were better than you. A hundred fighting a madman, and you lost."

Smythe ran his fingers through his beard, thoughtfully eyeing Fat Gut before saying, "Looks to me like *you* lost, mate. She kicked your teeth out? You know, there are a half dozen I could name that I'd rather see on that horse than you."

Creed said, "Now, I can agree with your blather."

Gut swallowed his spit, forcing his words out slow and dry: "I-am-a-good-fighter. Always-do-wath-my-cousin-saith."

Smythe said, "You can't even defend how worthless you are. Ride on, I'm not taking you in."

"You're justh a pristhon guard! You got nothin' to thay about nothin'."

"I was a guard, and what I am now doesn't matter. What you've got to remember is that whether I'm wearing a uniform or a hood, I'll kill you just as soon as sneeze."

Fat Gut tried a busted-teeth smile, to show he wouldn't be backed down, so Smythe drew a Colt six-shot with a worn handle from his red tunic. "I said, ride on. Or be dinner for the wolves. Either way."

"Whath abouth my thare of gold?"

Creed said, "You're family, I carried you. But the prisoners' escape is on your head. That's what happened to your share." Creed turned his eyes to the sound of Fat Gut's heavy breathing. "I had other plans, but these men are saving your life. You should appreciate that. Now get the hell out."

Gut was about to say more, but thought better of it, as he brought the nag around, spurring her side too hard, and taking off at a run. Heading into Wyoming, leaving the rest behind.

Smythe looked down at Hector, who was amazed at the events of the previous minutes. "You're gonna catch flies in that mouth, you don't close it."

Creed, settled into his Pride, said, "He needs a ride."

Smythe said, "That horse's your eyes?"

"Better."

"Okay, boy-o, let's see what mama feeds ya."

Smythe extended his good arm, and pulled Hector onto the back of his saddle with a single, sweeping motion. Pain gripped him, but he didn't give it away. Fire Rider Smythe angled his skeleton-horse around, heading back toward the horizon, as Hector settled in. Creed's Pride followed, the captain holding the reins easy, with Fuller behind the bunch, keeping everyone in his sights.

No one was in a hurry against the snow and the darkening sky.

Smythe smiled at Hector. "You look like a veteran. Been with the captain a long time?"

"Pa rode with him, and he got killed, so he took me in. I'm his eyes and ears sometimes. Other times, he ain't too happy with me."

"I imagine you'll have a few more years together, yet."

"If I can ask, how you know each other? You don't sound like anybody else who rides with him."

"No, you can't ask that. But I'll tell you I hail from the coast of England. You know where that is?"

"Across the ocean someplace. That's how come you talk like you do?"

"Right."

"And does everyone there paint up their horses?"

Smythe reached behind his back, giving Hector his red hood, "In my business, sometimes it works best if people are a little scared of you. Throws 'em off their game."

"I never seen nothing like this before."

"When I was your age, my dad told me about the demons of Romney Marsh. You never heard of that one, right?"

"No, sir."

"They were pirates, did up themselves and their horses like demons, raiding French ships for booty. Come riding right out o' hell, scaring everybody to death, sometimes taking a shipful of goods without firing a shot."

"What happened if anybody tried to fight back?"

Smythe made a slashing motion across his throat. Hector's voice was small. "And you're the leader here?"

"Not the leader boy-o, but the painting-up was all mine."

Hector nodded, as a sting of wind rushed by his ear. There was a sound like bee wings, and a tiny pain. The snow blew heavier, and he brushed the cold from his ear, coming back with bloody fingers.

"H—Hey, I think I been shot!"

Fat Gut's second and third shots were distant puffs of smoke that ended in ground strikes. He pressed the nag full-out, galloping toward Creed and his men, with two pistols firing. His hands flailed in all directions, sending the bullets every which way.

Creed called out, "Hector!"

"I'm okay, sir! I can still do my duty!"

"Good. Sniper!"

Fuller had the Morgan-James, his thumb locking the hammer in place, steadying his shot.

Fuller said, "He's a mighty big target," before pulling the trigger, and exploding Fat Gut's chest. The slug passed clean through, hitting the trunk of a bare tree some yards behind him.

The nag carried Fat a while longer, before he slipped off her back and hit the ground, eyes locked open.

Creed said, "I could hear it. That was a clean shot."

Fuller lowered the rifle. "Yes, it was. And at a good distance."

"Hector! Report!"

Hector was blotting the blood from his ear with Smythe's hood. "I'm fine, Captain. Had to earn my wound sooner or later."

"You're a good boy." Creed gently nicked Pride to start again. "Sniper Fuller, why didn't you take the target when I asked the first time?"

Fuller eased alongside Creed. "The fat bastard never shot at me before."

The snow was gentle in the air, large flakes dancing around Bishop and White Fox, as they rode along the edge of the stream, thin bits of ice cracking under their horses. The sun was dipping, bringing a snap to the cold coming out of the woods, but Bishop didn't shield his face with collar or scarf; he wanted to feel the purity of it. The clean.

Bishop said, "That was a good thing you did, helping that child."

"Ugly child."

He laughed. "Like a two-snout pig. Never argue with a father."

White Fox smiled. *"Néhnéšétse."*

"Yes, I guess it was both of us."

"She needed a doctor, not just me."

Bishop let that thought hang for a moment, and then: "We helped her, and a few hours before, we killed a man. More than one. A hell of a lot more."

Her voice was flat. "Your journey became a war."

"And you knew it was going to happen."

Bishop looked at her. "We're riding in the wrong direction. We need to go back to the Goodwill."

Fox didn't return it. "This is right.

*Anôse.*"

"It isn't right. We don't know where the hell Beaudine went. We almost did."

Fox finally met him. "Their horses had an army brand."

"So, they were rustled."

"There's a man, past the deep trees, who'll know about the stolen horses, and the red ones. Everything."

*"Ma'êhóóhe."*

Fox didn't respond to her given name, she just repeated, "Everything."

They leapt across a small, leaf-filled gully, to an open break in the woods where a row of pines had been cut into a semicircle, their branches bent back, tied to stakes in the ground. The cones that had fallen around the trees were neatly stacked beside them.

Bishop brought up the bay, looked around. "Did we just cross a line?"

Fox turned, about to call out, when a large branch whip-snapped from the side of the largest pine, slamming Bishop in the chest, and knocking him hard, backwards off his horse. It was a trip-wire cannon shot that had the bay rearing, front legs chopping the air.

Bishop's head slammed onto the flat of a rock. He turned over in sharp pain, trying to find his way back to full consciousness, when the heavy rope slipped around his ankles, hoisting him into the air.

He was spinning.

He heard Fox's voice: distant, screaming, in Cheyenne. They were twisted half words that Bishop struggled to figure, if he could just hang on to the edge of the light. And stay there.

That's when the dark swallowed him.

# CHAPTER TWENTY-ONE:
# BLOOD ON THE CLAW

There were five talons to it, each pointed at the end and sharpened raw along the side. They were attached to a metal wristband by precise welding, with just a hint of a bump where the iron pieces were joined. The bumps actually looked to be knuckles on someone's hand, and not sloppy workmanship.

The spots marking the sides of the talons could have been blood, or flecks of rust. Bishop's eyes weren't focused yet, and he couldn't tell. The claw was mounted on a cut-stone wall just feet from where he was lying, between a Cheyenne warrior's shield crossed in black and white hide, and several long-knives, each in its own colorfully beaded sheath.

Bishop moved his head, and water tear-drizzled down his face. He bolted up, the bear rug covering him falling forward, as he pulled the wet cloth from his forehead, tossed it aside.

Noah Crawford picked the cloth up from the hard-dirt floor. "I keep a clean house, goddamn it!"

Crawford's voice was an explosion. His face, something carved from the side of a mountain, was surrounded by an acre of matted, grey hair. Brows were wild tufts over two lumps of coal, his mouth and nose shapes hammered to fit into this mess that'd been blasted apart, and put back together wrong.

There was a hogleg tied down to one thigh, and a Colt Lightning in his belt, almost covered by his wave of a belly. He slapped Bishop's feet to the floor with saddle-sized hands, "You took it hard, but I've had worse. What are you drinkin', and don't say well water."

"Anything."

Muttering thick in Cheyenne, Crawford lumbered to the other side of the rounded dugout, stopping to sniff at a cook pot in the fireplace. The curved ceiling and sides were rough-cut logs, cemented by sloppy mud and straw, while the wall Bishop rested against was bare rock, protected by animal skins crazily quilted across it.

Crawford said, "Sorry about the trap, but a man's got to protect his patch."

Bishop threw his legs over the bed, catching the edge of a spear with his foot. War clubs, bows, and blades of mountain tribes were all within reach, propped against the wall or under the furniture. By the door, there was a cabinet with ten books, all worn cloth binding, placed neatly on its top shelf. A double-blade fighting axe took up the rest of the space.

White Fox handed Bishop oily whiskey in a small bowl. "You can drink." She touched Bishop's hand, lifting the bowl to his mouth. He drank. She looked to Crawford, who brought a large knife down on a slab of salted beef he was cutting, the meat not pulling from the bone.

Crawford swore, and she said: "I'm needed outside, *ného'éehe.*"

Fox moved to the door, taking one of the books from the shelf before leaving.

Bishop waited for her to leave, then said to Crawford, "I know what that means."

The sun was actually showing its face as White Fox sat on a rail of the corral fence, *Tales of the Grotesque and Arabesque,* by Edgar Allan Poe, open on her lap. The corralled horses nickered and nudged, and she would absently stroke a mane, but stayed lost in the pages.

Crawford stood against the planked front

door, watching, before looking down to Bishop, who was beside him, finishing the whiskey in the bowl. "Always the same book, always the same place on the goddamned fence. That's how she learned to talk, that book."

Crawford waited another few minutes for a look from White Fox that never came, then stomped around to the back of the dugout, grunting at the Morning Star and five-talon claws painted on its walls. Bishop followed him to the smith's shop tucked in the back. It was a clean space, with bricked stove, crated scrap, and tools of all types, some for finer work, neatly laid out. It reminded him of his medical office, not a place to forge horseshoes.

"I didn't even know all this was back here 'til a month after I settled in."

"I thought you built this house."

Crawford took down a hammer and tongs. "Hell, no. I been living above the Platte River for a couple of years, and come down to get away from the goddamned Indian wars. Came out of them woods, saw this place and thought it damn nice. I figured to kill whoever was inside, and take it. These other boys beat me to it, hanged the foreigners what built it. So I took care of them, moved in. I guess the foreigner who put it up was a smithy, so after drinking everything in the house, I wandered back here and learned myself. Come on, use that one hand you got, give it some air."

Bishop pumped a small bellows to feed the coals in an iron scuttle. Crawford watched him. "You get why I'm tellin' you this?"

"I think I do."

"I know she never says nothing about me; what about her mother?" The coals began to glow, and Crawford inserted the tongs and several iron punches into the heat.

"She doesn't speak about herself."

"Well, she's back on that fence, and if I believed in anything, I'd say that was a miracle."

"She came here on her own, to talk to you about horses."

Crawford's beard shifted with his face, almost revealing a smile. "I think you're here for this." He dropped the blasted-open shotgun rig on the workbench.

"I know what happened to you. That son of a bitch she married build this thing?"

Bishop couldn't hide his surprise. "Yeah. I told him what I needed."

"A new arm." Crawford inspected the weapon, before shoving the barrel into the hot coals. "Piss-poor job, but I ain't surprised. Worked for me right here. That's how come she knew him. When he said he wanted to marry her, her mother said no, but I figured it was better than the other trash that was hangin' around."

Crawford turned the rig over, as the barrel started smoking. "How many times you sew her up, Doc?"

"Twice. Set a few broken bones. My wife always helped."

Crawford pulled the rig from the scuttle, breaking apart the last of the barrel and breach, the pieces dropping. "If I'd known what was going on, I would've had a great time killing that streak of piss."

"She did it all right."

"He suffer?"

Bishop's silence was answer enough for Crawford. "Nice to know she took something from her daddy. This how you firing these barrels?"

Crawford held out the rig, so Bishop could grab hold of the leather harness and pull it away from the scorched remains of the gunstock. Crawford snatched the leather back. "I don't like this trigger line. Get tangled, move the wrong way, kill the wrong man."

Bishop said, "It does the job."

"Not good enough, and you know it. I'm

a whitesmith, too. Work in cold metals, and damn good at it. I'll rig it new."

"I've seen your work. They still call you *Vóhpóóhe?*"

"She's teaching you, right? Painted them symbols on the side of the place when she was a kid."

They both looked back at Fox, who remained buried in Poe's words, never glancing up. Her father continued, "Before I ever married her mother, Crow warriors would come down, snoop around, and I gutted a few. That's when the Cheyenne started with that White Claw. Had to get special permission from the chief for the wedding, but we got it because I'd killed his enemy. Nobody's bothered me since. Helps to have a reputation."

Bishop said, "Yeah, it can."

"I already know your'n. You made that breather for her. We ran out of medicine to help with that when she was a kid, but you figured something out. Probably saved her."

"She gave it to a little girl she thought needed it more."

"Gets that from her mother."

Crawford threw the pieces of the double barrel onto the scrap pile. "Doctor, I'm going to build you a weapon you can use."

■ ■ ■ ■

Howard held old man Kirby down, one massive arm across his chest, and a hand tight on his mouth. Kirby twisted and kicked as Beaudine withdrew his blade from the man's belly, while Chaney pretended to check the dynamite wagon. He sorted through a few boxes of fuses and caps, found a dead mouse and tossed it — did anything not to hear the last bits of that old man's struggle.

Kirby finally went slack, and Howard let out, "Was he stronger than I thought, or just being stubborn?"

Beaudine said, "I gave the right order, not to shoot. Who knows who'd hear it? It was good strategy."

"Damn, it took a long time for Kirby to give it up."

Chaney stepped up to the wagon's driver's seat. "All he had to do was drive us, didn't have to fight."

Beaudine took a place beside him. "That wasn't Kirby's way. I've known that old man a lot of years, and he'd want paying, or go to the law. He always had his hand out."

Chaney said, "His dynamite sure helped the fight."

"As long as I was throwin' it." Howard counted the cash from Kirby's pocket, stretched out in the back of the open wagon, comfortable between two dynamite cases, his legs dangling over the side. "And those idjit buddies he sent us all got dead."

Beaudine slipped the cleaver beneath the driver's seat, "Kirby lived his life in the rough country, and this is how he knew he'd end. I feel good not to disappoint him."

Howard said, "Hey, he's got a plunger back here! Use that instead of them damn cigars. Made me sick as hell."

Chaney looked to Beaudine. "Now what? Who do we throw the dynamite at? Or shoot at?"

Beaudine measured his words. "Lem always claimed you to be a gambler, but you don't know strategy. You must not be a very good one."

Chaney said, "Lem mouthed off. A lot. This capture did not go as planned, so I want to know about the new plan. Major."

"It's simple. We are the target and Bishop wants us. So we'll let him come, and be ready to meet him."

"Like all that craziness that just happened? What about them riders?"

"You don't get that many attacking for nothing. That's more proof the gold is there for taking."

Chaney pressed. "By who? And when?"

Beaudine shut his eyes. "If you want out, we can leave you with Kirby."

"You're not answering the question. Try and game me now? I'll kill you."

Chaney looked at Kirby and didn't answer Beaudine, who was now rubbing his temples, his head rocking back. "If you're driving, Mr. Chaney, head the team for the next town and wake me when we're near a clean bed and hot food. And we'll strategize to your satisfaction. I believe you want to be going northeast."

Chaney snapped the reins on the two mules harnessed in front of them, heading the wagon down a half-frozen trail leading out of the foothills.

Bishop dipped into the cook pot, trying to balance a clay bowl on his knee. Fox swatted him away. "You're no help, so sit and enjoy it."

Bishop settled on the floor in front of a small tree-stump table, tucking his shirt behind his back, then running the palm of his left hand over his clean-shaven face.

"A man shouldn't hide behind a beard."

"I've had it for so long, it feels strange."

"Because you've changed."

Bishop couldn't deny it. His fingers told him the soft roundness of his face was gone, the scar from Chester Pardee's knife as much a sign of who he was now as the shotgun rig on his right arm.

Fox smiled. "From now on, you shave yourself. Do you want my vanity glass?"

She ladled jerky soup and dumplings into clay bowls with intricate designs of deer running around the edges.

"This is all he lives on. All he ever lived on."

Bishop took his bowl. "And whiskey."

"And whiskey."

Bishop said, *"Vé'ho'émahpe."*

Fox sat opposite. "That's right. You can eat."

"Shouldn't we wait, for your father?"

Fox set out a plate of cornbread. "He's at my mother's grave. He'll be back in the morning." She held out her right hand. "You can give thanks."

Bishop squeezed her hand, and they gave silent thanks, for the food and the warmth. Bishop squeezed her hand again, and Fox broke his grasp, started eating.

"Why didn't you tell me about Edgar Allan Poe?"

She said, "I read to learn, and haven't learned it all. Yet."

" 'Morella'? I go back to that one most."

"Still, not perfect."

Bishop smiled. "You don't speak so you can find out what everyone else is thinking."

Fox cast her eyes to Bishop, ate a dumpling from her spoon. "When I'm perfect. When will you be perfect?"

Bishop grinned. *"Nenóveto?"*

"Good. Then soon, we can both talk the way we want."

"Did your father buy those books for you?"

"No." Fox broke a piece of cornbread, put the rest in front of Bishop. "He killed a man for his horse. They were in his saddlebags. My father is *not* like your father."

Fox's words dropped off. Bishop gave her time before saying, "He knows about your life."

"Memories of what *náhko'éehe* said."

"Your mother told him, about when your husband hurt you."

"Right before she died." Fox poured the last of the soup into Bishop's bowl. "You saved me. And I will do for you. Until I can't."


The lantern cast stale yellow on the two grave markers. One was flat steel, polished, with fine scrolling and the Morning Star hammered into its surface. Just below the star were the words, ARCHISHA. MOTHER AND WIFE. SHE LIVES ALWAYS. The other was a wooden cross with HORACE SMITH burned onto it.

Crawford stood before the Morning Star. "You won't believe what happened, Chisha. Hell, you probably knew before I did." He punched the ground in front of Horace's marker with his shovel, quick-turning the earth only a few inches before hitting the coffin.

Crawford tossed the shovel aside, pried the lid until it opened.

Batting the smell away from his nose, he scooped a pile of moldy hats and blood-stained jackets with his giant hands, tossing it all on Archisha's grave beside him. He added a tangle of kerchiefs, monogrammed things, and a sheriff's badge cut by a bullet hole to the pile, before yanking up the coffin's false bottom.

The coffin was actually built deep enough for four men lying on top of each other, which meant that Crawford could store at least fifty rifles and as many pistols as he could tuck in around them. Each weapon was wrapped in oilcloth, and he checked them carefully, searching for a specific shotgun he'd taken off a Swede who had been passing through years before.

Crawford found the Shuster double-barrel, and remembered the kill: the Swede was a family man, and surprised as hell when Crawford peeled two slugs into him after he'd just paid to have his horses shod.

Most of the others had fought back. He'd been chopped and shot, but one way or another Crawford got them, their horses, or their wagons. That's when he was White Claw, ripping through whoever came his way. Other times, he just did his work in the smith shop, lived a righteous life. It all depended on his mood.

He packed away the guns and clothes of the dead, covered the coffin up again. Tucking the Swede's gun under his arm, he picked up the lantern, and said to his wife's marker, "I'm giving *Vóhkêhésoa* a gift. She always heard you — get her to take it."

Bishop watched Fox from the rope-mattress bed as she knelt by the fire, pouring water for tea. Her naked legs were long, meeting her waist a little high on her body. They were muscular, the sinews working too close to the surface of her skin, as they did on her upper arms.

Her toned strength was almost masculine,

except where it melted into the flat of her stomach, or the full curve of her breasts. Her hair fell in front of her face, until she threw it back over her shoulder, glancing back with a smile for him alone.

Her smile was so rare it felt like a privilege to see it. It always started with her eyes, warming from cold to welcoming, letting him inside. She stood, carrying the tea to the bed, walking proud, and just as fine exposing the multiple scars on her left side as she was with the flawlessness on her right.

Bishop sat up in bed, propped on his one arm, as she settled under the bearskin, holding out the tea.

"It surely tastes better than the whiskey."

She sipped after he did, nodded, put the cup aside, and then wrapped herself around his body. He could feel her scars among the softness, the rough flesh left behind after his surgeries and the signs of recent violence that were healing.

She murmured, running her fingers across his chest, lightly kissing to his shoulders, across them. Bishop's half-arm pressed against her back, holding her tight to him. All she felt was his strength, not any sort of compromise. Her hands traveled back across his wounds, brushing his nose with a giggle.

Her laugh was something Bishop had

heard only a few times, and he didn't want it to stop, but her smile was fading, and a different feeling was taking over her eyes.

He kissed her, and they lost themselves in each other again.

Bishop shifted to the other side of the bed, curling under the bearskin, reaching for Fox in his sleep, when the distant thunder jostled him. There was a second strike, and Bishop sat up and saw that he was alone, except for a pot of coffee boiling over.

Bishop stayed in bed until the blast faded, his thoughts about his wife and son.

Outside, Crawford shucked the spent shells from the double barrel, checked the dead oak he'd used as a target. The buckshot spread was good, and the damage severe. He set the gun on his workbench to adjust the special triggers he'd made, when Bishop limped around the side of the dugout, struggling to put on his left boot.

"So that's why God gave us two hands!" Crawford was still laughing when he grabbed the bootstrap, pulled it up. "Doctor, I guess there are still some things you need help with."

"A few, thanks."

"Your boots, not shooting this here."

Crawford moved to his bench, held up the

new shotgun rig with tired, toothless pride. "Say somethin', damn it."

The weapon was swivel breeched-open to the side, with the stock cut shorter to fit flush into the amputee cup. Jointed metal supports kept the gun steady in any position, while a catgut line looped around both the triggers, and was knotted to a small chain bracing across the cut-leather shoulder straps, and then anchored to the left arm at the wrist.

"That's fine workmanship, Mr. Crawford."

"Told you I was going to do it."

Bishop slipped his half-arm into the padded cup as Crawford fastened the new leather rig across his back. "This is a damn sight better than what that son of a bitch fixed up for ya."

"Did Fox see all this?"

"She's running her horse."

Crawford brought the trigger line from Bishop's right arm, and fastened it to a small, Cheyenne-silver band that he slipped on his left wrist, giving the line a little play. Bishop buttoned his shirt, rolled down his sleeves. He nodded; the rig was perfect under his clothes.

Crawford said, "This needs saying: we're not on terms, but I'm still her pa. Any kindness I'm doing? Because of her." Crawford held up two twelve-gauge shells. "So?"

Bishop loaded both barrels, snapped the breech shut.

"That's a Shuler swivel-breech for a quicker reload. And these barrels can take anything. Straighten your left arm."

Bishop straightened his left at his side, the chain from his wrist snapping tight across his shoulders, instantly bringing the shotgun rig on his right waist-high and steady, twice as fast as before.

"Position and shoot. So, who're you going to face down, Doctor?"

Bishop turned from Crawford, brought back the hammers, and snapped his wrist pulling the trigger line. The first barrel blasted the oak dead center like a man's chest, the metal braces absorbing the gun's recoil into Bishop's body.

Bishop said, "It really feels like a part of me."

"Over here!"

Bishop half-turned, and the rig reacted, swinging in the direction of Crawford's voice, and locking, but not firing.

Crawford laughed, "She won't do nothin' you don't want her to. Go ahead, shoot. The line's tight, use your shoulders."

Bishop spun on his heel, as if taken by surprise, and shrugged. The second barrel ripped apart two limbs. Bishop swung open the rig, popped the shells.

They clattered to the floor, black-powder smoking.

Crawford said, "That's faster than a lot of men can draw. And I made you this here."

Crawford held out a small bandolier, sized to fit Bishop's arm. "It'll hold six, so you ain't fumbling for shells. I also got a loader for you."

Bishop regarded Crawford. "If you've heard anything about money I'm supposed to have —"

"Because I'm White Claw? I know you had to get that insulting shit out of the way, but forget it. She picked you, Doc, and this rig's to keep her safe as long as she's with you. If you ride on alone, this pays back all you done for her."

"I wouldn't be alive if it wasn't for her."

"I settle my own accounts." Crawford stepped back to admire his work. "Either way, them dogs you're chasin' won't know what hit 'em. It ain't flapdoodle — I'm damn good."

Bishop checked the sights. "We came close to getting the leader."

"You'll get him, you'll feel the revenge for your family. But that'll go, and you'll go after more. Killing a man ain't nothing more than flipping a switch, and there's always some that's asking for it."

"I'll finish what I have to do, then put it behind me."

"The hell you say. You've already crossed the river. Look at the way you handle that rig. Like God's own power, ain't it? Some days you'll be the doc, other days you'll be the shotgun man. Then one day, you'll only be shotgun. And I hope she ain't with you when that happens."

Bishop said, "Maybe," the truth punching him.

He bent his elbow, bringing the rig up to him, as if it were on a precise gear-set. He moved his body, and the double barrel adjusted its height and position to compensate. "You have skills, sir, and at this moment, I'm a doctor and I need them."

"A week."

"What?"

"Rifled your saddlebag."

"Not much there, Claw."

"I saw what you sketched out for that breather box. She needs a new one, gave the old one away? One week, and it'll be better than what she had. But don't tell her it's from me, 'cause she'd rather choke to death than use it."

Crawford held out two more shotgun

shells. "Ain't you gonna reload, Doc?"

White Fox ran the painted through the woods, heading for the clearing where her father had set his traps. She had a long blade tied to her thigh, and a vision of red hanging in front of her eyes like blinders.

It was dark red, as dark as the night sky above it, and spreading wide against the snow. It was the first thing Fox had seen as she'd ridden toward the little house with the porch and rocking chairs. She'd had a present for Dr. Bishop's son tucked under her jacket, away from the evening weather, and had been rehearsing a birthday song when she saw the circle of blood around the two bodies lying in the yard.

Fox pushed the painted harder, thinking of how she'd run to Amaryllis, who had been shot twice and had still been cradling her son. The boy, his face buried against his mother, had had a single bullet wound to the head.

They had been holding hands, gently.

The painted broke to a full gallop. White Fox was pushing against the images of Bishop's wife, but they kept coming. She remembered touching the side of her face, color gone, her skin turning with the cold, frozen tears on her cheeks. Fox had taken a blanket from her horse, draped it over mother and son.

That's when she'd heard John Bishop's voice from the house. He had crawled inside, arm gone, and had been trying to get to a rifle behind a shattered china cabinet. Bishop had pleaded about his family, but Fox hadn't known what to say to make him understand. She hadn't had the words.

He was dying in front of her.

She'd brought the painted right to the front door, helped him climb from the chair onto its back, where he'd collapsed. She'd swung on behind him, holding him on, and they'd galloped away from that ruined house, leaving wife, son, and a birthday present lying in the snow.

That was a year ago. She'd had the same painted then, running the same way, and she was now on her own mission to revenge that night. Her revenge. The Cheyenne word is *óoxo'eéh,* and it was the first she'd taught Bishop to say — the first he'd wanted to learn.

This moment, it was all she could think of as she got closer.

She leapt the small gully before reaching the clearing, and Fox stopped the painted feet away from the trip lines around the pine trees. She cut rope after rope with the long blade, releasing the tied-back branches, hurling packed snow and ice like flaming bales from a catapult.

She rode beyond White Claw's traps, to a small slope leading to a split of two tall-grass hills damped with snow, a stream running between them — a tiny valley. Fox heeled, and looked down into the split at fifty or so horses, all good stock, held behind a barrier of fallen trees. She pulled the lasso from her saddle, and headed toward them.

Bishop was packed and saddled, when Fox brought the painted down the small trail to the dugout, a second stallion tied behind her. There were small cuts and bruises on her hands and face, and her expression was dark. Bishop stayed by the bay, as Fox rode her horse to Crawford and stopped just inches away, looking down on him from the painted's back.

Crawford's beard and bearskin coat buried him in hair, with only his two black eyes showing through the tangle. Staring at her. "Thought you might head out to Wyoming."

"Don't know anyone there."

"That ain't always a bad thing. I got your man outfitted with a whole new deal."

"Don't call the doctor that."

"Doubt that he minds." Crawford opened the gate to the corral, looked beyond Fox to the horse tied behind her. "Catch one of my strays?"

"No stray, and not yours." Fox finally turned to Bishop. "Ready?"

"Whenever you are."

"Which way should we go? Follow the river? It's of no matter." Fox looked to her father. "Were you going to warn them we were coming? Have us killed?"

"You got it wrong, daughter."

"I did not want to return to this place." Fox got off the painted and moved around it to the horse she'd roped in the hills, pointing to an FD brand on its rump. "The men in red hoods had this brand, and I knew it was you. An army horse, the kind you always stole. Two are in the corral."

"I've got customers coming. Not them red hoods, though."

"And you hide the rest in the same place you did when I was a girl. I was just there. You'll always be White Claw, and I'm forever *tanehe*."

Crawford said, "I know you're ashamed, but before you start jumpin', take a ride. I've got something that'll help you both." Bishop had the shotgun aimed, as Crawford threw his hands up. "If you don't like it, the doc can always use the new rig on me."

Bishop said to Crawford, "You built this thing to cut a man in half."

Crawford shook his head. "Oh, I know, Shotgun. Well? *Vóhkêhésoa?*"

The shadows of the grave markers grew longer as the winter evening settled in. The sound of the distant river was carried on a cold breeze that blew back Fox's hair, and the fringe on her leathers. She stood by Morning Star, but kept her eyes averted from her mother's name.

Bishop held fast by the horses, letting father and daughter settle their business, the hammers on the rig cocked, the bandolier with six shells tight on his arm.

Fox said, "What is this gift, *nomáhtsé'héó'o?*"

Crawford stepped to the other side of the markers, said to Bishop, "Did she teach you that one yet, doc? It means 'thief.' "

Crawford held up a large bundle, wrapped in an old blanket and tied twice. He tossed it with one hand onto the snow-wet ground of Horace Smith's grave. Heavy as cast iron, it sunk in. Fox and Bishop eyed the bundle, but made no move.

"It's only right that White Claw's daughter

recognize the branding on a stolen horse."
Fox met Crawford's face as he continued:
"I know it pains you to say it, but I'm your
pa. A thief, and a killer, and every other
damn thing you ever dreamed up."

She said nothing. Crawford blasted,
"White Claw. Goddamned White Claw, and
you're *my* child!"

White Fox would not shake. She rested
her hand on the tip of her mother's grave
marker, keeping her words low and flat.
"What about the horses?"

Crawford yanked a bottle from his coat,
drank half of it in one swallow. "There's a
foreigner, he runs a bunch call themselves
the Fire Riders. And I be dealing with
them."

Bishop said, "Are you with them?"

"Hell, no!"

"Then what?"

"They're about money, new U.S. cur-
rency. And anyone who don't do business
gets their house burned and their throat cut.
Ain't no politics here. And they dress up
crazier than a pack of wall-eyed mules, scare
most folks to death. Reputation, right, Doc?
That's how come they can do what they
want."

"What about the law, the Marshals in this
territory?"

"They love them Fire Riders, 'cause all they do is come down on scofflaws like me! Take a train, they want a piece. Rob a bank, you gotta pay!"

Crawford threw the finished bottle to the sky. It shattered someplace. "The foreigner's an Englishman. Never saw his face, just heard him. I've been supplying horses for six months, Army mounts from Fort Davis. The branding you recognized, daughter."

Fox said, "We fought them."

"Sure as hell did, and lived to tell the tale."

"It was a bloody war."

"That's what they do. I don't know if them Fire Riders are mixed up in your business, Doc, but that's really stickin' your head in a rattler hole. If I hadn't gotten them mounts, I wouldn't be here now, claw or no."

Bishop said, "You know I'm going to hunt down the men who killed my family. These Red Hoods know who they are well enough to attack them."

Crawford looked to Bishop, and the barrels leveled on him. "You don't have to threaten me, Doc. I'm the man who built you the best chance you got. I'll tell ya, they ride the Wyoming border, come in for raids. Paradise River don't have no river, but they got a rail station, and they've been hit more than once. Somebody'll give up that foreigner, if you swear to kill him."

Bishop lowered the rig as Crawford reached out to Fox, but didn't touch her. "This is too dangerous, daughter. You were lucky once — it may not happen again."

Fox kept her hand on her mother's name. "I can't stay here."

"You can go anyplace you want, but it don't have to be with the doc."

Bishop said, "You already saved my life."

Fox let her hand fall from the marker. "I told you I would be with you until I couldn't. That was my mother's way. That's my way."

Crawford crouched by the bundle, untied it. "I made these a couple of months ago, when I knew you two was riding together."

He threw back the blanket to reveal two more grave markers, one with DR. JOHN BISHOP written on it, and the other, VÓH-KÊHÉSOA — BELOVED DAUGHTER.

"That's my gift: freedom. If they think you're already dead, you can do whatever you want. And if anybody comes lookin', this should stop 'em. Or I will."

Crawford stood and looked to his daughter, who simply nodded. He said, "You better make tracks. I'll get these up in the morning."

Fox turned away from her father, running her palms over her face. Bishop stepped up, extended his left hand.

Crawford's giant hand smothered Bishop's. "Better that one than the other."

"You did a lot for us."

Crawford was still holding on, grip tight as hell. "The Cheyenne's a strong spirit, Doc, so you protect her, even if she hates you for it."

# CHAPTER TWENTY-TWO: GOOD DEEDS

Crawford pulled the punch from the coal scuttle, then pierced the edge of the breather box, before rounding the corners with small sections of sheet silver. Large fingers manipulated the cold-smith tools, fashioning an air portal around the pierced metal surface. Each move was precise, and the tools never slipped.

He was cutting the padded leather sections for the side of the box when he saw the small wagon with the flat top rumbling down the trail, and pulling up by the corral.

The Brakeman, all blond moustache and braggart's mouth, dropped off the driver's seat with a wave to Crawford as he walked out of the smith's.

"You ready to do some business, Claw?"

"I don't like that coming from you, but if you got money this time, I'll let it slide."

"Sorry, Noah. Them the ones you talking about?"

Crawford brought one of the stolen horses out of the corral for the Brakeman's inspection. He was making a show of checking the teeth and hooves, but actually knew damn little about horseflesh.

Crawford said, "Why you bother with that every time? I know you're gonna take 'em out on the trail and sell 'em."

"Not to blind men. I want to pay a fair price, but I have to make mine too." The Brakeman ran his hand across his moustache. "These still got the brand on 'em. I'm taking a risk."

"A hundred extra, I'll change the brand right now."

"One fifty for both, change the brand, and I'll give you a free turn."

The Brakeman nodded to the wagon, and a petite Chinese woman threw open the canvas in the back and peeked around the corner. She was in her early twenties, but had additional age beaten on to her. Her nightgown hadn't seen a recent washing, but she tried for beauty with a torn paper flower behind one ear.

"Ain't she left you yet?"

"Hard to get a divorce in the wild country."

"I don't want no time with your wife, but I'll settle for the price, if you take a package to general delivery up to Paradise River."

"Who's it for?"

"What the hell's the difference?"

The woman watched from the wagon, waiting for White Claw to tear into her husband, holding her breath and crossing her fingers.

The Brakeman said, "I'll do anything, Noah. I just don't want to get picked up. I've got a job in a couple of days."

"For my sister. My daughter passed away, and wanted her aunt to have a few things."

"I sure am sorry to hear that, Noah. I ain't gonna up my offer, but I feel for ya."

Crawford handed the Brakeman the reins on the horse, as his wife dropped back inside the wagon, the canvas flap falling shut behind her.

Crawford said, "I'll heat the irons for the horses, you'll wait for the package to take."

"Whatever you need. We're amigos."

Crawford peered at the wagon. "She all right in there? Got jerky and dumplings."

The Brakeman shrugged. "She's fine. And don't never eat. That's one of the things I like about her."

Fox and Bishop had been riding in the Colorado silence for hours when they saw the buckboard coming from the opposite direction. The road they were on was well traveled, cutting along the base of some smaller mountains, but today, they had had it to themselves and the wind, until they saw the couple.

The husband was waving at them in a friendly manner, but the wife sat statue still, with her hands folded in her lap.

They pulled up.

Fox had seen it first, and she gave Bishop a look as she peeled away from him, riding the painted to the side of the wagon where the wife was sitting.

The husband tipped his hat. "Good 'morrow, friends! This is a lonely stretch. Are ye travelling far?"

Bishop kept his rig arm down, the sleeve of his coat covering the barrels from the husband's view.

"We're on our way to the next town, going to meet a friend, actually."

"The next town is Paradise River, and aptly named she is."

"How much farther is it?"

"Less than a day's ride, friend. We've just stocked up ourselves, this sky tells me we'll be seeing a long winter. You look a little light on food. Perhaps we can leave you with something."

"That'd be appreciated. Truly."

The husband tipped his hat, still smiling broadly when he reached behind the seat.

The rig blasted, tearing the husband in the side, hurling him off the wagon, onto the road. The pistol in his hand fired when he hit the ground.

The wife burst into tears, screaming, "Kill him!"

Bishop jumped from his horse, moved to the husband, and kicked the pistol out of reach.

"Sorry friend, but you're not going to make it."

The man was still showing long, perfect teeth. "Should have killed you before we stopped. What'd you get me with? How'd you know?"

Bishop tilted his head to Fox. "She knew. Your pocket."

The man felt his jacket, and the hood that was sticking out of the top of his side pocket, like a red warning flag.

"Did you really come from Paradise River?" Bishop asked.

"You know how many of us there are?"

"What about a man called Smythe?"

The man's smile was locked, and not going anywhere, when he said, "Dyin' isn't as hard as I thought it would be. Piss on you, brother."

Fox said to the wife, "What about your man?"

"He's been shot, left by the side of the road."

Bishop said, "How long?"

"Not half an hour ago."

"You really coming from Paradise River?"

"Trying to leave forever, because of those damnable night riders. My husband's a deputy sheriff." She choked on her words, but her face was calm now, and lovely. "And he was quitting."

The wife turned the wagon around, running the team back toward Paradise, with Bishop and Fox alongside.

# CHAPTER TWENTY-THREE:
## FORTRESS OF THE DEAD

"What's it looking like, boy?"

"Like a castle from a picture book, Captain. A burned castle."

Smythe laughed out loud at Hector's description, grinning at the boy over his shoulder, but not contradicting him. Hector craned his neck to get a better look at the grey ruin rising out of the Wyoming badlands in front of them: Cannon Mountain Territorial Prison.

The walls were more than thirty feet high, and sloped outward, with tons of smashed, jagged boulders protecting the foundation, like an ancient moat. Iron spikes with bent, speared edges lined the top of the walls, with stretched barbed wire connecting them.

Parapets stood as sentries at each corner, with eye-like windows for the sniping guards facing both the outside and the prison yard. Stout anchor chains hung from the windows, ladders for the men to climb into position.

And it had all been burned.

Scars of the fire disfigured the place, destroying large sections that were now falling in on themselves. A few men on horses broke around the charred front gate, riding toward the group at a full gallop.

Smythe said, "Nobody draws. These blokes'll kill you, even if they know you."

The men rode up, and gave a signal to follow.

A body dangled by the neck from one of the few bare and twisted trees near the place. Its hands and feet were bound with red cloth and a sign that read "He Didn't Pay!" had been fastened to his chest with a small dagger.

Smythe said to Hector: "That's to show the scoflaws that we mean business."

Passing through the front gates to the main prison yard, with riders and guns on all sides, Hector kept speaking to Creed, describing everything: the corpse, debris and rubble piled high enough to climb; twisted-apart cell doors stacked against the scorched remains of a guard's turret; and behind it, what had been the stables, now a pile of ashes and trash.

Hector watched as men in red moved

among the wreckage with purpose, carrying weapons, furniture, and food supplies to tents that had been set up along the inner wall, forming a compound. The injured Fire Riders were laid out around the tents, waiting for a medic to fix them or pronounce them.

He stumbled in his telling, as this new, savage army prepared itself for some kind of war. Hector looked to the far end of the yard, and the entrance to the cellblock, where old cannons were being repaired, ammunition stacked, and a Gatling gun was being set up in the back of a freight wagon.

Hector said, "Sir, you've shown me a lot, but nothing like this."

Creed took in the prison with his dead eyes. "That's fine, son, but you don't have to go with the report. I can hear what they're doing. I know what's around me."

The remains of an iron fence served as a hitch rail, where Smythe, Creed, and Fuller tied their horses. Hector dropped from the saddle to help the captain.

"You don't know it, son, but these are your brothers in arms."

One of the riders who'd brought them in noted Fuller and his rifle. "There's some new beauties. You're going to want to move up, if you fight with us, boy."

Fuller kept the Morgan-James on his shoulder. "I haven't decided yet."

"Maybe it'll be decided for you." The rider turned to Smythe. "He's busy now, but he'll want to know why so many got left dead at the silver mine."

Smythe held out his slinged arm, "And I'll tell him. What's he busy with?"

The rider spit, pointed to a multi-colored Conestoga wagon and its team, hitched to a post by the old cells.

Warden Allard had broken his chair more than once, and Devlin Bishop felt lost in its warped back, and overstuffed seat. He adjusted himself several times as Albert Tomlinson opened a ledger on the hand-tooled leather-top desk that separated them.

Tomlinson admired the desk. "Nice piece. I understand this is already paid for, Mr. Bishop."

"I didn't pay for it."

"Regardless, it's a luxury, and if you get used to such things, it can make the adjustment of paring down difficult."

Dev's shirtsleeves were cleanly rolled up, revealing a tattoo of the flag of Virginia on his forearm, and his collar was buttoned to his Adam's apple. He sported suspenders and trousers cuffed above new, laced shoes.

His prison manner had neatened with his wardrobe, but the casual threat behind his eyes was permanent.

Dev had Tomlinson's complete attention: "Tomlinson, this is the beginning of a great business, the first of its kind in the west, and it's important that it be run like a business. Now, I don't have a lot of formal learning, which is why you're here, to make sure our money is going where it needs to go."

Matching Dev, the timid, Arkansas scarecrow was now a seasoned professional, without a trace of stammer. Tomlinson took a pair of bifocals from a tortoise-shell case, slipped them on, and ran his finger down a column of numbers on the ledger page. "When you refer to monies, that's a problem, because your cash situation is, uh, compromised."

Dev leaned across the desk. "You understand what this is? We're robbers, Tomlinson."

There was a moment, as Tomlinson considered his response. "You're my employer, Mr. Bishop, as long as you want me. I pride myself on discretion. This business is a tad unusual, but I have two growing girls. You know how that is."

"Fine, then. You've worked for thieves before?"

"Well —"

"Railroad? Steamship company?"

"Yes."

"Then you've worked for thieves, just
none honest about who they are. But they
all have money to start with. We don't. Our
investments are goods. We bring in a wagon,
it ain't filled with cash. But the rifles, and
tomato plants, the clothes, and Grandma's
piano all have value, and I've got some
pirates who're very good at trading."

"That's difficult to enter. I'd have to ap-
proximate, after seeing all the stores. Or
wait, for the cash deposits to vault. Or whatever."

"Let's say whatever."

Dev leaned back in the large chair, finally
settling in. "The cash is going to flow, and
it's going to be a hell of a lot. Because every
thief in the territory is going to be paying
us tribute."

"Really?"

"If they don't want to end up dead, or
worse, a place like this here."

"I saw the example outside."

"The men have left a few around the territory.

Tomlinson sniffed, "I'll be ready to make

those entries," before turning the ledger around on the desk for Dev to inspect. Dev just looked straight at the accountant.

"What about gold?"

"Your gold is your foundation."

Bishop said, "That's good. Good to know, because I've gone through hell for that foundation."

"Uh, it would help a great deal if I knew how much gold there was."

"I had some, but that all went to bringing these men, this place, together. Very little left, but the total's about to go up. I'll give you a figure next week. We'll also be getting regular protection payments from a gal who'll be running some whorehouses between here and California. That'll be good money, and good company."

Tomlinson's head bobbed in agreement. "This is going to be colorful."

"You should see this."

Dev stood, revealing a bullet hole in the back of the chair. "That's where the slug went through Mr. Allard, came out his back. You didn't know him, but that's a hell of a trip. Now, I didn't fire that shot."

"I'm relieved."

"But I danced me a jig when I found out, not fifty feet from here."

"May I ask where you were, sir, when this

all happened?"

Dev kicked the burned remains of the door aside. "Guess the territorial governor forgot to tell folks they was storing lamp fuel and powder under here. Figured if it blew, who'd miss this bunch of cow pies? Well, it did and nobody gave a tinker's damn."

Tomlinson stood beside Dev in the commons area, with its roof now burned through, the cells twisted apart by heat, and the stains of the dead scorched to the floor.

"We're just a burned-down nothing, until somebody from the territory decides to notice. Which they never will."

Tomlinson said quietly, "I've never even been in a prison before."

"This is a hell of a one to start with," Dev chuckled. "And hell it was."

"You were a prisoner, now it's your fortress."

"The warden was a snake; took a payoff to fake my execution, then double-crossed me when he wouldn't let me out of the cells! I paid him off to stay inside!"

Dev let it settle. "I was the king fool for trusting him, and there wasn't a guard or prisoner who didn't hate his guts. But we got him."

Tomlinson asked from the back of his

throat, "Did you set the fire?"

"One of them jackass guards was sellin' black powder to a Sioux war party, so they could blow up a piece of the railroad. Got into a fight, set the storage on fire, and brought this whole place down. Lotta men killed, and the ones that were left had nothing."

Dev Bishop ran the toe of his shoe over the scorched outline of a prisoner who had been trapped at the bottom of the iron stairs, now collapsed.

Dev repeated, "Nothing."

Tomlinson stood up straight. "You had gold."

"A little. From a Union pay master. Never did time on that one, don't know if they've forgotten about it yet."

"They don't forget. You could end up in a place just like this again."

Dev faced Tomlinson. "That ain't gonna happen."

"I surely hope not."

"If you've got something on your mind, bookkeeper, you better say before we go any further."

Tomlinson stepped closer, his voice as low as he could take it. "I think I can work for you real well, but I need something extra."

"How much?"

"It's my wife. She's in the wagon. My eldest got into it with her, hit her hard, while we was on our way here. She's kind of stuffed in a dresser in the back. We've been traveling with her."

Dev took a breath. "You want her buried?"

Tomlinson took his step back. "Well, yes. I wasn't going to leave her in the woods, and the way she is, we can't take her to no Methodist cemetery without questions. She was Methodist."

Dev patted his shoulder. "I can have that taken care of."

Tomlinson heaved a sigh that came through his entire body. "That's a real burden lifted. Thank you."

The old whipping post blew apart on the floor, charred pieces flying, when Smythe kicked it over. Tomlinson was startled as the Fire Rider strode across the common area with a guard's swagger, his arm in a sling and his fist balled.

Captain Creed had Hector lead him in, right behind.

"Tomlinson, this is Captain Creed, and Smythe."

"I'll note they're a part of this organization?"

"We'll see."

Smythe loomed over Dev and said, "Oh,

you have something to say to me, boy-o?"

"In the old place."

The kid at the telegraph was thinner than a homeless dog, hunched over the receiving key, downing his third cup of belly wash, when he heard Smythe's voice. He turned as Dev, Smythe, and Creed made their way down the metal stairs to the Tomb.

Creed said, "The stink of death."

Smythe leaned in with, "And more than a few. Your kid thinks he's in a bloody haunted house."

"Hector!"

Hector descended the stairs, inches at a time. "Sir?"

"Stand with me, boy."

Hector found his place with Creed as Dev slapped the telegraph operator on the back. "It's all right, Lemuel. We won't get no messages in the next few minutes."

Lemuel mumbled, "You never know," and took the stairs two at a time to get out.

Smythe stood by Dev's old cell, which was now being used as a store for old single-shot rifles. The other cells were filled with crates and stuffed burlap sacks, the metal bunks stacked with supplies.

"I was right here while you set up your

brother, boy-o. That was quite a bit of business."

Dev said, "And why didn't you follow on it?"

"Because I was keeping me eye on the lot of you, in case I had to beat somebody senseless."

"And you always liked that. So what happened to your arm?"

Creed's voice was first: "He was ambushed, because he was following your orders."

Dev moved between Creed and Hector. "Captain, you're the one who truly failed. You wanted to settle a score with John, and still let him get away."

"We followed protocol. Let you know as soon as possible."

Hector said, "Yes, sir. I was at the key."

Dev said, "And the message came through right here. Failure is your word, how you described letting him escape."

Creed said, "And to make up for it, you sent all those men to slaughter. All you want is your brother and Beaudine dead, and you can't manage it."

"You're really overstepping yourself, blind man." Dev walked into his old cell, touched the ceiling with his hands, his palms flat against it.

345

"It really is like being buried alive. It's because we were in the Tomb that we weren't killed in that explosion."

Smythe blocked the cell door with his enormous frame. "You don't have to remind me, boy-o. Just like you don't have to remind me what a hog screwing we took at that silver mine. Beaudine's crazy, but it's what keeps him alive. That place was rigged like you couldn't believe."

Dev said to Creed, "Rigged — expecting you, Captain."

Smythe cut back, "You can't predict him. You should know, all those letters you had him write. What you figured he was going to do."

Dev said, "He was my voice down here. And I knew as soon as I put it in his mind about me and John and some robbery, he wouldn't be able to let it go."

"Your brother never had anything to do with anything."

"Of course not, but he had to be gone if we were going to build this empire."

Smythe said, "You should've stopped him, boy-o."

"I couldn't raise a hand against him myself. Never once, even when we was kids. Thought Beaudine would take care of it for me. Or you, Creed."

Creed said, "Your brother owes me, and I will collect that debt."

"John survived the conflicts, Beaudine's attack, all of it. One thing you learn in here, some men die easy, and some don't."

A small voice said, "With that special shotgun of his."

Dev stepped from his cell. "The boy has something to add?"

Hector coughed, looked to Creed, who put a hand on his shoulder for assurance. Hector finally said, "Just that I've seen him use that gun. I'd be real, extra careful, sir."

Dev said, "That's the smartest thing I've heard today."

"All she must do is say the words. She must."

The Brakeman grinned at Beaudine. "She's a chink. Don't know no English, buddy. Just do your business. She don't care."

The canvas walls of the tent wafted as the Brakeman stepped outside, leaving his wife alone with Beaudine. She sat on the edge of a tiny, wooden-slat cot, Beaudine before her, suspenders off his shoulders but still dressed, including his boots.

He said, "You can't say you're Nellie Bly? You have no idea, you poor idiot."

She smiled politely, and shrugged, reaching up to unbutton his trousers. He swatted her hands away.

"I do lose myself, sometimes. You have to help me, and you can't. Or won't. If you're refusing me, that would be an insult, wouldn't it?"

Her smile continued, even as he raised his hand. She did not flinch or turn away.

Outside the tent, Chaney and Howard sat on the empty dynamite wagon, counting the last of their money, all coins. Chaney's shirt was caked with blood, and he had a bandage wrapped around his ribs. Behind them, the muddy trail stretched for miles, and in front of them was more of the same. The bursts of wind from the Colorado north felt like broken glass.

The only thing for miles was the Brakeman's tent, and them sitting beside it.

"Everything we got from old man Kirby wasn't worth salt for peanuts."

"And you choked him for it." Chaney shoved the change back in his pants. "This working out the way you thought? You made more hammering coffins. Hell's fire, I'd join you."

"I was set, and you all came in and turned me upside down."

"Along for the ride. That was Lem."

Howard shook his head. "It wasn't Dead-eye. Don't be saying that."

Chaney winced. "Beaudine's holding a bluff hand, and we fell for it. Now we're an 'Army of Three,' whatever the hell that means. Now what? Gonna keep following that maniac? He's got to get his bell rope pulled, and we're out here freezin' to death. At least the cold makes my side feel tolerable."

"You said you'd kill Beaudine. Seems like that's your bluff."

"You'll find out."

"Maybe I should have let you die back there. You ain't my friend. Lem was."

"Well, I sure wish he was with us now."

Howard said, "I never seen who shot him."

Chaney pulled at his bandage, adjusting it, not missing a beat. "It was that Bishop, but I blew that double barrel to pieces."

"Looks like he did more to you."

"The Cheyenne! And just what are we gonna do about all that?"

They looked up as the Brakeman set out a stack of jars of milky-white grain shine, and a few with moldy preserves floating in sugar-clouded juice. He arranged them on an old ammunition crate beside the torn canvas, with a large sign declaring A DOL-LER FOR ALL HAPYNESS YOU CAN STAND!

"Thirsty? If you don't have the dollar, you don't have to answer."

Howard said, "I like store bought."

"Store bought ain't got this kick, and I don't see no saloons nowhere."

Chaney took a deck of cards from his jacket. "Would you play for it?"

The Brakeman ran his fingers through a thick blond moustache. "The lady of chance is a whore I don't favor."

Howard grabbed the last stick of dynamite from one of the crates. "It's gettin' damn cold. You just gonna let us sit here?"

The Brakeman said, "You don't have a primer or a fuse for that, friend."

"You know your TNT?"

"Work with it all the time on the Colorado Line."

Chaney said, "This ain't your work?"

The Brakeman laughed, "Her? That's my wife! We travel these teamster trails, set up for a week, then move on when the railroad needs me. You'd be surprised how many she can handle in a day."

Howard said, "Lotta money. Sounds like you could spare a drink."

"It does, don't it?"

"So what is your trade, friend, other than your wife?"

"Stand-by brakeman."

"On the Colorado?"

"That's what I said. I don't repeat."

The Brakeman took a sip of homemade, while Howard was rubbing his arms to keep warm. Howard said, "Which work do you like better, that or this here?"

"The same. She pays, they pay. And sometimes the Colorado kicks it up a bit."

"When's that?"

The Brakeman checked his watch. "Your friend has three minutes."

Chaney said, "Won't let us put anything on the cuff, so what's the harm in talkin'? I'm looking for work. So when does the Colorado kick it up? You ever work a run from that mint?"

The Brakeman took another sip. "Not that they ever told me."

"Friend, you could be a couple of train cars away from a fortune."

"I don't think about that. I do my job."

Howard said, "When's your next run?"

The Brakeman pulled a folded schedule from his pocket. "Whenever they say. We're packing out of here tomorrow. Either of you want a crack, best speak up."

Beaudine stepped from the tent, holding a small package, addressed to MRS. BISHOP. He shoved it at the Brakeman, who grabbed for it.

"How the hell'd you get that?"

Beaudine kept it out of reach. "It was by the woman's bed. Who is this for?"

"Your time's up!"

Beaudine tossed the small package to Howard. "Look at that name. Where did you get this? Believe me, you don't want to set my blood to boiling, friend."

The Brakeman screamed, "Lotus! Get your ass out here!"

Chaney tossed Beaudine his long cleaver, and he advanced on the Brakeman, turning the blade. Chaney and Howard both had their guns out.

Beaudine said, "All I need is the truth. Who is this Mrs. Bishop?"

The woman stepped from the tent, but made no move for her husband. She stood, watching.

Beaudine brought the cleaver to his throat. "The truth, or you will spill on this ground."

"I don't care who it is, goes to general delivery in Paradise River before I take the train out. My old buddy's got a daughter, and she died, and he's sending something to family."

Chaney said, "Is that daughter a Cheyenne?"

"How'd you know that?"

Beaudine said, "And where is this friend?"

352

The Brakeman straightened, met Beaudine's stare. "Now information like that's gonna cost. In fact, these last five minutes are going to cost."

The woman said, "I know him."

Chaney shot the Brakeman in the chest with the Derringer. He fell back, busting some grain shine jars, then slopped into the side of the tent, ripping part of it to the ground.

He sprawled, gurgling. "Bastards . . . do anything for money . . ."

Beaudine said, "No, that would be you."

Chaney hopped down from the wagon and went through the dying man's pockets. He found a razor in his belt, a wad of singles, some coin, and a rail worker's schedule. He pocketed the schedule, peeled twenty dollars, and handed the rest to the woman.

Beaudine said, "If you hurry, you can get him to a doctor. But you'll have to tell me what I need."

The woman said, "No, I won't hurry."

Chaney fired one more slug between the Brakeman's surprised eyes.

The woman quick-stepped around Beaudine to where her husband was lying in a mess of canvas, 'shine, and icy slush. She bent down to look at him closely, neatened his moustache with her finger, pausing for a moment to feel his breath. There was none. She stood back up.

Beaudine said, "Miss Lotus?"

"My husband would get lost. We have a map."

Howard said, "He must've been a lousy railroad man."

She went back into the tent.

"Howard, take the map, see who this is. Gambler, you're coming with me to Paradise River."

The woman handed the map to Beaudine. She pulled the paper flower from her hair, dropped it on her husband's chest, bowed to the three men in the dynamite wagon, and said, ever so quietly, "My thanks."

Dev Bishop was careful with the last of Allard's whiskey, pouring it into two glasses on the desk, the final drops hanging on the lip of the bottle. The soldier was dead, and Dev corked it. Smythe sat in front of him, raising his glass.

Dev wasn't returning the toast. "Smythe, how bad was it at the Goodwill?"

"You lost a lot of men, most to the dynamite Beaudine planted. And that was all done for the meetup with Creed. Beaudine wanted to make sure nobody walked out of there."

"You said most, how did we lose the others?"

"Your brother. But you know that, don't you?"

Dev took a drink. "We've got something big coming up in Paradise River in two days, and it can't be thwarted."

"That train job could really set us up, boy-o. We need it."

"It's always tough to get started."

"Or reconstructed." Smythe laughed as he took another pull, leaving the last bit. "I know my history, Dev. New country can be a great playground, but only if you get in early."

"That's what this is all for."

Dev unfurled a map showing sections of the Colorado Line, and its stations, including Paradise River. The railroad was a curving snake of red across miles of green and blue mountains.

"And there's the problem," Smythe said. "How many miles? What you want to do is already being done in New York and by my old man in London. Villages and cities, mate. You can control that with a few men on every street. There's too much land — how can you keep track?"

"That's why we need an army."

"The one we almost lost."

"I kept you on the road. All you got is that scratch."

Smythe snorted. Dev continued, "You'll heal. That accountant's going to help us get organized. The money from this train will get us men, equipment. Maybe even buy us a sheriff or two. Whatever we need to stay in control, and you're going to be the man in the towns and villages, making sure everything's running right."

"The Indians might have a thing or two to say about these plans. And the real Army."

"Wouldn't it be something if the tribes lined up on our side?"

"Oh, big dreams, boy-o."

"This train is no dream."

"That's a hell of a job you're handing me."

"You're important to this."

Smythe finished his drink. "Because I shot the warden?"

"Because you listened to my ideas."

"And you're paying me well for it, but it doesn't mean I agree with everything."

Dev leaned forward, his injured arm resting on the edge of the desk. "One more Goodwill, and we're done.

"John doesn't know I'm alive, and wants

Beaudine dead. Let 'em tear each other up, and we'll take care of the man left standing. But nothing comes before these plans."

The bounce-back of a rifle's report moved Dev to the window, where he looked down into the prison yard. Fuller was drawing down on targets beyond the front gate — loading, shooting, and hitting straight, every single time.

Captain Creed sat his Pride near Fuller, with Hector by the stirrups describing the shots. Dev watched for a few more moments, then turned to Smythe. "Creed's got that buffalo soldier. Good sniper. We can use him."

"What about the blind man himself?"

"This is going to be done right. Cut him loose." Dev drank the final drops of the warden's fine mash. "We're taking this train."

"Never thought any different, mate."

# CHAPTER TWENTY-FOUR:
## BAD DEEDS

"I've been shot before, and can't say it ever gets any better."

Miles Duffin tried a smile, but failed, as Bishop and Fox swabbed the bullet wound just above his hip. He was lying on a stack of blankets in the back of a buckboard, surrounded by suitcases and packed boxes, the bay and the painted tethered to the side.

His young wife was driving, and not looking back at her husband as he tried again, "I wish I could say the other fellow looks worse."

Bishop said, "He does."

"You get him with that Shuler double?"

Fox took cotton from the medical kit, combed it out, before pressing it onto the bullet wound. Miles screamed, and his wife looked back. Her face was streaked, but didn't give up a word. Fox bound the cotton tight; the wife kept her jaw clenched.

"You two are the doggonedest doctors I

ever seen. But dying men can't be choosers. I'm truly obliged."

Bishop smiled. "You talk too much, Deputy."

"Not my only failure. I was serving papers when this happened, wish I could say it was a shoot-out."

Miles's wife looked at him again. Furious.

Bishop said, "Be glad it wasn't, and you really talk too much. You've lost a lot of blood, and half the slug's in there. You know the doc in Paradise River?"

Miles's wife spoke from the driver's seat. "Yes, we know him. He's worked on Miles. A lot."

"He's going to be working on him again. It's not deep, but it's got to come out."

Miles whispered, "Okay. If you tell me how you got that all fixed up."

"I lost the arm a year ago, and her father made it."

Miles turned to Fox. "Real good job. Don't make you look like a doc, but I sure as hell wouldn't mess with you!"

"We're tying to find other men like the one who shot you. The Fire Riders."

Miles's wife said, voice rising, "That should be easy enough. They've raided the town half a dozen times, and I don't know how many they've killed."

"Rachel, it wasn't that many times, or that many people. And I took down a lot of 'em. Give me a little credit, honey."

She said, "Fine. And they kept coming back, with more men. And now look at you."

Miles said to Bishop, "We best drop it," while scribbling a note on a piece of a wanted poster, with a pencil he had in his pocket. He pressed the note into Bishop's left.

Rachel guided the buckboard into Paradise River, following the one road that turned into a main street that met three more streets in the center of town. Paradise had a worn look, with shingles missing from roofs, split glass in store windows, or railings broken on hotel balconies. Yet, it was all freshly painted, as if the entire town had been dressed up for some quick influx of people or money that hadn't happened.

Paradise was a spinster, still waiting for a beau.

The one building that was newly built was the rail station, with a full loading area for cattle, and a water tower. There were no cattle. A few people lounged on the platform.

Fox and Bishop climbed from the buckboard, and grabbed their horses, as Rachel drove on to the doctor's down the street.

360

Miles waved his best and shouted his thanks, which only made Rachel snap the team to drive faster.

She had given Bishop a look of gratitude, but nothing else, and he understood. She hated that her husband was lying with a bullet in him, and wanted no part of this kind of life. Not anymore. He'd seen that look in a woman's eyes before and, following Fox into the shabby hotel, wondered about seeing it again.

"We don't usually accept . . . unusual guests."

Bishop looked from the deskman, trying to focus on his small, pink rabbit eyes, then to Fox, and then to himself, before saying, "So who's unusual?"

"I don't know how comfortable you'll be here."

"The ground's frozen, and there's a storm heading in. You've got a lot of keys on that pegboard. You want to ask me about my arm? Ask."

Bishop dropped the double-barrels in front of the deskman with a loud thud. Rabbit eyes jumped back.

"Believe it or not, I'm a doctor, so I can tell details of the operation, but most folks just want to know if it actually works. Would you like to see? Maybe that old couch?"

He turned, the shotgun snapping into position, when the deskman grabbed a key from the pegboard. Fox snatched it from his hands.

The bed was too large for the room, the door hitting it when you entered. There was a nightstand with a cracked pitcher and washbasin, both painted with blue roses, and one ragged towel. There had been a mirror on the wall sometime, but it was long gone, with only the dirty outline of it remaining.

Bishop put his saddlebags and med kit on the floor, and reached for something as Fox splashed water on her face from the basin.

"I'm sorry about that."

She turned to him.

"I don't like to act that way, but he was being stupid."

"He was."

He held out the note that Miles had slipped him. "That's the train that's coming tomorrow night. It's a gold transfer for the bank."

"Dev's gold? The treasure that everyone wants?"

"That's not real."

"The pain it's caused you is real."

"This shipment might bring out some of the men we're looking for. You saying I should leave it alone?"

Fox just said, "Things do not stay the same."

"They have to for a little while." He took the copy of Poe from his bags, and placed it on the bed. "You left that behind."

Fox regarded the book, but didn't make a reach. "Let's do what you need done. Then we'll see."

Bishop said, *"Hó'ótóva,"* wanting Fox to agree and say, "Yes. Someday." But she didn't.

Instead, she handed him the bandolier of six.

Howard was on the ground at Crawford's feet, holding his stomach that had been ripped by the iron talons of White Claw. The metal contraption was still fitted to Crawford's hand, spattering red whenever he moved. Howard screamed, but it only made it worse for him, intensifying the pain, as he felt his lungs and throat with his cries.

His face was slashed, and one arm taken down to the bone. Every move that Howard made, Crawford blocked with his boots, holding him down, making him squirm even more. And cry out again, to nothing, but the woods.

Crawford kept walking around Howard,

kicking small piles of snow against his torn face, bringing the claw close to him, pressing the sharp edges against open wounds.

"Think you can come onto my place, threaten my daughter? Because you're a big fella? That ain't the way it works. You're talking about harming *my* blood, which means *your* blood is gonna run! You're gonna die here, and then I'm gonna feed ya to the next thing that comes down out of them woods! Because you needed me to talk? Brother, that's the mistake that killed you."

He slashed again, opening Howard's back through his jacket. Howard crawled, face pressing into the muddy snow. Crawford bent down, and snatched the deputy's badge from his shirt.

"I don't know if you're a real lawman, or just stupid, but I'm keepin' this."

Howard rolled onto his back, staring into the sky. Crawford held Howard's gun above his head. "Gun ain't a threat, if you don't know when to use it. And you sure don't."

Howard couldn't speak, and tears erupted from his eyes to his mouth. Everything else was soaked red, and burning.

Crawford aimed the pistol at Howard's head. "If you shot me a few times, at least you could'a gotten the hell away. I ain't gonna do anything more to ya, though. Now, I bet you wish I would, just to get her done. You made your choice to come after my family, and you're gonna die with it. And wherever you end up, remember, it was White Claw what sent you there."

Beaudine let the match's flame edge the tobacco of the cigar, heating it just right, before drawing deep. It was fine leaf, but tightly rolled in several layers. That made it last and gave it a firm ash, but it was difficult to light.

Chaney stood with him on the platform of the Paradise River station, watching the cigar process and checking his watch. The sun was red behind the mountains, and Beaudine had to shield his eyes when he spoke to him.

"Mr. Chaney, the window doesn't open for another three minutes. You should enjoy this time."

"If we get that money, the shares are a lot larger than when we started."

He drew on the cigar, and studied it. "Yes, I've done my calculations. Our earlier efforts were derailed by other forces. I always said the best way was to have Bishop come to us. Now he has to, or he doesn't get the little package, does he? Or even the bang-tail. We just have to have patience."

"That's getting short in supply."

"So you keep threatening."

The ticket window opened, and a pair of thick glasses peered out, with a man behind them. Beaudine gave the ticket clerk the package for general express, then unfolded the Brakeman's schedule.

The clerk said, "You work for the Colorado, young fella?"

"A good friend does."

"That's paperwork only for employees."

"He's trusting me with this information. Can you tell me about this train? Is it express?"

The clerk laughed. "Better not be. It's got to stop here and make a gold transfer to the bank. And the only reason I'm letting you know is —" The clerk brought a Colt 45 up from under the counter and pointed it out of the cage. "And mister, there are soldiers on that train, and they're carrying something a damn sight bigger than this."

# CHAPTER TWENTY-FIVE:
# KEEP MY COFFIN OPEN

The bonfires were set in three separate places in the prison yard, spreading a moving light that allowed the men to check weapons and horses. Some tried for night target practice: quick-drawing service pieces, or cracking off as many as possible with a Winchester.

Dev and Smythe moved among them, noting the weapons and their variable abilities. One rider tried long-shooting with a Colt, missing the wooden target three times out of six. Fuller stepped in, obliterating it with two perfectly placed kill shots.

"You're putting all these fellas to shame."

Fuller checked the hammer of his Morgan-James, blew it out. "Well, that's not my intention, Mr. Bishop."

"Just the same. You going to be riding tomorrow night? We could use you, and I'll see that your share's double these others."

"Double?"

"Triple."

Fuller looked to Creed, who was standing with Hector, brushing down Pride by the firelight, the flames literally dancing in the reflection of the horse's muscled, black coat.

"What about the captain? That's who brought me in."

Dev said, "I'll talk to him. He wants the best for you."

He walked over and put a hand on Hector's shoulder. "Watch the captain, son. Learn how to do things right."

Creed continued with the grooming. "What are we doing about your brother, Mr. Bishop? Is finding him part of the mission tomorrow night?"

"The mission's about money. My brother's close, Captain. And when he pops his head out of the ground, we'll chop it off."

"You agreed that would be my role."

"Not tomorrow night, sir."

"I have the finest horse here, and Hector for my eyes."

"It's not enough. There's too much at stake."

Creed stopped brushing and followed Dev's voice so he could be directly in front of him. His dark glasses looked like eyeless sockets in the firelight, transforming his face into a skull.

"You remember who you're talking to? I have more right to kill your brother than anyone. I helped you organize this ragtag, because I was told that I would get to exercise that right."

"And we followed him after his accident, so you'd know where he was for the capture. But he's not here, is he, Captain?"

Creed turned away, slipping the grooming brush into his saddle. "If we're a burden, then we'll ride."

"Mr. Fuller's staying on."

Creed stepped around his horse, Hector taking his arm as he tripped over a pile of stones and rotting wood. He stumbled almost to the ground, then stood, jerking away from Hector. "Fuller! Is this true?"

Fuller said, "I need money for my family, Captain. That's what you promised."

"Do you know what will happen if I find Bishop?"

"Yes, sir, I do."

Fuller extended his hand to shake, but Creed turned from him. "I had my hand out for you, Captain."

"I know."

Hector guided Creed to his horse, then stood away, as he swung onto Pride's back. Pride lowered his head, helping Hector climb on behind. Pride snorted, ready to run, but Creed sat the animal for a moment before walking Pride around the bonfires, circling the yard and the men in red and then breaking to a full run out the front gate.

From the back of the Conastoga wagon, Tomlinson's daughters began to sing. Their perfect-pitch voices carrying over the sounds of the prison yard, as Smythe, Dev, and Fuller watched Captain Creed and Hector ride into the enormous darkness beyond the gates. And then they were gone.

They said nothing when Smythe held out a new .56 caliber Spencer carbine. "Ready to go to work?"

Fuller took the rifle, hefting its weight.

"Feel good?"

"A fine weapon. Balanced. Never shot it before. Looks like I'll be practicing." He slammed home an ammo magazine.

Dev said, "After the raid tomorrow, you'll be able to give your family a future. Better than these others. Money in the bank, and it's only going to get better. You're a Fire Rider, now, sniper."

"Maybe, but —" Fuller picked up a red hood from the ground, tossed it on the bonfire, and watched it burn.

White Fox was curled up on top of the bed,

not even a blanket covering her, as Bishop sat in the corner, checking the motion of the rig. He snapped his wrist, and the barrels responded instantly. He turned, the gun turned. Every move, and the weapon responded. He let the hammers drop. Click.

Fox murmured, and Bishop tucked a blanket around her.

The break of morning was shrouded by blowing snow that moved thick in the air, the heavy powder of the mountains being swept up by cold bursts of wind. For Smythe, it was like grey evening, as he tied his horse and walked around the side of the Paradise River Rail Station, noting the platform and tracks.

The station was deserted — no crew or distant whistle of a locomotive. Just the cold that deadens the back of the neck, which is why he didn't feel the barrel of Beaudine's Colt against him.

Beaudine kept his voice steady, though his hand was shaking. "Mr. Smythe, killing you the worst way possible has been one of my dreams, since we were in the Tomb. But I think I'll allow you to stay above ground, while we discuss our new partnership."

"Oh, you're making a whopping mistake, boy-o."

"My mistake was not killing you all those times I had the chance."

Beaudine nudged Smythe with the pistol, and they both moved off the platform, toward the cattle pens.

White Fox woke in the room, stretching her arms, and wiping her eyes. For a moment, she felt that someone would be next to her. But she was alone.

Rachel Duffin tried to hide her displeasure when Bishop knocked on the doctor's door, but she was unsuccessful. Her face was newly tear-stained, and her expression, dark.

Rachel said, "We're not staying in this town. I don't want you saying anything to change my husband's mind."

"I won't do that."

Bishop wanted to extend Rachel a bit of comfort and tell her that she reminded him of his wife, when Dr. Benson stepped from the back room and introduced himself. He was pleasant and old school, and probably had a drink or two with his breakfast. Benson walked Bishop to a small side bedroom where Miles was recovering. Bishop kept his arm down, his duster hiding the barrels of the rig.

Benson gave Bishop a sidelong look over

his glasses. "Miles told me you fixed him on the road. Where did you serve?"

"Out of Virginia."

"That was a good field dressing, doctor."

Benson's office and the patient's room were clean. Organized. And he carried himself with that rare combination of sawbones and educated physician. There was a little more small talk, but he knew when to leave. Another good sign of a good doctor.

Bishop sat by Miles's bed and told him so. Rachel stood in the doorway, arms folded, struggling.

Miles said, "I'm glad to hear you think he knows what he's doing."

"You're the best judge. How do you feel?"

"Like hell. But less like hell than I did yesterday."

Rachel said, "This is the best thing for him, but he can't get overtired."

"Honey, I sure would like a cup of coffee."

"Tea."

"Fine. Anything for you, Doctor Bishop?"

Bishop turned to Rachel and said, "Tea sounds very fine, I haven't eaten this morning."

Rachel left, but didn't shut the door. Bishop tapped it with his foot, nudging it almost shut. "I need to know about the gold train."

"You gonna rob it?"

"Not me, but someone might have plans."

"That's what the soldiers are for, I guess. They didn't really include me in it, except as an extra gun, when they carry the money to the bank from the station. They've only done it twice before, and nothing happened."

"With the money or the town?"

"Both. They deposit here because shipping companies keep threatening to build, and they need loans. The mayor gets excited for the boom he's been counting on for twenty years, and then nothing happens, and they pull the deposits. Last time it almost wiped the town out."

"What about the sheriff?"

"Up territory someplace. I heard he has another wife. Anyway, he's not around much anymore, so when I get laid up, it can be a problem."

"And what about your wife?"

"She don't like what I do, and something like this makes her hate it."

"She might not be wrong."

"Doc, I have considered that about twenty times a day."

"Miles, no one can hit that train at the

station if they've got men on it."

"I know a little spot, just a gopher hole about ten miles down the tracks. That's where I stake out. Perfect view of the Fire Riders, if that's what you're talking about."

"One man, one badge, huh?"

"That's why we're lame ducks. If you can find anybody from Paradise to help, you're a better man than me."

Bishop stood. "Doubtful, but here's some advice. Do what she wants, and go build your life."

"But, ere long the heaven of this pure affection became darkened, and gloom, and horror, and grief swept over it in clouds."

White Fox read the line from "Morella" aloud several times, the words coming easier and easier to her, even if their true meaning didn't. She said, "Not perfect," to the empty room, flipped through some pages, and let the cover drop shut.

The knock on the door came immediately afterward. Her hand turned the knob; then she was thrown back hard. Chaney had shouldered the door into her and was now slamming it shut behind him.

Chaney flicked his gold tooth before speaking. "Where is he? And don't look at me like a squaw pissing in the dirt."

Fox separated her words: "I — don't — know."

Chaney's Derringer was out of his jacket, and he brought it up to her temple. "We know about that little package from your pa, and I paid three clerks to let me know if they saw you. I stacked the deck a little, especially since you cut my rib in half with an arrowhead."

Fox let Chaney lean in close; she could taste his breath, even as he kept the gun pressed into her, leaving a mark.

"Your man has money, the railroad has money. Everybody but me, and we're going to fix that right up. Tell me where he hides his cash, or I'll kill you. Understand? Or do I have to talk in dog-tongue?"

She closed her eyes. *"Tó'ovenohtsé."*

"Not an answer."

Fox locked eyes with Chaney, staring. He almost smiled, as she reached over her head for the water pitcher, and shattered it against his skull. The scream of the breaking china and the scream of the gambler were a garbled one as he fell to the floor.

She lunged across the bed for her saddle, grabbing a sheathed knife, as Chaney came up shooting wild, blood washing his eyes from the cuts on his head.

The slugs hit the wall behind her, as she

threw the knife. It hit his chest, but broke off at the tip. Chaney fell forward, catching himself on the edge of the bed.

"God, get me some help, and I won't do nothing else to you again. I swear. Just help me, please."

Chaney lurched as Fox took a step toward him. The knife blade in his gun's pistol grip jutted out, and he slashed, catching her arm. Fox smashed him back with both elbows, the bone punching his face, then brought up her knees to send him slamming against the wall.

The knifepoint was pushed deeper into Chaney's chest. He dropped to his knees, and then collapsed. The room seemed darker for a moment, as Fox sat on the edge of the bed. Chaney was nothing now, just an empty shell lying on the floor. It had all taken less than five seconds.

Fox wiped at the tears she hated.

The roof was nothing but an overhang, but it kept the now steady snow off Smythe and Beaudine. Smythe's hands were tied, and he was sitting with his back against a wall, long lengths of chain and butchering hooks hanging behind and above him. Sledgehammers to knock out the cows were gathered in a large barrel by the door that opened onto the always empty cattle pens.

Beaudine settled on a bench, holding the long cleaver.

"Another business in Paradise that isn't doing well. Ask anyone in town and they'll be happy to tell you. I understand their need, as I have it myself. Money comes so easy to some, and the rest of us can chase it forever, and not catch a dollar. What do you think, Smythe? About money? Do you know anyone who has any?"

"Come on, boy-o. Doc Bishop's got nothing! All that gold talk was a trick to get you to go after the brother, so Dev could work his own thing."

Beaudine studied the blade, letting the light from an oil lantern bounce off of it, into his eyes. "You keep saying that, Smythe."

"Because it's the bloody truth. He's got big plans."

"I was closer to him than anyone, helped him."

"But he played you, mate. He didn't want you anywhere near this."

Beaudine took a few steps with the blade chest-high, as an executioner would hold it before going to the chopping block. "Yet, he trusts a prison guard, and not his own cellmate?"

"So what do you do now? Kill me? Or go after him? You've talked to the station master, you know what's happening with this train."

"Those men in red who attacked me, they belong to Devlin?"

Smythe threw away, "They're his men, yeah."

Beaudine lowered the blade. "That can't go unpunished."

"There's money on that train. Real money, not some kind of trick. I don't give a damn about Dev Bishop, but you can't take it alone."

"I don't trust you a bit."

"I'll show you, then you decide. I'm not running, boy-o."

Beaudine hauled Smythe to his feet with a grunt. "You know this is going to end in his death."

"And I'm in for shares, Major?"

# CHAPTER TWENTY-SIX: DEAD MEN KILL, TOO

The tracks of the Colorado Line ran through a narrow gorge that opened onto flatlands on the other side of a small grouping of mountains, before reaching Paradise River. It was like a natural tunnel, heavily treed, and a beautiful cousin to the Rockies if seen during a new spring.

But the first snows settled and stayed, slicking the mountainside, and weighing the trees until they bent almost to the ground. The gorge was covered with jags of ice, from frozen rain and water coming down from the higher range, only to be captured and paralyzed here.

Dev Bishop and Fuller stood by on their horses, just above the gorge, watching as dynamite was bundled to the trunks of some tall pines just above the tracks.

Fuller said, "That stuff almost killed you and your men once."

"Well, now you're riding with us, so you

best pay attention. What position are you going to take?"

"You want me to hit the engineer?"

"Just take care of what the trees and the boiler don't."

Someone yelled, "She's goin!" and all broke for their horses, riding quickly away as the first charges exploded, throwing tree trunks in the air, and breaking them into huge pieces, tumbling down onto the tracks, blocking them.

A wave of snow and ice followed, rolling from the hillside, covering the blockade. After a few moments, the air calmed again, as the last bits of wreckage found its place.

Fuller said, "Now, that was a hell of a noise."

"There's not a train due until the one we want. This bunch will take care of anyone who comes sniffing around. You're too valuable for guard duty, stay with me."

Chaney's body was covered with a blanket, one of his hands peeking out from under. Spots of blood had soaked through across his chest. Miles walked around the side of the bed with the help of a cane, lifting the blanket for another look, then dropping it again.

Bishop and Fox stood by the open door,

the rabbit deskman with them, his arms folded as tight as his expression.

"I knew I shouldn't have given them the room. I'm not letting this go. She's gonna feel the law!"

Miles said, "This is a killing, and you're going to have to go to trial, miss."

Bishop said, "Chaney tried to kill her."

"Miss, you self-defended this one all over the room and I'm sure a judge will see it that way."

The deskman said, "But you'll be rotting in jail until then!"

Miles stepped to Fox, his voice low. "I understand what this is about for you two, so if you swear you'll appear, I won't arrest you."

White Fox said, "I swear."

"I'll do up the papers for a territorial judge."

The rabbit said, "That's it?"

"For right now. If she don't come for trial, I'll have a warrant sworn out."

The deskman was still fuming, his forehead changing color, as Bishop and Miles moved into the hallway. Miles hobbled toward the stairs, his voice low. "I should be doing a hell of a lot more."

"I know. They'll probably take your badge."

"That's not the worst thing to happen. Doc, I couldn't be more grateful to you and the miss for what you've done, but please, don't test it. You have to come back and face this. I won't be the law anymore, but you don't want this hanging over you."

Bishop said, "Miles, if we're able to make it back, we will."

"One last bit of advice? You're a civilian. Let the troops do their job."

Bishop gave Miles a shake with his left, before turning to Fox. She started down the stairs ahead of him, walking across the street to the livery, her eyes dry and fixed ahead.

Bishop fell in next to her and said, "You don't have to go. Now I'm giving you the out, if you want it."

Fox said nothing. Light, fresh snow stuck to them both as they moved to their horses, checking for the weapons they'd need. She held out a knife, the same size as the one she'd used on Chaney. Her hand started to shake.

Bishop didn't see it, and said, "Have it ready."

He filled the bandolier with shells, and more in his pockets, then slipped a small-caliber Smith and Wesson into his jacket, and gave Fox a Colt. She checked the weapon; all their moves were measured, just what he thought they should be. Automatic.

Bishop said, "I'm ready. Are you? Last chance."

Fox swung onto the painted's back.

They broke from the livery, running the painted and the bay down the road parallel to the tracks, heading for the trail in the hills above them. The snow was coming harder now, blowing heavy, and sideways.

"It would be unwise to fabricate."

Smythe was on his horse, riding alongside Beaudine, his hands still tied behind his back. "I'm telling you this is the place that we've chosen. They've already brought down some trees up the tracks, and here's where we'll ride out to take the cars."

Beaudine maneuvered farther along a ledge high above the tracks, ice patching the rock, before taking a spot next to a sparse blue fir.

Smythe said, "What about me?"

He didn't see the gun in Beaudine's hand, or hear the shot. He saw the muzzle flash, and then it was too late.

The distant shot echoed, as the Fire Riders gathered at the edge of the woods, some taking their attack positions above the railroad tracks, while others towed more split trunks and giant limbs into place. The wall they'd built was over ten feet high, and beyond the height of the engine's cow-catcher.

Fuller watched as they worked, all wearing their crimson tunics, and a few, their hoods. All the sniper could think about was family, and money, and the worth of the risk.

One of the Riders barked at Fuller, "Hey, how many times you kill for money, son?"

Fuller didn't answer, checked the action on the Spencer.

Dev Bishop called out, "We've got less than ten!"

Down the tracks, the train whistle called out, and echoed back through the hills. The snow was now a thick curtain, whiting everyone's vision.

John Bishop and Fox rode their horses up from the tracks to a small space in the rocks, looking down on the gorge. Deputy Miles's cigarette makings littered the ground where there was a tin cup solid with ice, and flat stones for a small campfire.

The whistle called again.

Bishop looked to Fox. "We can't stop this happening, but we'll avenge my wife, my son."

She finally said, "That's what we're here for."

The train whistle became a pained cry, and the crash that followed was so loud the bay and painted buckled at the knees.

The gold train was five cars long, led by a Baldwin steam engine, powering through the storm. The engineer had pulled the brakes half a mile back, but the downward grade and icy tracks pushed the train faster, with its large power wheels throwing hot, yellow sparks as they skidded, fighting to slow. Failing.

Half the trees and rocks were blasted out of the way on impact, but the rest held fast, jammed beneath the rails and pushing against the boiler until it exploded. Bleeding iron. The rest of the engine crumpling into itself, blowing off the wheels, sending them still-spinning into the frozen mountainside.

Bolts were bullets, blowing off in all directions, while the brass fittings twisted from the engine and ripped back through the cab, killing the engineer and fireman.

It was all screaming metal and steam, as the rest of the train spun wild off the tracks, the cars tumbling, colliding with each other, glass and metal erupting before smashing into the snow drifts — dominoes thrown by God.

Bishop and Fox charged the small cut through the hills, down to the tracks. Metal was still bending, whining, as steam exploded from safety valves and brakes. The falling snow cooled the boiler, which sizzled as the winter fought to put it out.

The soldiers in the passenger and mail cars cried through bloody injuries. Bishop and Fox climbed on top of the mail car, peering into the door that had been ripped open like wet paper. Two young soldiers were huddled in the tipped-over corner, bleeding and wide-eyed, clutching their rifles, but not knowing what or where to shoot.

Bishop called to them, "Boys, we're here to help! Stay down!"

Slugs ripped at Bishop and Fox. They dove off the car, the shots tearing close.

In the trees, Fuller's position was good, as he lay cover fire for the Riders. He drew on Bishop, and fired. Bishop rolled, the slug ricocheting off the rig, and the steel taking it. Bishop grabbed Fox and dove from the wreck, as the shots tore into the train cars around them.

The sniper fire kept Bishop low, behind cover, as a Fire Rider bore down on him.

Bishop jostled his arm. The rig was instantly up and loaded, and he sprang, blowing the Rider clean out of the saddle. The Fire Rider spun with the impact, then landed dead, on hot-metal debris.

Before his body tumbled into the snow, another Rider charged, and Bishop let fire with the second barrel. He shucked the shells, pulled down two more, and turned on another, who was coming up over the wood tender. He fired, turned, fired again.

The Riders lay wounded and dying, the snow offering a new shroud as they bled out.

Four Riders rode fast along the tracks, leaping around wreckage, and hurling Ketchum Hand Grenades. One, two, blasts sent ice, mud, and fire into the air.

Two young soldiers dove from the wreck of the passenger car, scrambling to get a good shot, as a grenade landed between them. One panicked a throw, tossing it into the air, where it exploded through the falling snow.

Bishop shot two Riders with a pull of the trigger line, sending them sprawling from their horses and still shooting as they hit the ground. Bishop reloaded from the bandolier, and wounded one more as he rode by.

White Fox got the last one, hurling a knife into his gut.

Bishop called out to the mail car, "Boys, you okay in there?"

A soldier yelled back that he'd been hit, but was all right.

Bishop worked his way to the top of the car when the Gatling gun cut loose from the trees. The thousand rounds hit the train wreckage, beating hell out of it, as Bishop and Fox took cover behind the old boiler. A few of the young soldiers shot back from the passenger car, which was riddled with bullets.

The gun stopped as two Fire Riders hurled dynamite, blowing off the back of the mail car. Hot metal and fire sliced the air. They kicked their way inside, grabbed a large strong box, and shouldered it out to a wagon. The Gatling laid cover fire as the horse team bolted, carrying the Riders and the strong box away from the battle.

Bishop signaled Fox.

He ran around to the far side of the locomotive, keeping behind the wheels, bursts of steam still gutting from the engine. The Gatling let loose again. Bishop made for his horse.

Fox worked back to the wood tender, and the fireman's station. A drum of coal oil hadn't burst in the wreck. Its seams bulged as she rolled it into the half-ton of firewood that was spread from the tender. She grabbed a fireman's ax and cut open the lid, soaking the wood with oil.

The snow was falling solid now, frosting the wreckage, and the dead. Wet. Cold.

Fox watched, as Bishop climbed back toward the trail, trying to reach the ledge where the Gatling was protected. Fox ducked as another burst of fire raked the metal and glass.

She grabbed the brakeman's lantern, lit it, and waited. Bishop got to the ledge, dropped silently from the bay. Fox smashed the lantern into the wood tender, lighting the pools of coal oil, and the wood. The flames ate the oil, spewing black.

Thick plumes of smoke instantly choked the sky around the locomotive, then blanketing the train. The Gatling opened up from the hills, shooting blind.

The smoke rolled from the train, as the wood fire grew. Bishop kept low, moving on the Gatling, the grey smoke mixed with the snow his cover. Both barrels were ready, the Fire Rider feeding the ammo into the machine gun, raking the train over and over.

The Rider had no time to react when both barrels of the shotgun lifted him off his feet, and tossed him down the icy side of the mountain, to the wreckage below.

The last sounds of the machine gun died in the distance, and Bishop stood, listening to the final reports. The snow was thicker, a curtain of white beads, as it began dousing the flames around the train. Bishop pulled the firing mechanism and ammo clips from the Gatling when a voice said, "I could have killed you a dozen times."

Bishop turned to see Fuller step from the trees, with his Spencer rifle in his hands, but not aimed at him.

"Why didn't you?"

"You see all that down there, doc? I guess I've had enough for a while. How about you?"

Bishop brought the shotgun rig up.

"I never was after you, but you and Creed stopped me from finding the men who killed my family. That's all I wanted."

Fuller said, "If you'd let me, I want to get back to mine. You'll never see me again."

Bishop lowered the rig. Fuller turned and walked back to where his horse was tied in the trees. He got on it, his rifle on his back, and gave Bishop a last nod before riding into the deeper woods.

John Bishop took some deep breaths, the rig now weighing him down. He stepped around the bodies of the Riders he'd dropped, and looked at the burning damage below, the field of battle.

Bishop made his way off the ridge and rode toward the mail car, as the soldiers began climbing from the wreckage. He got off his horse, and walked it to the other side of the wood tender. The fire was now smoldering, but the smoke from the coal oil was still thick, and choking the air.

Bishop couldn't be sure of what he was seeing as he moved through the cloud of grey. He stopped, the cloud breaking apart. It was a man, holding a woman, with a large blade pressed against her throat.

"Dr. Bishop, wouldn't it have been so much simpler to give me what I wanted a year ago? Think of the lives you could have saved. You're still a doctor, correct?"

Bishop's answer was to take a step, the rig snapping into place. He pulled back the sleeve on his right arm completely, to expose the gun and the extra shells: two chambered, and two ready.

"What do you think this is going to get you?"

Beaudine held the blade tight. "My fortune."

"They stole some."

392

"Your brother promised me a fortune in gold."

"You should have gotten it from him before they hanged him."

Beaudine laughed. "They never hanged him, you fool."

Bishop took another step, the smoke and snow shifting in front of him, making him ghostly. An apparition. The shotgun rig shifted with his every move, keeping its aim on Beaudine's chest.

"Take that blade away."

"And what will you give me? You know what happened last time, and I have no problem doing the same thing again."

"I don't have any gold. But I can give you your life."

Beaudine was fixed on the figure in front of him, advancing.

"You asked if I was a doctor, and I'm really not. I'm something else, that is going to kill you in ten seconds if you don't let her go." Bishop extended the rig. "We both have something the other one wants."

"I know."

Beaudine said, "I'm the man who turned you into what you are, and I think that deserves compensation."

"You're right."

Fox brought her heel down, breaking

Beaudine's foot, before smashing his windpipe with her elbow. He stumbled, the cleaver blade falling away. The first barrel caught him in the leg, dropping him.

Bishop moved on Beaudine, screaming in the snow.

"Why did you say my brother was alive?"

"Because he is! Oh, sweet Lord —"

"Tell me!"

"I don't know much — !"

"You've made me very angry."

The next barrel blew half of Beaudine's right arm off, leaving it to dangle. Beaudine screamed, and prayed. Bishop loaded the weapon again.

"I'll leave you in the snow to die unless you tell me everything."

Beaudine looked up; he was choking now, Bishop's figure in front of him darkening even more behind the smoke and snow.

"The Riders . . . You're not who you were. . . . You're the Angel of Death."

Bishop fired two more barrels into Beaudine. Fox turned away, started to run for her horse. Bishop ran for her, grabbing her with his left, and spinning her around.

Fox twisted away. "Let go of me!"

"I deserved that! You know what that man took from me! You've been with me for a year, leading to this!"

Fox looked at him, said, "I told you I would help you until I can't. Now I can't."

The young soldiers had finally climbed from the wreckage, laying some of their comrades in the snow while wounds were tended to. A young officer took a head count, while the two soldiers from the mail car handed over the cache of gold.

Bishop watched all this from a distance. Fox had climbed onto the painted, and brought the horse around. She looked down at him, and said, "Aren't you going to help them?"

Bishop said, "Yeah, I'll try, if I can."

"This is what you need to do now."

Fox eased the painted away, and Bishop watched her as she followed the tracks, before climbing a small trail that led into the mountains.

"Are you a doctor? We could use you over here!"

Bishop nodded, following the young man to the remains of the passenger car and the caboose.

The soldier looked at the shotgun. "I've never seen anything like that before."

"I had it made special."

The soldier stopped in his tracks, was peering into the distance, snow collecting on his face.

"What's wrong?"

"The guys in the Red Hoods, there are two of them on the ridge. If they go for another wave, that's the end of us. We've already lost the shipment."

Bishop looked where the young soldier was pointing to see two men on horseback, both wearing crimson tunics, one sporting a red hood, while the other was not.

The young soldier was calling his friends to arms, as John Bishop saw what looked to be his brother flanked by the other rider.

Bishop took a step, and Dev's face came more and more in focus. Through the snow and screams, he recognized him, and his name tore from Bishop in a demonic cry.

The rig snapped instantly into place. The hooded rider threw something, as Dev reared on his horse, and galloped away.

The grenade landed at John Bishop's feet.

Bishop's eyes opened, just as the Benson finished rolling his cigarette. He lit it and drew deep before saying anything to his patient.

"They tell me a grenade blew you ten feet in the air. You've got some bruises and a broken ankle, but I didn't find any sign of hemorrhage. Pretty amazing. There were a lot of dead men at that wreck."

"How many have you treated?"

"About twenty, shipped them out to an army hospital yesterday."

"How long have I been out? What have you been giving me?"

"Light morphine so you could sleep. Two and a half days."

Bishop edged his way onto his elbow, "Great. I'll have soldier's disease on top of everything else. How'd I get here?"

"A boy brought you on horseback. Said he was a friend, but that no one could know he helped you. He brought some of your things, too."

Bishop looked to the dresser by the bed to see the shotgun rig, his medical kit, and a worn volume of Edgar Alan Poe setting on top of it.

The doc moved to the dresser and picked up the shotgun. "That's quite a contraption. Had a hell of a time getting it off you, but you don't need it now, understand? You should, you're a doctor, too."

Bishop lay back in the bed, enjoying the feeling of the cold, clean sheets. He nodded his cooperation.

The doc said, "Sleep for another few hours, and we'll get you some good supper. You're lucky, my wife can cook."

Bishop smiled. "Yeah, I'm lucky."

The doc stepped from the room, pulling the door behind him. Bishop threw back the sheets and sat up, a jolt of pain hitting him. He caught his breath, and then looked to the gun, book, and med kit on the dresser.

John Bishop reached for one of them.